MW01007787

# Perfect!

## A Story of Love and Suspense

# Perfect Love

# Perfect Death

# Perfect DNA

Sharon Hickey Sterling

ISBN Print: 978-0-9969408-6-3
ISBN eBook: 978-0-9969408-3-2

Changing Lines Press
Tucson, Arizona USA

If you find your roots and nourish them
You will know longevity.
If you live a long creative life,
You will leave an eternal legacy.

<u>Tao Te Ching</u> By Lao Tzu

# PROLOGUE

Tallahassee Florida - July 1978

Holly Wallace walked down the concourse of the Tallahassee airport resisting the urge to run. I'mlate, I'm late! rang in her mind. It had been three dayssince she held her infant daughter, Laura. Her parentswere taking care of the baby, but how she missed that sweet little soul. And Lee, the baby's father. When would they be able to stop hiding, live together like a normal family?

In the employee parking lot, she found her Mustang convertible, sank down into the seat and threw off her stewardess uniform hat. It was a ridiculous little thing meant to look pert yet also business-like. Her hand went beneath the neck of her blouse, to the necklace wrought in eighteen carat gold. The chain held one word in script: *Perfect.* Her fingers trembled with the desire to jerk it off too, and fling it out the window. The word was an embarrassment to her. The necklace felt like a noose rather than a valuable piece of jewelry. Gunther expected to see herwearing it. Always. Her life might depend on wearingit--and on keeping the secret of the two people she loved most in the world.

She let her head fall back against the headrest with a sigh. She had worked flights from the airline's base in Miami to Brazil, then back to Miami for a turnaround flight to Argentina. Most of the passengers had been charming, amorous men easy enough to rebuff. The toughest leg of the trip was the last, non- working flight from Miami to the Tallahassee airport.

She sat on the small jump-seat at the rear of the plane, an employee stand-by seat she had begged for. Since she had returned from Canada and was rehired by the airline,

1

her manager again suggested she move to the airline's hub in Miami. She refused. Gunther would either move there too, or turn her over to another handler who might be even more dangerous.

She put the Mustang's convertible top down then reached for the seat belt. It didn't pull down. She tried again, looking to her left at the belt retractor. Something must be wrong with it but she couldn't determine what. She tried once more. Most people didn't use these new car seatbelts. Anyway, it felt too much like being strapped in during take-offs and landings.

She turned the key in the ignition, wound her way out of the parking area and pulled the car onto Interstate-10, welcoming the sun on her face with fresh air tousling her hair. Her shoulders settled. Soon the white of her knuckles on the steering wheel eased to pink. The words of a song, a love song, came to her. She began to hum. After hours in smoke-filled plane cabins, she cherished this ride home to Oak Bayou. She had bought the sports car before she married Lee and gave birth to Laura.

She considered selling the car in favor of a station wagon but with the price of gas more than half-dollar a gallon and her home an hour from the airport, driving a small car was cheaper.

Her mind leaped ahead to her meeting with Lee and joy filled her. Earlier today, Lee had paged her at the airport. She hurried to the airline's desk phone, her heart racing with panic. Was something wrong with the baby? Thank God, no. Someone had broken into Lee's apartment and searched it. Nothing appeared to be missing, but he said they would no longer be safe there so he would find another place. Today she wouldn't be able to go to him, make love. Instead, they would meet at their chosen restaurant a block from the highway, usually not busy or crowded. There, in a secluded corner she would embrace him, kiss him, talk with him. Then, finally at home, she would hold their precious baby in her arms again.

#

# PART ONE

## Present Day--Oak Bayou, Florida

**Chapter One**

A man's voice startled her, "Wake up, Sugar. Let me see those pretty green eyes." A hand on her shoulder. She started. Her eyes popped wide. Oh! Wayne...the old house. Yesterday, Wayne Kelley had come to help her move from the house she had lived in all her life. Now this. She rubbed her face with both hands and turned to look up at him. "I am not your Sugar. Did you forget my name is Sage? And they're hazel, not green." She sat up. "What are you doing in here anyway?"

A Southern drawl softened his words, "Aren't you lonely under the covers? Let me in. I'll keep you company."

"Not on your life!"

He grunted in disappointment and sat down on the bed. His weight depressed the mattress to bring her body closer. He reached for her breast. She rolled away and scrambled out of bed on the side opposite him, standing to face him. She wore only an old t-shirt and pajama pants that drooped low over her hips. She saw his eyes lock on her belly. It was probably the first time he had seen her navel. If his avid stare was a compliment, it didn't please her but triggered her defenses. She glared at him through strands of hair hanging over her eyes. Then she hiked up her pajama pants, shrugged her shoulders and pulled at her t-shirt to lift it away from her breasts. He continued to stare, folding his large hands against his waist: a tall, solid man wearing jeans but no shirt. "So why can't we get better acquainted? This morning's as good a time as ever."

4

"We're as acquainted as we're going to get. You came to help me move furniture, remember? A simple job for you. A favor for me. Not a lover's retreat and sure not a dirty dick visit."

His eyes narrowed. "You locked your door on me last night. Now you're insulting me. I'm tired of hearing no, *Sage*." He loaded her name with sarcasm.

"Of course I locked.... How did you...?" She spotted the old hook and eye latch on the carpet in the open doorway. Her spine went rigid. She flexed her knees and folded her hands into fists. She waited, staring at him and asked, "Well?"

"Well, what?"

"Are you going to make a move?"

"Move?" A pause. "Ah, you think I'd try to force you?"

She gestured at the lock on the floor. "You forced your way in. That is beyond trashy behavior, Wayne. I don't know what to expect from you next."

His face flushed, intensifying the strength of his features. He took a step toward her. "I didn't break in. The latch popped when I tried the door. My behavior is not *trashy* enough to include rape. I don't hurt women."

She took a deep breath, sweeping hair out of her eyes.

He shook his head at her with a grudging half-smile. "If some ignorant redneck tried to get rowdy with you, you'd make a move on him with that *Taikwando* stuff."

"Damn right, and I could beat you."

A smile crept into his eyes. "Like hell you could. You got the power to hold out on me Sugar, not the skills to beat me in a fight. If it ever came to that."

Sage gritted her teeth. "You agreed to use your truck to move the furniture with me, not fight me. And sure not hook up like oversexed teenagers. It's not going to happen."

"Well damn, I guess it's pretty clear by now. We've been dating two months. It's never going to happen, right?"

He didn't wait for her answer. "What the hell are you saving it for?"

She stepped forward, her knees pressed against the bed frame, arms rigid at her sides, fists still clenched. "Enough! Get out!"

He misunderstood. "Happy to. I'm going to make breakfast." He turned and clomped down the stairs to the kitchen rather than out the front door, as she intended for him to do.

The tautness in her arms and legs eased slowly. She took a deep breath then went to shower. Feeling refreshed and wide awake, she dressed in clean jeans and a t-shirt. Standing at the top of the stairs she heard him singing while he moved around in the kitchen, his untrained baritone voice disrespecting a popular tune. The normalcy of the moment brought a wisp of self-reproof. Why had she feared him minutes before in the bedroom?

During the past months she had been aware he wanted a sexual relationship with her, but had never before been crass or demanding. Nothing about him had ever made her wary or fearful, and she had known him for years. His easygoing personality complimented a pleasant face with an easy smile. Reddish-blond hair he kept a little long looked as natural, as uncontrived, as the rest of him including his tall, fit body shaped by a laborer's muscles.

In Oak Bayou, this medium-sized town in the panhandle of Florida, folks thought well of him and his family. From the family's reputation alone, a person would conclude he was harmless.

She came down the stairs. He smiled at her as if nothing had happened. He wore a plaid shirt with rolled up sleeves and a long tail hanging over his jeans. Yesterday afternoon when he grew tired and overheated, he removed his t-shirt, revealing smooth tanned skin over powerful sinews. It was an image of healthy virility which she had

6

noticed without a spark of desire, desire as lacking now as then.

He glanced up. "Grits are almost done. Bacon and eggs are on the table. You can't say I don't cook like a good-ole' country boy."

"I would never accuse you of that." She looked everywhere but directly at him. "I will say you've been great with the furniture pieces I'm keeping for Mom. Some of those antiques weigh a ton and we didn't break a thing." She went to the old percolator coffee pot and poured herself a cup then refilled his, adding the right amounts of half-n-half and sugar. She sat down at the table.

He turned from the stove to plunk down a chipped enameled pan filled with steaming grits. "Evidently I'm more skilled at moving furniture than people." He pushed over the saucer holding a stick of butter then sat down across from her. "Are we about done here? Have you found everything you need?"

"Not quite everything." She picked up her mug to sip coffee while her other hand rubbed at a damp ring on the worn oak table. "I have to go up to the attic. There are some old photo albums and a few other things I have to take. When Mom recovers, she'll enjoy looking through them."

"*If* she recovers."

"*When* she recovers she'll enjoy her favorite things at our new place."

"Have you told her yet?"

"I have lots of news for her. When she's ready."

"It's been over two months now."

"Yeah. If her rehab takes much longer, I'll already be at the Academy."

"You *haven't* told her. She deserves to know."

"She was in too much pain, too confused. Maybe still is."

7

"She should be confused. I sure am. It scares hellout of me imagining you with a gun at your hip. Can't stop chewing on that dream, can you, Sugar?"

Her lips tightened. "Do not--do *not* call me Sugar. Besides, it's not a dream. It's a goal. There's a difference."

He raised an eyebrow. She thought the expression far too sophisticated for his grounded, pragmatic personality. Her palms flat on the table, she leaned toward him. "The difference between a dream and a goal is work--and real possibilities."

He shrugged, taking another bite of grits. He had peppered his to a cloudy grey mass, with a yellow ring of melted butter swimming around the top.

Sage returned her attention to her own hearty meal, wondering why he would criticize her ambition to join the police force. The ambition had sparked in her middle school social studies class when they read and discussed newspapers stories. The ones that reported racial prejudice and demonstrations of violence against Black men and women ignited her capacity foroutrage.

She had told the teacher, "Some police are bad, sure. Some are racist and cruel. But I think the good ripples out farther than the bad." She told herself if she was a police officer she would never assault or shoot someone because their skin was different from hers.

Her parents took it for granted that after high school she would go on to college before pursuing her goal. She had applied and been accepted by two top-tier colleges but a month after she graduated from high school, her father died of pancreatic cancer. She felt distraught, disoriented, but her mother's grief was more direct, more intense. Sage couldn't bear the prospect of going away and leaving Laura alone in thebig, empty house. Thus, the immediacy of death and grieving obscured her visions of the future and put them on hold.

8

In early August when she would have been in flurry of preparations for college, a friend asked Sage to join her to become a barista at the local coffee shop.

By then her mother had reached a less intense stage of grief and needed her daughter less. So why not?

At first she enjoyed being on her feet active many hours at a time. The customers came from a dizzying range of backgrounds and revealed distinctly different personalities. She was fascinated. She studied their actions. She speculated about their motivations.

After two years behind the counter, she tired of even that. She felt her mind was in danger of going numb from a limited range of uses. Her ambition had been to work in urgent situations with troubled people; her customers' issues were usually no more urgent than whether a latte or a cappuccino would please them most.

After talking it over with her mother and a close friend, she chose ambition over expediency and enrolled in a Criminal Justice curriculum at the local community college. Two years later, after earning her associate's degree, she applied and was accepted to the police academy in this part of the State. The six months' Academy training would begin in late August. When she finished--rather if she did finish instead of washing out--she would apply to the Police Department. Getting hired would not be a shoo-in. She would have to complete a long application, a background vetting, then pass muster in two interviews to succeed. When she mentally reviewed the process ahead she wondered if the self-confidence she felt was her ego showing its face or simply a correct assessment of her abilities.

She took a last bite of toast, sat back in her chair and looked up to smile at Wayne. He cocked his head at her and surveyed her body where she sat. Her chin tilted upward.

She knew his look; he was about to revisit their earlier conversation.

He said, "A police officer. All five-feet-five inches, a hundred-twenty pounds of you against the bad guys. Even your *Taikwando* is no match against bullets. Face it, Sage. You couldn't intimidate a hard-core gang member if you were holding a hand grenade. And what about the other Po-po? Won't they be thrilled to have a cupcake like you to back them--all that stands between them and some douche-bag's bullet?"

Sage dropped her fork with a clatter. "Do not use that slang for police. It's disrespectful." She gripped the table edge and stood abruptly. Her chair tipped perilously back, then thumped down. She headed for the door, stopped, turned back to face him. "We have known each other since ninth grade, Wayne. In what demented fantasy of yours am I a cupcake?"

He didn't answer. Again, the eyebrow.

"I get it. You don't approve of me working as a police officer but when you talk to me that way, it doesn't discourage me. It makes me angry. What I want--what I need--is for you to encourage me, be my friend, not just my boyfriend." She grabbed her coffee mug and dropped it into the sink with a pronounced clink.

He stood. "I am not your boyfriend. Evidently I'm just a friend--*without benefits*!"

"Oh! Is that the most important thing to you in a relationship? Sex?"

He remained silent while she watched conflicting emotions move over his face. Then he tilted his head slightly. "Aw, don't be that way, Sage." His voice was much softer than hers had been.

"Well, thanks for calling me by my real name for a change. Tell me, what *way* would you like for me to be?" She didn't let him answer. "No! You can't tell me how to be.

10

You can tell me what you would like for me to say or do, but no one can tell me how to be. I'mfine being exactly the way I am. Not you, not anyone has the right to tell me to change." She strode throughthe back door out to the yard.

She paced for five minutes, working off her anger before she sat down on the back steps. Their confrontation in the bedroom had been at least partly her fault. Yesterday, ten hours of lifting and carrying furniture had left them exhausted. At the kitchen table they drank glass after glass of water before they started on the pizza-with-everything she had ordered. They ate incomfortable silence, without need for conversation.

Finished, Wayne sat back nodding his satisfaction and approval. She smiled. "I think we deserve dessert." She took two cans of cold beer from the refrigerator. Cold air swept towardthem. Wayne tilted his face to it, smiling.

Sage popped the top of hers, then reminded herself what she was here to do. She went to turn off the refrigerator and prop open its door, just another last chore before leaving the house for the last time.

Minutes laterWayne drained the last drop from his can of Coors and plunked it down. Seconds later his eyelids drooped and almost closed.

"Hey, don't crash on me now."

He opened his eyes, blinking to clear them.

Uh-oh, she thought. He's really out of it. If he drives home like this, he could fall asleep at the wheel or get stopped by traffic patrol. They'd smell the beer on his breath and give him a DUI. She said, "You're too tired to drive home, aren't you?"

He compressed his lips as if pondering the question. More evidence in the affirmative. "Hey, you don'thave to go home. There's the empty guest room upstairs."

"Yeah, sounds tempting but I keep a sleeping bag nthe truck. I'll go use."

"In the truck? I assume you'll sleep on it instead of inside it since it's still ninety degrees out there."

"Yep." He rose, tossed the empty pizza box and two beer cans in the trash.

"Will you sleep in the cab or in the bed? Wayne, if you sleep in the cab you'll sweat to death. If you sleep in the open bed, the mosquitos will eat you to death. The AC is still on in here. Toss your sleeping bag in that empty bedroom upstairs."

"Sounds like a plan." He paused to yawn and stretch then went to his truck to get the sleeping bag. On his way up the stairs with it, he nodded thanks to her.

Now she rose from the back steps, telling herself she might have anticipated what happened this morning. Working and eating together, the physical closeness of the sleeping arrangement had been suggestive, even seductive. Her annoyance at his earlier comments still lingered, but in spite of it she wanted to talk their relationship back to civility.

Inside she found him preparing to leave with their argument unresolved. "Wait," she said. "Now we're calmer, let's put it to rest."

He turned to face her full-on. "Yeah. I was a clod. I had no right. I'm sorry. Can you forgive and forget?"

"I think so. Hell, yes." They agreed they had had their last argument. Minutes later she eased the front door closed behind him instead of slamming it. She listened to the sound of his truck until it faded to silence. Then allowed herself a fist pump.

#

**Chapter Two**

Sage walked through the almost-empty house to take stock of all they had done. Satisfaction faded into thoughts of Wayne. She sat down on a metal folding chair, the only one left in the house. Sure, Wayne had apologized for his attempt to push their relationship to intimacy, but a painful thought occurred. She should have said to him, "Wayne, it's me, not you." That lying cliché so often used to placate a rejected lover was, in this case, the bare truth. Her life was too complicated to admit the energies of romantic love or even lust even though, at age twenty-one, she had welcomed and valued those experiences before.

In any case, they had agreed their romance--friendship--whatever it was--was over. Again. Back in high school, how he had made her laugh. At times in conversations on heavy topics, which they believed they understood, he was serious beyond his years. At other times he willingly played the clown.

As they walked home from school one day, he tried to sing an Elvis song, her oldies favorite. Unfortunately, he was at the brief age when his voice struggled to transition from tenor to baritone.

She was laughing by the time he stopped. She told him, "You sounded like a howler monkey with a sore throat." They laughed, exchanging insults until weak-kneed and breathless, they stopped to sit down on a neighbor's lawn.

Back then they didn't date, not exactly. During infrequent school dances they found each other across the room then furtively kept track, eyeing one another but never dancing together. Afterward they'd meet to sit in his truck talking about music and about the other kids. They

13

experimented with kissing. They hesitantly touched each other but never went beyond that level of intimacy. He had never pressured her.

The conflict that erupted this morning was greater in measure than any time back then or in recent months. His arguments against her being a policewoman implied she wasn't capable of doing the job, of taking care of herself. It was a dangerous job; anyone in law enforcement was in danger of being killed on the job, or worse, made invalid in some way. She could handle that grim but unlikely possibility, so he should have been able to also.

She shifted in her chair, trying to dispel the tightness in her chest and at the small of her back. Her nails dug into her palms. Then she unclenched her fists and shrugged her shoulders. Besides, she couldn't die on duty. It would mean abandoning her mother to a life alone, since Dad died. Sage was an only child, as was Laura. Laura's mother died when Laura was an infant. The identity of Laura's father was unknown. There were no close relatives.

It occurred to Sage then, that her mother Laura was one of the bravest women she knew. They had both grieved their loss of Steve, her dad and Laura's husband, but Sage was shocked at the extent of the devastation it inflicted on her mother. And the need for courage to recover was thrust back on Laura after her recent hike on a mountain trail that ended in a long tumble down a cliff.

The accident fractured her skull, the most serious of many injuries. Doctors initially warned Sage that her mother, a formerly bright, healthy woman in her mid-forties, might remain mentally or physically impaired. Sage's life filled with fear and stress, the words and tune of a tragic song. A myriad of wants and needs for her mother obscured thoughts for herself. No wonder she lacked interest in sex with Wayne.

She brought herself back to the present and looked around the empty room. Without Wayne nearby, without her friends around, with her mother needing support rather than giving it, she was very much on her own. For the first time in my life, she told herself. It was a powerful concept.

She rose from the chair and stretched. Time to take action, her last chore in the attic, sorting family photos and other keepsakes to save them from the trash or the estate sale.

The entrance to the attic was a pull-down ladder in the ceiling of her room, where there used to be a narrow stairway. Years ago, her parents had the stairway removed to enlarge her room for the work- out equipment she wanted.

The attic ran the length and breadth of the house. Its peaked ceiling was high enough for an adult to stand upright. She thought it was the builders' compensation for not providing a basement. In these areas of Florida, the sandy soil and unpredictable water tables could produce sink holes. The occasional hurricane brought a risk of flooding, as well. Basements were not an option.

She took a stool from the closet and standing on it, reached to pull the rope that deployed the collapsible ladder. Sudden goose bumps chilled her arms. A serpentine quiver crawled up her back. What is this about? she wondered. She climbed the ladder slowly, telling herself that sorting through things up there would be easy, no comparison to the strenuous lifting and carrying they did yesterday.

She paused on the top rung, succumbing to her own resistance. Finally, she stepped onto the creaky floorboards and breathed in the stifling-hot air. A bare lightbulb hung from an overhead beam. She switched it on. It lit only the near end of the attic but at the opposite end, a window under the peak of the roof cast enough light to penetrate the far corners.

A movement at eye level caught her attention. A black widow spider hung in its web. The red hour- glass shape on its belly was visible even in dim light. She saw the spider crawl, the web vibrating. She hated to kill insects but this was different. She took off her shoe and squashed it. With an involuntary shudder of disgust, she pushed the body into a crack in the flooring.

Shoe back on, she walked over to the nearest box. Reaching for it, a web caught her hand with a faint crackling sound that made her start, then shudder. The web was old, unoccupied. It occurred to her then that spaces like this were not neutral. They held the shadowy residue of human emotions, past loves and hates, fears and hopes. She coughed then shrugged her shoulders as if removing a shroud. A shroud woven through with the dross of many lives lived under this roof.

She shook off her revulsion. Walking to the far end of the attic near the window, she found several decrepit cardboard boxes filled with moldy papers and clothing. Discards. Next, she found a trunk holding half a dozen hundred-year-old wooden toys. Bright paints carefully applied by skilled hands were now faded, but the toys had been cleverly made with intricate detailing, perfect for the estate sale.

A trunk bound with leather straps and large-head nails caught her attention. It held family photos from generations when cameras, rather than smartphones, took pictures. She opened the trunk and picked up a leather-bound album engraved in gold with thick cream-colored pages. Its photos were held in place by corner tabs of paper, a method used a hundred years ago.

She removed several of the older pictures and flipped them over. No names or dates. She didn't recognize the people; couldn't guess the year the photos were taken. Her mother would know. She placed the album back into the trunk and picked up a more recent photo on the bottom. It was Aunt Bertha, her father's sister and Sage's God-mother. The woman had been given the job of Sage's spiritual training when she turned five. Sage grunted in disgust at the woman's image. She threw the photo down. Her head dropped forward while she remembered her aunt's promises. Eternal damnation if Sage committed any of a half-dozen behaviors perfectly natural for a child. She grabbed the photo, tore it in half and dropped it, shrugging her shoulders to shake off the memories.

When she picked up the album again and flipped through it two pages stuck together. She separated them carefully with her fingernail. One photograph fell into her hand. A quiver of recognition shook her to the core. This was her grandmother, Holly Wallace, one of several mysteries in the family tree. Holly had lived large and died young only a few months after birthing Sage's mother. Sage remembered her mother telling her she looked very much like the pictures of Holly. Curiosity filled her, then an unaccountable pang of grief brought tears.

She put the photo back into the album, the album into the trunk. She swiped her eyes then rubbed her damp fingers on her jeans. This wasn't like her. She reached into the trunk to pick up the album and place it in a save pile. It opened again to the same page with the same photo. Okay, then. She took it out and held it carefully by a corner. There in the glossy five-by-seven color photo was beautiful Holly, barely out of her teens. It appeared the background was an up-scale restaurant or perhaps a cruise ship. Starched white tablecloths, ornate silverware and crystal goblets revealed the opulence of the venue.

The picture of Holly revealed her large green eyes, a smooth broad forehead and wide expressive mouth in a Mona Lisa half-smile. Her light blond hair fell in natural waves that brushed her smooth shoulders, framing the subtle swell of her décolletage. Around her pale neck, between her breasts lay a gold necklace. Its delicate chain ended in a single ornament; a word formed in golden script--the word *Perfect.*

Sage shook her head. How ironic. Holly did look perfect in this photo, her fresh young face untouched by guilt or grief. She couldn't have foreseen her early death; had no inkling of the shock and turmoil it would cause. If Holly was perfect, she was also ill-fated.

Sage opened her hand to drop the picture. It clung to her damp fingers, it held her. What else could it tell her? Something peculiar drew her attention--two perfect little stars in Holly's green eyes, no doubt a trick of lighting from a crystal chandelier above Holly's head. How very strange. Stars in her eyes. Photographic alchemy had transmuted a verbal cliché into a charming visual reality.

Through the rest of the album, there were no other photos of Holly or Holly's husband or partner--whoever he had been. Sage had seen her mother's birth certificate. The box for "Father" held one word, "Unknown." The place of birth was Quebec City, Canada. She asked her mother why Holly was so far from home the day she gave birth. Laura said she had no idea. This was a mystery too close to home for comfort. Sage put the photo aside to take with her and placed the album with others in a 'to keep' box. In the idle moment following, she registered the pain in her knees from kneeling too long on the parched wooden the floor. She sat back onto her heels, then onto the floor. She took her phone from her shirt pocket and checked the time. Four p.m. At the rehab facility, her mother's last physical therapy session was over and dinner was an hour away; Laura would be free to talk. Laura answered on the second ring.

"Hi, Mom. I'm in the attic. Can you hear me? How did your therapy go today?" A little later she said, "I have a few questions for you. About Holly. Do you mind?"

"I don't mind, but I don't know much about her, Sage. I've told you that before."

"I think you'll know this. Do you have a gold necklace with a word on it, the word Perfect?"

"What? Well of course not. Where would you get an idea like that?"

"I--I remember--I was around four or five years old. You gave me some of her jewelry to play with. Some beads, costume jewelry. On my eighteenth birthday, you gave me her jewelry box with her nicer things like the emerald ring I wear. But there was no necklace with the word 'perfect'."

"If there ever was such a necklace, I never saw it. Are you going through the photos there at the house? Is that what this is about?"

"Mom, one more question. You said Holly died in a car accident. Is there anything else you can tell me?" "Let's see....the newspaper said it was night and her little convertible sports car had the top down. She went off the road somehow. Hit a tree. She wasn't in the car when they found her. Gram and Gramps didn't talk about her, much less about the accident. It was such a blow to lose her with me only a few months old."

"Was anyone with her?"

"I'm certain there wasn't."

"Did they do an autopsy? Test for drugs or alcohol?"

"What a thing to bring up! Why, I'm sure they did. It's the law for sudden or unexplained deaths."

"Unexplained?"

"Of course it was an accident. Well, there was a newspaper article with something about it not making sense, something nobody could explain."

Her mother's voice took on a higher pitch. "Why are you asking me all these questions? I wasn't there. Well, I was only a baby." She sighed.

To Sage, it sounded like a tired sigh. "Sorry, Mom. I didn't mean to upset you." They ended the call.

Sitting in the old attic holding her phone, it came to Sage that nature had decreed the most influential person in a female's life should be her mother. Holly had perished before she and Laura could fulfill their essential relationship. How had the deprivation affected her mother?

She put the phone down beside her on the dusty floor. The weight of family sorrow and family mysteries pressed on her. She stretched her cramped legs and slowly reclined, surrendering her head and upper body to rough flooring covered with layers of dust. She looked up into the exposed rafters, then turned her head to the sides. No more spiders, no webs. She stretched her arms above her head then lowered them and relaxed into a meditation pose taught by her *Taikwando* trainer.

With a deep exhale of breath, tensions in her back relented and the pain in her knees ebbed. With tired deliberation, she slowed and calmed her breathing while words whispered in her mind, letting go...letting go. Awareness of her surroundings, of her body, faded into serenity. She floated in a nameless void, aimless and exquisitely comfortable. Into the void, the picture of Holly in the photograph entered. Sage and Holly. Sage who looked so similar to Holly. Sage *as* Holly. Their identities began to merge, slipping from one into the other. Sage no longer *saw* Holly; Sage *was* Holly.

The ears of a dreaming Sage registered sounds, riffs of smooth jazz, muted laughter and animated conversations, the clink of champagne-filled crystal flutes and fine China dinnerware. While she listened, cool air caressed her bare shoulders. Then she saw, saw through Holly's eyes, her hand grasping the stem of a wide-rimmed champagne glass. In the golden liquid, tiny bubbles burst in joyous abandon while the tingle of champagne lingered on her tongue. She

20

was aware of her body, the pressure on her toes from elegant high heel shoes made of the same rich, green satin fabric as her dress.

As Holly, she turned her head to look around. She felt the feathery touch of a gold chain around her neck and knew the golden word resting between her breasts. While she watched through Holly's eyes, the young man beside her stood, bent down to whisper something in her ear, then turned and walked away from their table.

What did he say? "Holly, you are so beautiful, so nubile."

Nubile? The word penetrated Sage's consciousness, popped the dream bubble and brought her awake. Her eyes opened with an instant touch of regret. She lay on the dusty floor of an attic. Gone was the elegant restaurant and the taste of champagne. It had been so real. So real she couldn't dismiss it. The word the young man uttered, "nubile", indicated a woman's readiness for intercourse and childbearing. What a strange word for a lover to say to his beloved!

She sat up, brushed powdery dust from the back of her head, shook out her pony tail, then stood. The whole thing wasn't merely strange, it was absurd. Her imagination had gone berserk. She had dozed off and dreamed she was her own grandmother.

She stretched and looked around grounding herself, taking in the photo of Holly on the floor, dusty old rafters overhead, weakening light leaking through the narrow window. Standing in the fading shafts of sunlight, she wondered if there really was a gold necklace and if so, where was it? And who was the young man with Holly in the dream? Was he Laura's father, her own grandfather? Most puzzling was what she learned from her mother. Why did the news article suggest Holly's death was not an accident?

The weighted past refused to lift. Unanswered questions gnawed at her, an un-deciphered legacy. Shutting down her questioning mind she checked in with her emotions. Sadness and confusion.

An idea, a sureness of how right it was, overcame her. She had to find out all she could about Holly and how she had died. She would investigate. If her questioning led to knowledge of who Laura's father, her own grandfather was, let it be, although that wasn't her goal. She blinked. What is my goal? Ah. To find truth, to bring peace to Holly's memory.

She took a deep breath. And sneezed. Again. A third time. Okay, my present reality is dust-motes in the air, the heat and humidity of a Florida afternoon in July, the scent of old things, old people, old mysteries.

She finished dusting herself off and pulled her dark hair up to retie her ponytail. Then she picked up her phone and the photo of Holly, closed the lid of the chest and went to the ladder to climb down into her own life.

#

## Chapter Three

On the way to the new house, she thought of Wayne again. Her mother's accident had effectively banished any thoughts of sex and romance. Yet strangely enough, it was Laura's accident that caused Sage to become involved with Wayne again after they had lost touch for many years.

For the few days Laura's actual survival was in jeopardy, Sage sat at her mother's bedside during the day; at night she slept on a hospital-provided cot. When the worst was over, orderlies still appeared at odd times to wheel her mother out of the room for a scan, an x-ray or another surgery. Sage's lingering fears brought worst-case scenarios to mind. Her simplest activities became grueling chores. Soon, she tried to work off stress by power-walking the hospital'sendless hallways.

The day she met Wayne again, he walked the hall in the opposite direction. They almost passed each other before he recognized her. "Hey, it'sNinja Girl."

"Says Sumo Guy," she answered, remembering her high school nickname for Wayne, who was a varsity wrestler. The brief verbal exchange did little to rouse her from the worried funk. She walked on. He did a neat about-face to walk beside her. "Where are you headed?"

"Oh, the cafeteria, I guess."

"I could use some coffee, too."

Sitting across from him at the table, she indulgeda pale curiosity by searching his face. He looked vigorous but as open and friendly as she remembered. They chatted a while. Sage's thoughts of her mom were a constant undercurrent; she soon lost interest and left abruptly.

During the following days, Wayne's attentions wedged him neatly into her life, to become the long- lost, newfound boyfriend. She was far too preoccupied, too needy to resist. His presence provided the comfort and distraction she needed. She was equally grateful for her work at the cafe to keep her focused on the present. She chose to be with Wayne when she wasn't at work or with her mother. The two women friends she was closest with drifted out of contact as involvement in her mother's care replaced new entertainments. Her social life dwindled to nothing.

Sage pulled into the driveway of the new house, amazed, again, at how things came together, enabling them to buy it. The title company had at first balked at the idea of doing the closing in a hospital but after Laura's doctor assured them Laura was a few days from discharge and a psychiatrist asserted she was mentally competent, they agreed.

Setting up and decorating the new ranch-style house provided an element of creative fun for Sage. She bought curtains and added other decorator touches to reveal the home's character, very different from the older, two-story home. Today she stayed long enough to hang the last two oil paintings she had brought, then gather a few magazines and an audio book for her mother.

At the thirty-bed facility rehab facility the social worker greeted her in the foyer. Together they walked down the hall toward Laura's room. "She's doing so much better this week," the woman told her.

"Therapy going well?"

"She finished speech therapy. There wasn't much dysfunction there to begin with. The neurologist said it was due mostly to shock. The physical therapists all tell us she's maybe a week from discharge."

Sage hesitated at the door of her mother's room, a hill over strategy from weeks before, when she dreaded what she would see. Her mother was often in pain, often struggling to talk or to move. Today Laura looked more normal, although she had lost weight; now she was nearly as slender as Sage. She wore the typical cotton hospital gown with her own floor lengthrobe belted over it.

"Hey, Mom. You look great."

Laura turned from her seat at a small table. She was brushing her dark brown hair with uneven strokes, carefully avoiding a small circle of staples in her scalp. Surgeons had removed a portion of her skull to ease brain swelling. Now skull and scalp were finishing theprocess of reattaching and healing. Sage noticed an inch of grey roots at the part in Laura's hair. She hadn't been able to color it since the accident.

"Mom, pretty soon you'll be able to fix your hair the way you used to, dress yourself, too."

"Sure. Dress myself as well as any smart five- year-old."

"As well as any five-year-old who fell off a cliff, for heaven's sake. Give yourself credit for what you've accomplished."

Laura smiled. "You're right. I have come a long way, Baby." She rose slowly, kissed her daughter on the cheek then moved toward the bed, careful of the cast on her right wrist and bandages on one knee. On her right foot she wore a soft blue house shoe and on the left a large orthopedic boot.

Sage resisted the urgeto assist her. Laura seated herself on the side of the bed. Sage sat beside her, taking her mother's uninjured hand.

Laura asked, "How are you doing with clearing out the house?"

"Yesterday we moved your Shaker knee-hole desk and the Pennsylvania dower chest. They fit in fine in the new place. I bought you a new bedspread. Lavender."

"Nice."

"Also, a couple more pillows. Your bedroom is all set now. Everything on one floor will be so much easier."

"I hope you don't come to regret selling the familyplace. You were born there."

"We discussed this before we signed the papers, Mom. *You're* the one who needs to be okay with it. You lived there your whole life, too."

"Well, you can't sell memories. I'll still have my favorite ones: life with Steve before he passed away, you, when you were a baby, then a little girl. My memories will make it home."

Sage couldn't think of what to say; she settled on agreement. "Sure, Mom. Now...um, I have some things to tell you."

"Good news or bad?"

"Not sure. Maybe one of each. First, I broke up with Wayne."

"Well, don't expect me to look shocked. Youbrought him by only once. You didn't seem that into him."

"How could you tell?"

"I'm your mother, that's how. You never told me he was the greatest guy in the world. I never heard yourefer to him with some cute nickname. So? He was nogood in bed?"

"Mom! I'm not going to talk to you about my sexlife. Uh...oh hell. There wasn't any sex life. That's thereason I broke up with him, because he was pressuringme and I...."

"Well kudos for you. I've always told you not to let anyone push you into anything you didn't feelcomfortable with." Laura's brown eyes searched Sage's hazel ones. "The other news?"

"Right. Well, remember I got my Associates degree in May? After that I applied to the Police Academy. They accepted me. I start August first. It lasts six months. By next year, I could be on the Derryville Police Force."

Laura was silent for a long minute. Then, "If it's what you want."

Sage didn't reply; she knew her mother intended to say more.

Laura finally spoke. "Of course I'll be concerned for you, but I'm sure you can take care of yourself. Your *Taikwando* will help."

"Mom, I doubt I'll do any spinning kicks or quickjabs. Police brutality isn't in the news quite as often these days. I certainly don't want to change that. The Academy will teach me some less forceful methods to take down the bad guys--and gals."

"You're right. You have spunk but you couldn't be brutal if you tried. Not in a million years or in any uniform."

"I guess I take after you. You enlisted in the Army. You were only eighteen. That took more than spunk." Laura shifted on the bed in a way Sage knew she wanted to change positions. She stood, waiting to see if Laura needed assistance. Her mother leaned back, lifted her legs onto the bed one by one then scooted back until she could prop herself up on pillows against the wall.

She continued. "Well, there's no point trying to escape danger. If it wants you, it will hunt you down, uniform or no uniform. I came through those years in the Army no worse for the wear."

"It must have been tough, though."

Laura snorted. "The military never sent me any place tougher or more lethal than Texas. I joined because my grandparents--of course they were my parents in a way, they raised me. Then they died within weeks of each other. I knew I had to take care of myself from then on. And I did." As if dismissing herself as subject, she looked into Sage's face. "Well, what else? You have other news for me."

"About DNA. Remember I told you I found a web site that was able to draw a family tree for us?"

"Oh. 23-Something, or Ancestry? Is that what you mean?"

"No, not at all. The one I chose is different. I did spit into a little cup for the sample, but this company analyzes genetic health issues as well as ancestry."

Laura sat up straighter. "You have some health problem you haven't told me about?"

"Of course not."

"Then what are you searching for? Are you trying to find your grandfather?"

"No. Well, not necessarily. I'm trying to fill in the blanks a little. We know nothing at all about your father, like what genetic illnesses he might have--if he's still alive--or that exist on his side of our family. Your father, my grandfather, is a big mystery. Aren't you curious about him?"

Laura sighed. "Being curious, if you can't find the answer, starts a person worrying. Being worried and not having answers makes a person unhappy. I gave up being curious a long time ago."

"Mom! Nobody can simply stop being curious."

Laura tilted her head to the side in a dismissive gesture.

Sage thought Laura's words made light of what must have been a profound decision: make no attempt to discover her father's identity. That unknown was especially significant since Laura's mother had died so young. A person's parents were role models for good or bad, vital limbs in a family tree. If those were missing, how could a person place herself in the scheme of things?

Holly was a beautiful young woman who worked as a flight attendant, but her partner could have been anyone from a talented artist to an ax murderer. The information void was a hole in the family tree, a mysterious hole begging to be filled. It gave Sage an ungrounded, worried feeling.

The start of a deeper conversation hovered on her lips. A tap on the door interrupted. The door opened. A head peeked around at them. Laura began to work her way off the bed. "Lee, come in. I'd like you to meet my daughter."

Sage helped her mother stand with an arm around her back, then went to open the door wider for the man, who entered tentatively. He looked to be about seventy years old with brown eyes and brown hair streaked with grey, an average-looking man whose shoulders drooped a bit on his average frame. He wore grey sweat pants with matching sweat shirt.

"Lee Pendfield," he said to Sage, extending his hand. "It's a real pleasure to meet you."

Sage took his hand without hesitation.

Laura said, "Lee arrived in rehab day before yesterday. We're already friends. We play scrabble and bridge." She turned to smile at him. "I wish you wouldn't try to take care of me, though. My daughter does a thorough job of that."

Sage turned to ask Lee. "You're a staff member then?"

"No, I'm here for a tune-up, like the other residents."

Laura shook her head at him. "Tune up? As if that's all *I* need. You're not the same as the rest of us. I haven't seen you in the pool doing hydrotherapy. I haven't seen you patrolling the halls in your sweats--you know, with the physical therapist holding you up by that big wide strap they use. Gait belt, they call it. I bet we look like mannequins. It's how I feel, anyway."

After a few minutes Sage felt she was in the way of their connection somehow; she left. Walking down the hall she shrugged her shoulders back, taking a deep breath. Such a relief her mother was almost back to normal, everything they had hoped for. Now Laura had found another friend at the facility to pass time with during her last weeks. Sage realized she liked Lee although she couldn't have said why.

\* \* \*

On the way back to the older house to turn off the water main and lock up, she remembered the three- generation family who saw the house, loved it, contracted for it after it had been on the market only a few weeks. Proceeds from the sale and from the estate sale would cover Laura's uninsured medical expenses, her recovery time, and Sage's six-month stint in the police academy.

If the house had been located a few more miles north of the beach, it would have been worth half as much as the price they got. Sage's math teacher had once pointed out the inverse relationship between distance from the beach to the price of real estate in Florida.

In the last fifty years, any location where buildings hugged the shore was a ripe target for development, repurposing historic homes as restaurants or other commercial enterprises. Here in the panhandle close to the Gulf of Mexico and the Bay, elaborate vacation homes, posh resort hotels, and defunct plantations reigned; private homes were few.

Twenty or thirty minutes north of the coastal glitz, modest middle-class homes like theirs formed the neighborhoods. Twenty minutes farther north, Southern good-old-boy cottages planted themselves on an acre of undergrowth and native trees. Roughly two hours north of the water, ancient mobile homes hid beneath towering pines, their decrepit aluminum facades, camouflaged by black mold and clamoring kudzu vines, surrendered into the earth.

#

## Chapter Four

Sage turned her Hyundai sedan down the street toward the old house. She switched off the air conditioner but not the blower; it would continue to release cool air for the few minutes it took to reach the house and park in front under the shade of the oak tree. For the last time. Unexpected regret hollowed her belly and weighed her heart, the feelings that accompany departures.

She noticed but didn't consciously register an unmarked white van that turned and fell in behind her. She parked, got out with only her keys and phone in hand, leaving her purse under the front seat.

The white van barreled forward with a screech of tires accelerating. It sped around her car and stopped three feet in front of where she stood. Another squeal from protesting tires shocked her; an acrid gust of burnt rubber immobilized her. The van's rear doors swept open. A man jumped out, a man with no face; masked. He grabbed both her arms. He pushed her, made her stumble backward toward the van.

Pure instinct, *Taikwando* training took over. She lunged back. Fists clenched, she jerked her arms upward to free them from the man's grasp. No room for a twisting, tornado kick. She whirled halfway round into fighting stance. Bent sideways, she lifted her leg then kicked it straight, aiming at his chest rather than a killing blow to the head. Force of impact on his sternum surged up her leg. He went down.

A movement inside the truck. A woman stood above looking down at her, a gun in her hand. Sage was hypnotized, looking into the barrel for a split second before she dodged from the back of the van toward the house. She sprinted away, across the lawn, vaulted over the side fence, raced to the back fence, vaulted over it. Panting, she dropped to her hands and knees on the hard packed dirt of a neighbor's back lawn. Gasping, trembling, she looked up. No one coming after her. She listened. The sound of metal doors slamming. The roar of an engine accelerating. She gulped air. Able to think again, she looked toward the back door of the neighbor's house. She expected someone to appear, demand what she was doing there crouched on their lawn. Nothing. The neighbors were at work.

She took stock of herself. A little winded but no bullet holes. She was unharmed. In her left hand, she held the ring with keys to her car and two houses. In her right she still clutched her smart phone. Only then the realization hit: someone tried to kidnap me!

She stood on wobbling, adrenalin-weakened legs. She headed around the side of the neighbor's house to let herself out through the gate. Then she hurried to the end of the block and around to her street. She reached her car, got inside, locked the door. Her phone still clutched in sweaty fingers, she called 911.

The dispatcher interrupted her first sentence. "Are they still there? How long ago did they leave?" Then, "Are you safe where you are? Are you injured...do you need medical attention?

After each answer, the man fired another question in a rapid volley. About the kidnappers' vehicle? Damn! She couldn't give him the license plate number or the make or model. She silently willed her phone to stop shaking before she knew it was her hand. Sweat ran into her eyes. How stifling hot the closed car was, even in the shade! She scanned the street again before she climbed out to pace the sidewalk while she answered the dispatcher's questions.

A squad car holding a uniformed office sped toward her. She told the dispatcher then keyed off. The officer climbed out and walked toward her while they inspected each other. She noticed remnants of acne scars on the officer's face over a lean body not yet filled out into manhood. He wasn't long out of his teens, she thought, with the appearance of a wanna-be instead of the real thing.

She lifted her chin, standing straighter as he approached. He blatantly inspected her body and face then introduced himself, although his name and rank were clearly displayed on his uniform. Yes, she was the 911 caller. He jotted her name and address on a small pad. "What year was the van? ...make and model? ...any signage on it? ...license plate number?"

"It was an older model GMC. No signs. I couldn't see any numbers on the license place because it was covered with mud." At that, self-reproach filled her. She cleared her throat. She would be doing exactly this kind of work before long. Would her victims be this devoid of usable information? She blurted, "Why aren't you going after them?"

"With the info you gave the dispatcher, we set up a bullseye perimeter on the roads leading to the Interstate. Two other officers are on it." He indicated the pen and paper he held, asserting this part was his. "So white van, tinted windows, no windows on the back doors, no ladders or other equipment on board? Right?"

"No. Uh, right." Her forehead wrinkled with frustration. He prodded. More questions. She remembered a dent in the driver's side rear fender--a decal of some kind on the passenger side window. The Officer touched the radio on his shoulder. "Six-Adam- Four-Five. Victim reports...." He repeated the new details to the dispatcher.

She was curious enough now to listen with avid interest. This was her first contact with police as a crime victim. She knew she would remember even the most inconsequential details forever.

The officer's questions turned to the man and woman in the van. No, she didn't recognize them, but she was able to describe their approximate sizes, hair color, clothing. Were there witnesses to the attack? They both looked around at the homes within sight. All the doors closed, the street empty and silent.

Officer Dugas scrubbed at his face with his knuckles. "Never mind. We'll canvas later. If we're lucky, at least one person will have a doorbell camera that caught something." He put his pen back into the notebook. He surveyed her from head to toe without a trace of subtlety. "You said you fought him off?" Doubt shadowed his face--or maybe it was curiosity.

"With *Taikwando.*" She turned and demonstrated the kick.

He nodded. "It wasn't enough to keep him down." He touched the radio on his shoulder. "If they were able to stop the van, I'd have heard. They probably reached the Interstate before we set up the perimeter. Won't get them the easy way.

He turned to look carefully at the spot on the pavement where Sage told him the man landed after her kick. "Did his head bleed when it hit?"

"I...I don't know. I didn't notice if it did."

He went to the trunk of the patrol car and returned with orange cones, setting them up to surround the small area where he believed the man's head struck. He said, "Oak Bayou doesn't have a full staff of investigators, but I'll call over to Alaqua County. They'll send a crime scene man to examine this area. Maybe there's a hair or a spot of blood they can process through CODIS." Sage crossed her arms over her midsection, remembering CODIS was the FBI's DNA database.

The officer squared his shoulders and shuffled his feet farther apart; it was a more official stance.

"I guess we're done for now unless there's anything else you need to tell me?"

She shook her head.

"All right, then. Stay safe. If you spot the van again or either of the two people you described, call 911." He wrote on a pad of paper then handed it to her. "This is your case number. You can call or go online to follow our progress." With that, he went back to the car and drove away.

She let herself into the house. It was cool here inside with all the blinds closed, even though the air conditioning was off. The empty house echoed her footsteps across the hardwood floors. It held a new scent of desertion. She went straight to the folding chair to sit and gather herself, to answer questions whirling in her mind.

Who would want to kidnap her, of all the people in the world? She was no wealthy trustfund gal with parents able to pay a hefty ransom. What did they want with her? Did the man intend to rape her? But then, the woman. Did her presence eliminate a sexual motive?

She needed to process this with someone other than the police officer. She couldn't think who. She couldn't tell her mother. Her mother had been dealing with her own fears since the second she lost her balance and fell over a cliff; yet fear for herself would pale next to fear about Sage's safety.

Normally, Sage would talk with a friend but her two closest women friends had backed off during the weeks Sage was preoccupied with her mother's recovery.

Could she talk to Wayne? No. He no longer fit the role of confidant. She turned to what she had come for. It took ten minutes to finish chores in the house. It was late, after six o'clock before she left. She closed the front door behind her and turned the key in the lock.

At the bottom of the steps, she looked up. Wayne's truck was parked across the street. She saw him get out. "Wayne. Why are you here?"

He turned, ambling toward her. He skirted the orange cones near the curb without questioning them. "Hey, Sage. I dropped my hat when I left this morning. I just found it." He held up the baseball cap by its bill. They were silent, waiting for the other to speak. He said, "I was...was thinking I might visit your mom at the nursing home."

"Mom? You met her only once. Why would you visit her now?"

"She's a nice lady. I liked her. I'd like to her to tell her we broke up."

"I let her know. You don't have to."

He started to say something, hesitated, then said, "Okay, no sweat." He swiped the baseball cap back and forth against his thigh while he studied her face. Then he turned, walked away, climbed into his truck and was gone.

She looked after him, shaking her head then entered her own vehicle. She sat motionless, as if paralyzed. The Beach. It was the only thing that would calm her, restore equilibrium, wash away the dust and drama of this strange day. This overwhelming need for the beach happened to her often. Never this intensely before, but frequent enough so she kept a bathing suit, towel and blanket in the back seat of her car.

It was only a fifteen-minute drive to the bay in the Gulf of Mexico. Halfway there, she stopped at a convenience store to pick up a bottle of water and an apple. She stopped again at a red light on heavily traveled Highway 98. A prickling sensation on her scalp startled her, a feeling someone was watching her or following her. She looked around, searching other cars, the people they carried. No white van, only the usual mix. Local residents' American-made cars, workmen's pickups, a few panel trucks, and many foreign-made SUVs with out-of-state license plates. Most of them carried sunburned tourists. She soon convinced herself no car was tailing her.

First today, her eerie experience in the attic had spooked her, then the near-successful kidnapping. Now she told herself she refused to spend the rest of the day in fear or anxiety.

Traffic was sparse on the beach access road. Because it was the end of the day, she found a parking spot easily. The women's restroom-cabana was empty. She changed and emerged wearing a one-piece suit. She put her purse and street clothes in the trunk of her car.

With a towel and small blanket over her shoulder, her sandals in her hand, she walked down the wooden steps leading to the beach. The warning flag was yellow today. Rip tides as usual but not as dangerous as a red flag would indicate. She saw the curving shoreline was almost free of sunbathers. Natives knew this stretch of shore from Valparaiso to Okaloosa Island as the Emerald Coast. Its waters gleamed pale aquamarine near the shore but farther out lay a deep, hypnotic emerald green.

On the last step to the sand, she saw the aqua surf was clean and transparent in the shallows. Her eyes were now held captive by the ocean. She padded down toward the shoreline, enjoying the soft white sand caressing, soothed her feet. Finally, she stood in the surf up to her knees, threw back her head and uttered an open-throated sigh of relief.

A movement from the lifeguard's stand drew her. He still sat restlessly in his raised wooden perch. She glanced at her waterproof watch. His shift would be over in five minutes. She watched as he gathered his few belongings and climbed down from the wooden platform. He turned to smile and wave at her. Damn, he was gorgeous! Most

37

lifeguards had great bodies but all of them appeared to be deliciously handsome as well.

She waded into the surf. The setting sun had almost touched the glowing seam where sea met sky. Sage loved water, all of it, from puddles she splashed in as a child, to the alligator-infested brown soup in the bayous. She recognized the beauty, the power inherent in bodies of water. To her, these salty waters held a potency far greater than those of a placid blue lake. They were infinitely more mysterious than the soil- infused waters of a river.

Foamy surf eagerly lapped at her ankles. Then she was calf deep. She lay down on the sand, relaxed her muscles, surrendering to the push and pull of the tide. A slurry of sandy water engulfed her. She allowed the tide to roll her over then back. She laughed out loud. The ocean was tumbling her, polishing and refining her like a fragment of glass. She would emerge smooth, transformed, and feeling lovely.

At last she tired of the buffeting. She walked out to deep water, swam still deeper, dove deep then emerged without her coating of sand. Treading water, she dunked her head to remove the last few grains from her ears and probed beneath her bathing suit until she felt clean again, smooth and sleek as a sea otter.

With her mind in serene stream of consciousness mode, thoughts of Taikwando practice entered. How different was this experience! Taikwando demanded movements to be quick, even violent, bent in unnatural, machine-like angles. To kick effectively she must lift her hip high, with her leg level enough to form what her trainer called a "table." Here, no need for effort, no need to bend her body to violence. Rather than opposing her, here, the deep waters slowed her movement into grace, yielded to and soothed her.

#

## Chapter Five

By the following day Sage had almost convinced herself to let it all go. Let police do their thing, deal with her attempted kidnapers. They had probably made some kind of mistake, confused her with someone else. She would forget about it.

She greeted her coworkers and manager at the coffee shop as usual. Everything about the day was reassuringly usual. By the end of her shift, she thought only about her scheduled training. *Taikwando* lesson! Her mood brightened. After a day behind the counter her fatigue always drained away the minute she stepped through the door of the *dojang*.

The *kwan*, the school, adhered to the philosophy and regulations of the American Taikwando Association but its Korean origin and influence was evident throughout the interior of the building. This particular *dojang* was large enough to contain a dressing room, which few others provided, but didn't have showers or individuallockers.

In the main room a mirror covered the entire backwall. A Korean flag dominated one end wall. Bright posters decorated the other. Interlocking squares ofblue padding on the floor brightened the area, serving the building's athletic purpose and emphasis on safety. Her *sabum,* her instructor Mr. Kim, greeted her.

"Hey, Sage. Ready to spar?"

"Who's my opponent?" she asked with narrowed eyes, as if suspicious or reluctant, a private joke between them. Her instructor always carefully matched her with a man or woman with her approximated skill level, as well as close to her height in height and weight.

"Ah, we have a new student. Experienced but new to us. Here he is. Sage Stevens, meet Taylor James."

She didn't bow since they weren't suited up. She held out her hand while she tried not to stare at him. Taylor looked young although he carried himself with a more confident, experienced bearing. He was wiry and fit, only an inch taller than she and probably weighed five or ten pounds more. His eyes were deep he with a fine black rim around the pupils which intensified their color. She tried not to stare but his lashes were long, black and curved upward, his eyebrows full. He had bound his long black hair with a leather cord.

He smiled at her, showing the whitest teeth she had ever seen. A frisson of arousal shot up her torso, hardened her nipples, then rushed upward, dispersing in prickles on her scalp. It was enough to turn her fuzzy-headed.

"Nice to meet you," she said, then turned and fled to the dressing room.

Wow! Why this rush of physical excitement at the mere sight of the man? She was ashamed, then inwardly defiant. Memories swam into her mind, detailed memories of her last encounter with her first and only lover. She noticed a corresponding surge in her private parts. No, this won't work. I have to stop thinking about it completely!

She had entered *Taikwando* training in highschool then dropped it after a few months because of the cost to her parents. A year ago, she reminded herself she could pay for it herself. The physical fitness regained would enhance her performance at the police academy as well as in the police force--if her application succeeded.

She turned to check a vocabulary list posted on the wall. She still hadn't mastered Korean pronunciations of words for many of the commands, postures, body parts, and attack techniques in the curriculum. She had learned and immediately embraced the Theory of Power. The Theory was an assertion that in striking an opponent, speed is more powerful than mass. It favored those like herself, quick and agile rather than large and muscle-bound.

During her time as a newbie, warm-up exercises had been brutal. They required extreme stretches of arms, hips and waist. Along with other strenuous elements of the curriculum she practiced, they transformed her body. She was as limber as a gymnast, arms and legs as strong and quick as a soccer player's. Her concentration, center of balance, and breath control were honed to a previously unimagined skill level.

After she viewed the word list, she put on her white cotton top, wrapped her brown belt around it then donned white slacks, helmet, torso protector and the other paddings she would need for an informal match.

Barefoot, she returned to the floor. She stretched, warmed up then went to the center of the floor. Taylor had warmed up. He waited for her there with Mr. Kim. They stood together facing Mr. Kim, who said, "Are you ready to spar? Can you compete with control, with honor?"

In unison, they voiced the required reply, "Yes, *Sabum*, with respect and justice." They bowed to him, then to each other.

They walked to a padded floor area to face off. With a spinning motion, Taylor kicked her in the side, punched her sternum, and then did a spectacular jumping kick. The inside of his foot lightly touched the side of her helmet in what could have been a stunning blow. The instructor would approve. It demonstrated his striking skill, gauge of distance and impact, all without harm to her.

Sage regained her equilibrium and focus enough to block his next strikes successfully. She landed a few punches on his torso and several kicks above the waist. After fifteen minutes, they must have looked equally winded and fatigued. The instructor called it a draw. He had paired them evenly and well. The match ended as it began; they bowed to each other. Their instructor then walked between them to give his analysis of the performance, adding a few words of praise. They bowed to him. He dismissed them, returning to his other students.

Sage turned to enter her dressing room. Taylor touched her arm lightly. "Let's get a drink later. I'll wait for you." He didn't wait for her reply.

While she put on her street clothes, Sage reflected on her attraction to Taylor. Besides the obvious physical attraction, she loved the confidence and quiet, mature acceptance he showed when he was pared to spar with a woman. Some students refused to spar with her, giving the instructor the excuse they feared they might harm her. Their arrogance didn't consider the equal possibility she might hurt *them*.

She emerged from the dressing room wearing the same shorts and collared shirt she wore to work that morning but she had changed from work shoes into sandals. She looked around. He wasn't there. Her stomach clenched as if punched. She walked stiffly to the door and reached for the handle. The door swung way from her, opened from the outside by Taylor. He *was* waiting.

"My car or yours?" he asked.

"Mine."

They said nothing more until they were on their way down a two-lane road. It was shaded by tall oaks draped with Spanish moss. The magnolias trees were almost as tall. They held waxy white buds the size of a large man's fist, preparing to burst into fragrant blossoms. Smaller roads in the Panhandle were often similar to this, tunnels of greenery, placid bowers of transit so unlike the palm tree studded four-lanes farther south.

Sage glanced at Taylor, wondering. "Are you twenty-one?"

"Past it. I'm not twenty-anything. Are you legal?"

"Yep. So, you're thirty-something?"

"Don't use it against me like that."

"I won't. Let's go to The Landing. Their rum drinks are delicious."

"Whatever moves you. I'm your thirsty passenger. By the way, where did you get a name like 'Sage'? Are there cooks in your family?"

She turned and caught his expression. The rude question was a test of her sense of humor. She said, "It was given by my mother. She intended me to be wiser than her mother."

"If I ever want sage advice all I have to do is--ask Sage?"

"I never thought of it that way. All my advice is sage advice, then. What about you, Taylor James? Your parents sewed a lot? Or maybe your mom had a crush on James Taylor?"

He laughed. "I appreciate a woman with a healthy sense of humor."

"So do I. Currently the ones I believed were loyal friends aren't in the picture. They think I'm paying too much attention to Mom. I guess you'll have to do."

He laughed. "That's not a great compliment, but I'll take it. For now."

At the restaurant they sat on the patio to sip their drinks, watched the pale sky darken into blue satin studded with sequins, tiny yellow stars. They talked.

Taylor had turned thirty before he moved to the area for a fresh start after a business failure in central Florida. His tanning bed hadn't appealed to the locals and there weren't enough tourists in the area to make it a go.

Here, he found a job as a night security guard at a lumber yard adjacent to the owner's hardware store. It was what he needed and wanted, he said--easy work, a break from non-stop duties and long hours fighting the inevitable failure of his business.

When Sage told him she worked at a coffee shop he asked for its name and location. She knew he would show up there before long. Wondering how he would take it, she told him she had earned an associate's degree in criminal justice, would enter the police academy in August. He appeared neither shocked nor disapproving. Relief joined her excitement. She had found a new friend, maybe even a new love.

He asked about her family. She switched the subject. It was too early in their friendship to involve him in the mystery of her background. He didn't press; he must realize there was something she didn't want to reveal. "It's time we head back," she said to him. "I have to work tomorrow, early shift again."

"I can't tempt you to stay and have dinner with me?"

She reached for his hand, aware of the tension between them, the sexual tension she would refuse to succumb to on this first day they had met. She said, "I'll drop you at the *dojo* to get your car. I'll give you my telephone number. We can have dinner some other time."

He looked at her with a smile that meant he was aware of how much she was attracted to him. Yes, so attracted it frightened her. He took out his phone, put her number in it.

#

**Chapter Six**

The next morning, Sage spotted him when Taylor entered the coffee shop. He smiled at her. While he ordered, he tried to talk with her but she was too busy to chat. He sat at a table near the counter to watch her work while he drank his coffee.

She saw him get up to leave but instead he came to the counter and slipped a note into her hand. *The Landing. Tonight at 6:30.* He had drawn a face with wide round eyes holding question marks. She smiled at him, nodding yes.

That evening she debated what to wear for this first date. For sure no shorts and probably no slacks. She chose a green sheath dress with simple princess lines that hugged her waist and hips.

She was pleased with her image in the full-length mirror until she turned sideways. Beneath her perfectly flat, empty stomach a subtle swell of bone revealed itself. Damn. A word from the dictionary came to her: *pudendum*, external signs of feminine sex organs. Her hand brushed over subtle swell as if to flatten it. The root word for *pudendum* was *pudere*, to be ashamed. Her hands clenched at her sides. A flush suffused her face. I am not ashamed!

That evening at the restaurant, they both chose the blackened red snapper New Orleans style, which meant highly spiced, crisp on the outside.

After dinner and coffee with a shared dessert, Sage said, "I'm tired of sitting. Let's take a walk." A pathway circling the back of the restaurant drew them. As they walked, Taylor looked her over in the dim light. "Nice green dress," he said, "like you--no fuss, no muss loveliness." The path gleamed white in the moonlight, paved with sand holding crushed sea shells. It led them

45

through a stand of hundred-foot-tall pine trees. Their footsteps crunched tiny shells and nudged against downed pine cones. They didn't speak, enjoying the balmy, scented air.

They entered a small clearing. Taylor put his arm around her waist, pointing with the other hand. "Look, Venus is there with the moon tonight." The upper part of the moon's orb was faintly visible, as if glimpsed through a veil. Beneath it the rest appeared as a slender crescent of dark yellow, a golden chalice that held the planet Venus, a gold star suspended in the moon's embrace.

"So beautiful," she said and turned to see him staring at her. She said, "You're a star-gazer. I'll bet you memorized the names of all the constellations."

"I did. Right this minute, though, I prefer gazing at you. Your face is beautiful in this light. In any light." He drew her close, kissed her lips. Her eager response prolonged the moment. Mouths and tongues met, explored. She felt his body press closer to hers, felt it needing her.

She broke away first, breathless, her heart pounding. She turned away from him to recover herself. How strange, to learn a man's body by kicking and punching it, to know it attacking and yielding, then realize a desire to know it in this way, too.

He stepped close again to embrace her from behind. He lifted her hair. She felt his lips on the back of her neck. Her breathy response encouraged him. His kissing became nibbling, then tasting with his tongue, while his hands slipped around her breasts.

"I want to make love to you," he whispered. His arms grabbed her shoulders; he tried to turn her around. She turned but stepped back, away from him. She started to speak but had to catch her breath. Then, "We can't do this. We met only yesterday. We're practically strangers."

He smiled, tense but restrained. "I know you, Sage Stevens. You're beautiful, strong, honest and ambitious. You intend to be on the good guys' team. You don't know you already are."

"Then you must be a good guy, too. I wouldn't feel this way about you if you weren't."

"That's enough for now then," he said. They embraced, kissing again. She turned in his arms to look up at the darkening sky, inhale the scented air and envision moonlight on the Bay. A scene from a very old movie flashed in her mind. She moved sideways, taking a few swaying steps as if in time to music.

"Ah, so you think you can dance. Let's see if it's true." He raised his arm and twirled her under his own arm, spun her around again until she was close and almost fell against him.

"I didn't lose my balance."

"No, you didn't. He grabbed her hands. "You are too amazing, too luscious to be true. Now, are you going to tell me again that we can't make love?"

She laid her cheek against the hollow between his shoulder and neck, wondering why she was comfortable in this defenseless embrace. Breathing in the maleness of his skin, she remembered the active birth control method she used. It was a conscious, logical thought in spite of the fact her body and mind were awash in the chemicals of desire.

She said, "Let's go. My car, my place. I'll drive."

They walked back to the car holding hands, silent. It took only ten minutes to reach her home. Before she could close the door, he took her in his arms, kissed her face many times, then rubbed his body against hers. The hardness of his erection sent electricity through her, an urgency of desire. She said, "Let's take a shower together."

She led him to the bathroom. They undressed face to face, silent, without touching while their slow, mindful removal of clothing spoke for them. Since their intimate coupling was now assured, Sage wanted to prolong and savor the experience.

They stepped into the shower. He took the soap in his palm and began to wash her body, spending a long time on her breasts, her buttocks and her small patch of red/brown hair. His teasing hands stimulated her to the point of climax while she tried to swallow her groans of pleasure. Her open-throated purr inexplicably erupted into laughter.

He said, "I didn't know that was a funny sensation I was giving you, woman."

She grabbed the soap. "It reminded me of my Aunt Bertha. Now your turn."

"What?"

"Aunt Bertha thought all bodies were...nasty. Forget it." She began to swab his body with the wash cloth.

"Hey, take it easy! It's not your dirty car you're washing here." When they had almost finished drying themselves, she grabbed his hand and pulled him into her bedroom.

Naked on the bed, they faced each other. She placed her palm on his hip, moved it slowly down to his knee, hooked her hand behind it to pull him close. He grabbed her hand. "Wait. We have some important things to discuss."

"What?"

"Like what position is best...do you want to be on top, for example. Some women climax best that way. On the other hand, would you prefer something more creative, more athletic? Oh, then should I spend some time first on that special little part you have that's so sensitive, before the main event? It's small, but I'm sure I can find it."

"Taylor! Why are you stalling? You're not some eighty-year-old with erectile dysfunction."

"Wait. A few more decisions. Are we going to talk while we do it, and if so, are dirty words allowed or does it have to be romantic stuff?"

"Shut up," she said, laughing. She grabbed and squeezed the thing she was most interested in. He grunted and growled, imitating a tiger. She turned onto her back. He fairly vaulted on top of her to enter her quick and smooth, without direction or assistance.

At work the next day, she had a hard time with customer service. Lack of sleep would usually slow her down, but today she was energized, so exhilarated it was hard to concentrate. How could she smile at customers, ask them nicely for their order, while her head recreated an image of Taylor--his blue eyes...intense blue eyes, his smile...his laugh...his lips    No, she couldn't go there, unless she wanted to deliver a macchiato with mint rather than caramel flavor. She told herself, I'm too mature for this kind of infatuation--no matter how wonderful he is.

Before the end of the shift, obsessing about Taylor shifted to shock at how things had gone last night. It could have been a one-night stand, her first. Except it wasn't. He sent a text at midnight and again this morning. He called to say he wanted to meet her for lunch tomorrow rather than an evening date because his shift at work was from late afternoon till daybreak. He would be working that night-guard shift most of the time.

* * *

Two days later, Sage began to straighten the house to make it ready for her mother's homecoming. She polished the dining room table while her mind wandered over thoughts of Taylor. Until she realized she had effectively put the attempted kidnapping out of mind. It was by far the most bizarre thing that had ever happened to her. Not only had she put it out of mind, she hadn't had nightmares or other symptoms of PTSD.

She called the police station. They had no news; had made no progress. The crime scene officer hadn't found usable DNA at the site of the attack. Surveillance cameras along the white van's presumed route were either not working or showed nothing of interest.

Yeah, much as she expected. As large an event as it was in her mind, it was an attempt only; she was a virtually unknown person; she had no ties to previous crimes or criminals. Thus, she was sure the case was very low priority from the police force perspective.

With no new information to spark her memory it was easy to stay present. She did errands and, in the evening near dusk, went to the beach again. The surf appeared unusually calm; the under-tow flag was green. She gazed far out.Several dark fins rose to break the surface then the archof smooth, black backs. Bottlenose dolphins leaping and playing. They were relatively common along Florida coasts but she loved every glimpse of them.

She waded out, then swam further into deep water. Perhaps she could get a closer look at one of thedolphins, or even interact with one.

Suddenly she spotted a dark shape under water. It moved fast, straight at her. Not a dolphin. A shark? Adrenalin jolt!Before she could draw up her legs to swim, it smashedinto her. She screamed. She jerked her legs up. Her arms began to stroke for shore. A quick, desperate look down. The shape twisted, turned. She held her breath, stroking harder. Something rose to the surface. It was...a human face.

The man blinked at her, wiping his eyes. "Damn! I'm sorry. Did I hurt you?"

Sage treaded water. "I...you...no you didn't. You scared the...you scared me!"

The face of the man in front of her looked as shocked as she felt, his dark eyes wide. She turned toward shore. Pain bloomed in her leg. "Ow!"

She didn't know he was behind her until he said, "You are hurt. Here, uh, let's get to the beach." He took one of her arms. She shook off his grasp and continued swimming. He swam close beside, watching her. They reached the shallows. Walking to shore, the twinge in her knee returned, making her limp.

"Oh, I'm so sorry," he said, still behind her.

"I'm okay. It's nothing." She tried to control the limp while she walked to her blanket and sat down. He came near and looked down at her. "I'll take you to the emergency room."

"Absolutely not. My knee will be fine. I will be fine." She looked up again. He was a head taller than she, more than six-feet, with a lean, muscular body and a face that was strangely generic in character. Except for his eyes. They were slate grey in color and his lids drooped at the outer corners like...like Paul McCartney's? No. More comparable to an actor she had seen in old films, a little man with droopy eyes and a soft, creepy voice.

She noticed again the pale skin of his body. He appeared strangely monochrome, like the man in the same old black-and-while films. The setting sun cast a blurring sheen over his image. His black hair and dark eyes contrasted with his upper body, so pale it glowed with a faint greenish tint.

She began to wipe herself down with the towel. "You're not from around here, are you?"

"No. I am such a clumsy fool to bump into you like that. But then I don't always keep my eyes open under water." He gestured toward the blanket to ask if he could sit down. She nodded.

"Is it my pale skin or my clumsiness in water thattells you I don't live around here?"

She stopped toweling her hair and smiled at him."Both. I'll bet you have a desk job in--let's see--Alabama or Georgia."

"It's Georgia. I'm outed. A stranger in a strange land. My name is Wagner, Otto Wagner." He reached down to shake her hand and said, "I heard you natives call this the 'Redneck Riviera' because of people such as me."

"We do indeed. My name is Sage—like the desert plant. But I can't say I'm pleased to meet you."

He laughed. "Perfectly understandable, my dear."

She couldn't help but smile. "So, I'm sure you're not a redneck. Let's see, you're here too late for spring break--not thecollege type anyway--and now it's tourist season."

"I am much too mature for spring break, Sage, unless I came to spy on an offspring, of which I have none. Regrettably, I don't have the excuse of being a tourist. I'm here on a business trip—a few weeks or so only."

He rubbed his face then cupped both hands over his scalp, pushing down to squeeze out the water, which trickled down the back of his neck. Watching, she noticed grey hairs among the jet black.

He said, "Look, it's late. I'll bet you haven't eaten dinner yet. Neither have I. If you won't let me take you to the emergency room then let me take you to dinner."

The faintest unease whispered caution to her. "That's nice of you, Otto, but I have to say no."

"Oh, I understand. You know nothing about me. I'm from Dwightsburg, Georgia. I'm with Denham Communications. You've heard of it?"

"I don't know the town or the company at all.

He laughed. "And why should you, Sage Stevens? But my dear, you feel safe here on the beach, don't you?" He gestured at several couples strolling in the shallows, fully clothed but barefoot. The beach was seldom empty of human presence. She nodded her agreement. She did feel safe here and with this man.

"Then I'll go find our meal--something we can dine on here. Let me do that, at least."

"Yes, okay. It's been a long, tiring day. Pizza and a coke would be great." It was assent enough for him. She watched him go with long strides to ascend the top of the dunes and out of sight.

His way of speaking during their conversation had been a little formal, with a barely perceptible but peculiar accent. There was a soft Spanish rhythm to it, with German force of delivery. Hum. She rose and went back to the cabana to take a tepid, sun-warmed shower and dress again.

He returned half an hour later carrying a pizza topped with pepperoni and mushrooms along with a six-packs of coke and one of beer. She suggested they climb into the lifeguard's elevated perch to keep sand out of the food. They sat on the wooden bench with the box of pizza between them while they ate, drank and talked little, of nothing much, until stars appeared in the darkening sky.

Sage felt the cool night breeze caress her sun-warmed body, heard it tease the fronds of nearby palm trees into a soothing murmur harmonizing with the muted percussions of surf. At one with the rhythms of the place, all else faded away. She was at peace.

#

## Chapter Seven

The next day Sage's knee wasn't bothering her much but it might as the day wore on, she thought. She wrapped it with an Ace bandage and although she usually wore khaki hiking shorts to work, today she wore loose cotton slacks to cover the bandage.

Entering the café's work area, she immediately noticed a cut-glass vase holding a large bouquet of pink roses commanding the highest shelf. They were impossible to miss.

Her coworker Kaylee came through the door. She grabbed Sage's arm. "The flowers are for you. I put them up there where we can all enjoy them." She grinned. "Who is he, when did you meet him and have you done the deed yet? Is this one of those 'spank you, then thank you' bouquets?"

Sage chose to laugh rather than let it annoy her. Kaylee was the youngest of the baristas, ever curious and heedless of personal boundaries.

"I have no idea who sent them. I'll have to look. After I get my shoes." With Kaylee following, she went back to the small employee room where workers hung their aprons and stashed their work shoes. With those on, she went back to the service area and took down the vase. Sprigs of baby's breath and fern completing the arrangement. She plucked out the small florist's card while Kaylee's hands moved among the stems. "Look," Kaylee said, "the florist screwed up. There are only eleven."

"No, they didn't screw up." Sage held the card up so Kaylee could read the message, "You're the twelfth.Otto."

"What does that...? Oh!" Kaylee grabbed her arm. "That's so romantic. Is he in love with you?"

"I only met him yesterday, Kaylee, and it sounds a little too smarmy for my taste. My mom would call it 'corny.' He's about her age. Well, closer to her age than mine." She lifted down the vase and hurried back to the employee room to plunk it on top of a refrigerator. Then she returned to take her first order of the day with Kaylee working beside her. Minutes later she turned to whisper to Kaylee, "Red roses are much nicer than pink."

\* \* \*

Eleven-thirty a.m., time for Sage's lunch break. Kaylee would go at noon. Before she went to the back room, Sage checked her phone. There had been a call from Otto then a text asking her to meet him for dinner tonight. She sent a short message to decline, saying she had plans. Then she went to the window to check the weather before she went outside. Was that the tailgate of Wayne's truck pulling away? Couldn't be. She would have seen him if Wayne had come in.

The door swung open. Sage turned, did a double take. It was Otto. She said, "Oh. Hello. I sent you a message to say I can't meet with you tonight."

"And I regret it." He glanced down at her legs. "I came to see how you are doing with your unfortunate knee injury."

"Otto, it was nothing. You're not still harboring guilt from our underwater collision, are you? Please forget it."

"As you wish. But I do like coffee. Sometimes strong and black, maybe an Americano or sometimes in the afternoon, a latte."

"We can certainly give you both," she said. "Thanks again for our dinner last night." He nodded but remained facing her instead of sitting down, then turned, looking toward the higher shelves on the wall behind the counter.

Sage guessed what he was expecting to see. "Oh, thank you for the roses. They're beautiful but I wish you hadn't."

He smiled and shook his head. "It pleased me to do it, my dear. Do you have a few minutes to talk with me? Outside?"

"Uh, sure. It's time for a break."

"Fine. I will come back afterward for coffee." She removed her apron and went to hang it up, ignoring the blatant curiosity on Kaylee's face as she darted glances at Otto.

It made Sage aware of his appearance as they walked out. His straight dark hair was slicked back off his face. He wore beige slacks with brown shoes too stylish to be anything but expensive, hand-sewn Italian. His shirt in pale blue cotton was meant to be worn outside the slacks, with subtle embroidery detailing on the button placket and straight hem. It was a common style in the tropics and semi-tropics.

They stepped from an efficiently air-conditioned interior into the stifling heat of midday, where a glaring sun assaulted them. Otto took his sunglasses from his shirt pocket to put them on. In seconds the lenses fogged up to a misty, opaque white. He grumbled, took the glasses off and tried to wipe them dry with his handkerchief. Sage watched. His handkerchief was damp; the air was humid; it didn't work. He grumbled again and put the sun glasses back in his pocket.

Sage looked into his grey eyes and smiled. "Welcome to Florida. You get eighty percent humidity along with the sunshine."

"It's almost this torrid in Georgia, at least by the coast. To answer your question, I no longer feel guilty regarding the other day's accident but I would be happy to improve our friendship after such a painful beginning. Please reconsider--have dinner with me tonight. A nice restaurant, maybe the Magnolia Inn?"

Sage hesitated. It was flattering, even a little embarrassing, the interest this virtual stranger was showing her. She did not have the same interest in him. "Otto, I have to decline."

"Didn't we have a pleasant time at the beach the other night? I'm sure you know by now I am a gentleman."

"Yes, I can see you are. I appreciate your courtesy."

He stopped, took her hand in his and patted it. "If you have a boyfriend-- you must, you're too young and too pretty not to--I am much too old to compete for such a role. I'm new in town. I confess I'm a little lonely--at a loss for what to do in my spare time. I would be grateful if you would show me a bit of southern hospitality--at my expense, naturally."

"Thank you, Otto. Yes, I am in a relationship. But yes, I do consider myself a hospitable person, always open to a new friendship. I've never been to the Magnolia Inn. Can we meet there at seven?"

* * *

That afternoon at home, Sage kicked off her sandals to absorb the coolness of the tile floors. She took off her bra, grabbed a soft drink from the refrigerator and sat down at her computer. Memories of her failed kidnapping had brought her a new awareness of the need for personal safety. She accessed the internet to Google Otto Wagner.

Otto Wagner's company, Denham Communications, specialized in cyber security for large corporations. He had been with the company five years frequently traveled to South America and the Middle East. She found a social media site to discover he was unmarried. His hobbies were playing tennis and golf. His mother's given name was Gerta. The site did not reveal her maiden name, probably for security reasons. She followed a link to another site which told her Otto's father, Wilfred Wagner, was born in Argentina but was now deceased.

One more step would help her feel comfortable with Otto, the stranger with a strange name. To check for a criminal record, she allowed Pay Pal to charge her credit card a small fee for a site with relevant information. No entry, no record.

Back on LinkedIn, she learned he attended high school and undergrad college in Argentina, where he received his bachelor's degree in computer science. He earned a master's degree in Georgia. It was all very unremarkable, boring but reassuring.

At dusk, Sage drove down a long, curved driveway in what had once been a large sugar plantation. Magnolias and ancient oaks with thick, angled limbs lined the road. Brown, crepe-like Spanish moss draped their gnarled limbs, dowager's drab shawls.

He waited for her inside the restaurant. A hundred years ago it was the elegant home of the sugar plantation's owner. Peach colored rugs on hardwood floors and mahogany woodwork separated seating areas into cozy alcoves. White linen covered tables which held beautiful place-settings with glowing candles.

After the host had seated them, Sage said to Otto, "This place is lovely. More posh than I expected."

"A beautiful backdrop for a beautiful woman. You look wonderful in white, my friend. The contrast with your tan and your red-brown hair is lovely."

The compliment was nice but personal. She didn't reply.

He was quick to read her. "Sorry." His mouth turned down in a self-conscious expression. It complimented the droop of his eyelids, like the expression of a comically sad clown. He said, "I suppose I am a little too South American in the way I speak to women. I grew up in Argentina.

There, one says those things to friends and family as well as to lovers. Again, I consider you simply my hospitable friend. So. What will we dine on tonight? What is your pleasure?"

Over dinner, Otto talked about Argentina, then about the things he had seen on his trips to Qatar, Dubai and the United Arab Emirates. In spite of her interest, he avoided specific details regarding his cybersecurity work.

Otto, in turn, asked Sage about her education. She told him her plan to attend the police academy. Their conversation eventually touched on her *Taikwando* and other physical fitness activities, including her background as a swimmer. She had been on the swim team in high school. As a result, she was offered a fullcollege scholarship to play the sport. He was too polite to ask why she had chosen police work over a tuition-paid college education.

After coffee and dessert, he walked outside with her to wait for the valet to drive her car around. Then he clasped her hand with both of his, smiled and thanked her several times for her company, ending with the hint of an old-fashioned bow.

#

## Chapter Eight

Sage brought in the mail and sat at her desk in the office she would share with her mother. In the oblong-shaped room, a large window on the right provided ample light. Their desks sat back-to-back, hers against the near wall, her mother's against the far wall. A large painting of yellow roses by Laura's best friend graced the wall above her desk. Photos Sage had snapped of the beach and of wild flowers colorfully decorated the wall above hers. Thus, the décor's theme of natural beauty evolved without plan.

Sage tore open a large brown envelope that had just arrived in the mail. An hour later, she called her mother. "Mom, I got my DNA report."

"Your report. That brings back memories. When you were in grade school, you'd come bouncing into the house saying, 'Look, I got my report card.' It was always good – and sometimes great."

"This is a report card too, in a way. Except I didn't work to earn it. All I did was get born."

"Well, I might have had something to do with your getting born. Is it my report card too, then?"

"Uh, sort of. Can I come over to show you?"

"Sure. We're having breakfast but by the time you get here we'll be finished." By "we" she of course meant Lee was with her, as usual.

Sage walked down the hall to her mother's room. Doubt suddenly hitched her stride and made her stop. How would her mother accept this new information? Would it provoke bad memories or curiosity? Would it make Laura more open to learning about her parentage, her ancestry? Well, why not?

Sage reminded herself she might be taking too much for granted. Was she too preoccupied with her own curiosity to make an accurate assessment of her mother's point of view? But then, the world had tilted on its axis in the last few days for Sage. The attempted kidnapping, Taylor, and then Otto.

The door to her mother's room stood open. Laura was seated in the only easy chair while Lee sat on a folding chair by her side. Their heads were close together as they talked. Her mother looked up. "There you are, Sage. Come say 'hi' again to Lee."

Lee stood to greet her, smiling. She offered her hand, something she seldom did when meeting someone for the second time but she felt strangely comfortable with Lee already. Perhaps it was because her mother obviously did.

They exchanged a few perfunctory remarks while her fingers traced the square edges of the envelope she held. Lee didn't leave as she expected. He sat down again.

She pulled another chair over to join them and placed the envelope on her lap. Tapping it, she said, "Mom, a lot of this DNA report is good news."

Lee started. He looked as if he had been struck by a disturbing thought or even a sudden pain. Sage noticed then dismissed it. She turned back to her mother. "I couldn't afford to have them do the family tree yet; this is the medical part." Maybe now Lee would leave to give them privacy. He did not.

She pulled out a sheaf of papers. Something smaller fluttered to the floor. Lee bent to pick it up. He clutched the thing, then stayed bent over in that awkward position, staring at it. His hand began to shake.

Laura put her hand on his back. "Lee. Are you okay?" He sat up slowly. Sage saw what he held in his trembling fingers. It was the picture of Holly she had brought to show her mother. Abruptly, he flung it onto Sage's lap.

61

"I'm fine," he said, his voice quavering. He gulped.

Laura took the photo from her daughter's lap. "Sage, what is this? Oh! This is what you were talking about when you called me from the attic the other day. I haven't seen this photo in years. There's that necklace I didn't remember. It does say 'Perfect'."

Lee rose abruptly. Color darkened his tanned face to a muddy hue. "Nobody is perfect." He turned to Sage. "Nobody is perfect! Remember it." He turned and strode out.

Laura struggled to rise from the deeply cushioned recliner, calling after him, "Lee!"

Sage went to the doorway to look down the hall. "He's gone, Mom."

Laura sank back down. "For heaven's sake. What was that about? What upset him so much?"

"Mom, is he your boyfriend?"

"Of course not! He's just a kind and considerate man. We enjoy talking to each other. He's a friend."

"Well, your friend was downright rude to me."

"I didn't know he could act that way--so--so abrupt. He owes you an apology."

"He certainly does."

"I'll talk with him later." Her fingers twisted around each other until she flinched at the responding pain in her broken wrist. Her lips bent into the semblance of a smile. Turning to the pages on her daughter's lap she said, "Now what is this DNA thing you wanted to tell me about?"

Sage shuffled through the papers, trying to refocus but still wondering what had provoked Lee's display of intense emotion? The word 'perfect'? It meant something extraordinary to him but what that was, she couldn't imagine.

"Sage?"

"Oh. Sorry, Mom. Back to DNA. It appears we have an interesting mixture of blood in our veins. We'll live to a hundred years or more."

Laura tilted her head at a skeptical angle. "Is it those mixed bloodlines that'll keep us going?"

"I'm not sure. It's the Iberian Peninsula, maybe Italian or Spanish, a mix of those for me, along with the rest. We knew Dad was English/Irish and you're English with some Scandinavian thrown in. Holly looked like she was part Swedish or Norwegian with her light blond hair."

"Why do you keep talking about her, Sage?"

"Well...so it's probably your father who gave me about ten percent Italian or Spanish DNA."

"Did you really need to know that?"

Sage bit down a rude reply. She grabbed the sheaf of papers and thrust them at her mother. "I also needed to know I'm free of all twenty DNA markers for the most devastating hereditary diseases--breast cancer, colon cancer, Alzheimer's and Huntington's Chorea. It means I can't pass anything that devastating to my children."

"Children? Sage, you're not...."

"No, I'm not. And I'm sure not planning on it for now. Trust me a little more than that, can't you?" She stood, walked from the rear of the room to the door and back. "Let's return to the subject. I have a gene linked to longevity. You probably do too."

"I confess that surprises me. Considering Holly died at twenty and her parents died in their late seventies."

"Holly died in an accident--or not-an-accident, I don't know. Great Grandma and Grandpa Wallace died from that horrible Asian flu going around that year. The longevity gene can't prevent accidents or contagious diseases." She sat down again. "According to this report, only one person in a hundred thousand has a combination of longevity genes along with freedom from all the worst hereditary diseases. They say I'm one in a hundred thousand."

\* \* \*

Later at the coffee shop, Taylor and Sage took their lunch outside for a quiet place to talk. They sat at a concrete table and bench under a shade umbrella, trying to ignore the street traffic whizzing past nearby.

Taylor put his sandwich to his mouth for a big bite, then hesitated and put it down on the white paper. "Someone saw you at a restaurant with some older guy night before last. A relative of yours?"

Sage shook her head, wondering who their mutual friend, the tattle-tail, could be. He leaned toward her over the concrete table. "You had dinner with some guy at the Magnolia Inn, some guy who wasn't your favorite uncle? Tell me you're joking."

"No, I'm not joking. And it's not that way at all. He's a friend. I met him the other day at the beach. I Googled him. He seems harmless. I was clear with him; I'm in a relationship with you." She picked up her sandwich and took a bite. "The food was wonderful. It made me miss my mother's cooking. I've been surviving on fast-food for weeks."

Taylor's blue eyes grew darker, his expression fierce. "We're not talking about food, about cuisine. We're talking about our relationship."

Her first reaction was to be annoyed, then she felt pleased by his jealousy. Their relationship. She echoed, "Our relationship. You're darn right. Not a casual hook-up. A relationship." As soon as it was out, she knew her pleasure at speaking the word made her vulnerable.

He grabbed both her hands in his and leaned forward to kiss them. "I'm yours, only yours."

She leaned back a bit, smiling at him. His gesture and words, so formal they almost embarrassed her, had caused a strange but tender sensation to soften the tension in her chest. She asked, "Can you come over in the morning tomorrow, after your shift is over? I have a day off."

\* \* \*

They spent the early hours of morning in bed, confirming and deepening their relationship with soft words and love-making.

Sage was first to rise, shower, dress and mention food. Taylor made coffee while she found bacon and eggs to cook. In minutes the bacon spattered, making her yelp. Taylor took the tongs from her and finished cooking.

They ate, put dishes in the dishwasher then went to the living room to sit on the sofa. Taylor leaned his head back, closed his eyes, and sighed.

They fell into a comfortable silence until Sage noticed Taylor was starting to drift to sleep. Since receiving her DNA report, Sage had been processing thoughts of Holly, of her ancestry.

Among all the other things she had recently longed to discuss with a friend, this was by far the most important, the most pressing. She leaned into Taylor, not sparing him the angle of her elbow until his eyes opened. She grabbed his hand. "I keep obsessing on this thing about my family."

"What? What thing?"

"I need to share it with you."

"Give it to me, Beautiful." He reached for her breast.

She batted his hand away with a grimace. When he relented, she related what she knew of Holly's sudden death. She didn't mention her own strange dream about the photo of Holly with the gold necklace.

He said, "What stands out in your mind most? Is it the newspaper article hinting it might have been murder?"

"That's what bothers me most. I've been thinking about talking to the reporter who wrote the story; I want to ask him why he hinted there was something suspicious about the accident. And what exactly that was."

"Where was the story? In the local newspaper?"

"Yes. I haven't actually read it so I don't know the reporter's name. The newspaper covering this area has been around since nineteen-fifty."

Taylor rubbed his face. "Then it should be easy enough to find their office, to ask questions. What else might be useful to pin down the story or the reporter?"

"It happened in nineteen seventy-eight, that summer. She was driving at night. Or maybe just the evening, with the convertible top down. That's what my mom said, but she doesn't knw anything else. Without reading the story ourselves, we don't have much to go on, do we?"

He tilted his head. "Warm weather, evening with the top down. What about the reporter?"

"He might not be with the newspaper any longer. He might nt even be alive."

"You didn't expect it to be easy, did you?"

"But there has to be a source we can tap into."

"We?" he asked pointedly. She shrugged, looking into his eyes. He grabbed her arms and drew her forward to kiss her lightly on the lips then said, "Right. I'll help. I'm in. Let's check online. If that doesn't work, we can find out if the article is on microfiche somewhere."

In her office, Sage sat at her computer which was almost new, with high-speed internet service. She found only the more recent issues of the local newspaper online. She called the local library to ask for access to newspapers from that summer. The librarian suggested they fill out a request on an inter-library loan form. It would potentially have to travel all the way up the system to the national archives for a response.

Taylor said, "Sounds complicated. Inter-library loan all the way from the national archives. Want do it?"

"Only if we want to wait for lightening to strike. It could take months. We need a faster, more accurate source. Let's skip detours and go right to the newspaper."

Taylor nodded, then looked at his watch. "I don't have to be at work for four more hours. Damn!" He smacked his forehead in mock dismay. "I have to think of an excuse."

Sage caught on. "The newspaper office is in the mall. I know it's not a man's favorite place to hangout." She swiped his knee with the back of her hand. "We're not going there to shop. Be nice or I'll drag you into Victoria's Secret with me."

#

**Chapter Nine**

Taylor's offer to help investigate Holly's death bolstered Sage's enthusiasm for the project. They left the house holding hands.

"Hey!" Her next-door neighbor stepped out from behind his Humvee, dropped his sponge in a bucket of water and walked toward the low fence which separated the properties.

She recognized the man but hadn't found an opportunity to talk with him. He appeared around forty to fifty years old with a deeply lined face and a buzzed-to-the-scalp hair cut. His body was dense and weighty, his posture rigid, although he walked with a faint limp.

He reached the fence, grabbed the top rail and demanded, "What's goin' on at your place?"

Sage lifted her chin in surprise. "I don't know what you mean."

The man swiped his hand on his khaki pants then extending it to Sage. "Excuse my manners. Ben Davis."

Sage hesitated, knowing her angry grimace hadn't faded, but she took his hand.

He turned to openly scrutinize Taylor then said, "Last night by your place I saw two vehicles hangin' 'round. Not this fella's car, either one. After midnight. Didn't stop in front but for a second. Drove around a bit then one parked down the block. I knew they were watchin' you."

"Why would anyone watch my house?" Before the question was out, a flash-back of her near-kidnapping froze her. Her body stiffened. Ben Davis looked at Sage, then back at Taylor, as if waiting for one of them to answer her question.

Sage recovered. "Describe the vehicles."

"One of 'em a red pickup. Cruised by at twenty-three thirty. Guy sat there a few then took off."

"What about the driver?"

"Didn't see him real plain. A big dude, I'd say. Young."

She inhaled sharply. "I might know who that was. Anyone with him?"

"No one else. Other one was a black SUV. A. Cadillac, it was. Came later, closer to zero-thirty. Drove by twice, real slow, looking. I was fixin' to call police but it didn't come back for a third pass."

"Did you get the license number?"

"Couldn't see the tags. Too dark." As if his next words would conclude the conversation, Ben said, "Ah, just so's you know--if you're doin' anything you shouldn't be doin', someone's watchin'."

Sage stepped closer to the fence, grabbed one of the white pickets. She gestured toward Taylor. "Ben, this is my friend Taylor." The men shook hands. She said, "This house belongs to me and my mother now. We're ordinary people. We don't do anything illegal--nothing at all to make law enforcement stake out our house. If you see anything like that again, go ahead--call the police. Or come knock on our door, and we'll call them."

Ben nodded. "Police aint my favorite cadre but they'll do in a dog fight."

"Uh, yes, I think so too. Thank you. Nice to meet you, Neighbor." She turned and strode to her car with Taylor following. She jerked the door wide, took the driver's seat, slammed the door hard. She punched the start button with her thumb, jamming her nail. She flinched, then flailed her hand trying to shake away the pain.

Taylor turned to her. "Hey, don't take it out on the car. Besides, it's probably nothing. The guy is a flake."

"A flake? I think he's a military vet. And he means well." She took her hands off the wheel and turned to him. "The guy in the truck--if it's who I think it is I can deal with it–*with him*--later."

Taylor said softly, "I'm getting an old boyfriend vibe, but we won't go there."

She drove, relieved that Taylor hadn't asked for more information. She found herself searching traffic for any glimpse of the red pickup, a black Cadillac SUV or even a white van: three possibles.

Had she ever before suspected someone was watching her, stalking her? She remembered a self-defense class she took before starting *Taikwando*. The instructor's repeated warning became her mantra: *always trust your gut.*

Now she thought, Okay, I trust my gut. It says someone is following me or watching me. What should I do? She considered it during the rest of the drive but no option solidified into a reasonable course of action. When they reached the mall she shook it off in favor of pursuing the immediate goal--her ancestor Holly's mysterious death.

The L-shaped strip mall held a grocery store, a beauty shop, a small clothing boutique and a greeting card shop. The newspaper office anchored the foot of the L in an end space near the exit. Its double doors were identical to those in the retail shops, glass with brass hand bars.

The receptionist, young with long blond hair, saw them coming. She put on her professional smile. When her eyes met Taylor's, Sage noticed a spark of sudden interest from the woman—and was that return interest from Taylor?

She ignored the passing impression and told the receptionist what information they wanted, including the year and probable months in which the article would have appeared.

"Well, that far back, I'm not sure," the woman said. "When the paper was new, they bound each edition in full-size binders with rings holding the pages for easy turning. Then, in--maybe it was the nineteen-sixties--the main library started putting the editions on microfiche. When the library stopped, the college took it up. It's probably your best bet. Check with the college."

Back in the car, Taylor said, "Look, the college is almost an hour away. Considering all the things I have to do at my apartment before work, I won't go with you."

"No problem. I'll drop you off." Fifteen minutes later when she stopped the car in front of his apartment, she expected him to lean over to kiss her goodbye. Instead, he stared at her silently. She stared back into deep blue eyes fringed by those long black lashes set beneath thick black brows. She asked, "Can we get together again soon?"

"Being your slave, what should I do but tend upon the hours and times of your desire?"

"Taylor!"

He winked. "It's Shakespeare." He bent over and bit her bare thigh. Without another word or action, he climbed out of the car and went inside.

Sitting in the driver's seat, waves of desire rendered Sage unable to move. Long minutes passed. Her eyes were closed, head thrown back against the head-rest. She waited for the tide to ebb and her brain to reboot.

\* \* \*

The college library was as she remembered it--a crash pad for students needing to snooze in quiet, a temple of arcane facts for scholars, and for the nerdish as well as those suffering from social phobia, a refuge from the hectic energy of campus life.

There, she had one lead to follow: newspaper editions from June, July, and August of 1978, the year of Holly's death. To her surprise, she found that back in the '70s, the area was far less populated and supported only a weekly edition rather than daily news. That would reduce the amount of newsprint she would have to visually slog through.

June and July gave her nothing. The first edition in August was the one. The tragedy had earned the front page. Although she was prepared, she felt a tightening in her solar plexus at the headline.

## LOCAL WOMAN KILLED IN CAR ACCIDENT

Northwest Florida Sun Gazette
August 10, 1978

William Jones

An Oak Bayou woman died in a one-vehicle crash Wednesday night on Highway 97. Holly Wallace, 20, was driving her Mustang convertible east near Fordham when she lost control of the vehicle, according to the Florida Highway Patrol. The car veered off the road into the heavily forested shoulder, where it struck several trees before coming to a stop.

Wallace was ejected from the vehicle and sustained critical injuries. According to FHP, she was transported to Mercy Hospital by first responders, where she was pronounced dead.

First responders, FHP and medical personnel declined to comment on what may have caused the accident but speculated that speed may have been a factor in the crash. Alcohol as a factor was ruled out. The report of a second vehicle involved in the accident was later found to be erroneous.

A reliable informant, who refused to be identified by name or official capacity, said failure of Steven's seat belt caused her to be ejected from the vehicle and thus sustain fatal injuries.

Sage read then re-read the words. Chills ran up her spine, surged down her arms and up through her chest. *Holly wearing the gold necklace; Holly at the table drinking champagne; Holly with the young man, "You are so nubile...."* it came back, Sage was there. She felt it, recoiling from it: brakes screaming, steering wheel jerking, body jolting, disoriented, darkness, dizzying motion. Impact.

Half-dazed, she sat back in the chair, rubbing down the raised hair on her arms. She reminded herself to breathe. She forced herself to turn to the business at hand. She transferred the microfiche image to the printer and the article onto paper.

There. A bit of her family's history on paper. This was reality. It would overtake and encompass her fears and suspicions to either deny or confirm them.

She read the article one more time. Then she sat with her eyes closed, listening to the rustle and soft-voiced business of the library continuing around her.

Holly had been murdered.

She opened her eyes again. The page in her hand was moist from sweat. A librarian near by was staring at her with concern.

\* \* \*

At home again, she microwaved a frozen lasagna, then sat down to eat. The first bite made her grimace. She had no appetite at all. She toyed with the pasta while musing that the meal was not like one of her mother's wonderful lasagna creations at all. She had never fully realized or appreciated Laura's cooking before now. It was true, she reflected; you didn't value what you had until you lost it.

Her mind returned to Holly. The news article had convinced her Holly was murdered with not a hint as to why and by whom. This must not stand. For more than forty years, twice the young woman's years on earth, her death—she herself--had not been honored with justice or retribution.

Thereporter. He must know more than he had revealed in the article. She had to contact him, talk to him. But how? Pondering, she went out to the deck, to the scent of pine trees and the muted hum of an ordinary day in an ordinary neighborhood to face an extraordinary dilemma. For half an hour she pondered her next action. It occurred that the person or people responsible for Holly's death might be gone himself or themselves by now. The challenge before her grew until at last she couldn't entertain it; her mind stalled.

Her earlier conversation with Ben returned with force. A red pickup truck. It had to be Wayne. She wipedher mouth on a paper napkin, loaded the dishwasher, then reached for her phone. She stopped. No. She hadto confront him to see the truth on his face because he wasn't devious enough to wear a mask of deceit. Finally, here was something that needed doing that she could actually accomplish.

His house was in an older neighborhood on the north side of town. She had been here only once beforefor a party when she was still a teen-ager. Today she stalked up the sidewalk and onto the steps of his porch as if she would claim it by conquest. He must have seen or heard her arrival. As she reached the top step he opened the front door. Before he could say a word, she demanded, "Have you been following me? Stalking me?"

He nodded.

"So, the time a few weeks ago when I came out ofour old house?"

He nodded.

"And outside the *dojang?* And the cafe?"

He nodded again twice. Her tone of voice ratcheted up to shrill. "And outside my new place at night?"

"Let me explain. Come inside." He gestured.

She backed away. "Not on your life. Explain it allright here, right now or I'm going straight to thepolice."

"Okay, okay. Let's at least sit down." He closed the front door and sat down on the wooden bench swing at the far end of the porch. He didn't swing. He planted both feet solidly onthe wooden plank floor, put his hands on his knees andleaned toward her. Sage stayed on the top step with her arms crossed over her mid-section. Then, in an easy, conversational tone he said, "My mom visited your mom today in rehab. We're so glad she's recovering."

"Don't change the subject."

"Then I'll start with the fact that we've been friends fora long time. I was uncomfortable with the way we ended it. Or that we ended it at all. I thought about it alot. I'd still like to be your friend. Without benefits is fine."

"So that's why you stalked me? Because you wantto be my friend?"

He ducked his head to stare at the floor then looked up again. "I had the stupid idea I would accidentally meet you again. I figured if I apologized again and we both remembered our history together, maybe we'd get back to a fine old friendship."

"We did meet again. I saw you outside my old house. You said you were looking for your hat."

"I lost my nerve. Like a dumb kid. Humble and contrite doesn't come easy for me." He tilted his head back and closed his eyes. The porch light reflected gold from the top of his strawberry blond hair. Then his chin dropped forward; he locked eyes with her. "Now I can say it again. I pressured you. I should have remembered that you aren't anyone's pushover. It was inconsiderate and insensitive."

She wouldn't let it go at that. "Yes, you were."

"I've had friendships with women before. I'm not a guy who has to have it X-rated or nothing."

Her glare didn't waver. She said, "Now you sound politically correct, I'll give you that much. We both know it's what a man does that counts, not what he says." She let out her breath and shook her head. Wayne, the most solidly normal, dependable person she knew had played a part in last weeks' extraordinary events.

She leaned toward him. "You still haven't explained why you were cruising by my house at midnight. Did you expect to 'accidentally' meet me in the middle of the damned road?"

"I... Well, it was obvious by that time you...uh, you have a boyfriend."

Sage clenched her fists. "What?"

He raised his hand as if to stem an outburst. "I saw a pickup truck parked in front of your place a couple of times in the early morning. The same truck, a man'struck. Hey, it's fine. I mean, it's none of my business. He's probably a stand-up guy. Before I figured it out, I was--let's say I was concerned. Concerned some jerk might not take your *no* for an answer."

"How big of you. I was fine when *you* couldn't take no."

"Yeah, you handled it. You can take care of yourself. But guys can play dirty--slip the woman a dose, a drug. An illegal drug like ketamine. I feared for you. But since that night I backed off because you're in a relationship."

"What does that have to do with anything?"

"I know you don't need a guy's protection, Sage. But having someone steady, nearby does provide some safety."

She considered it. Yeah, enough truth in that. Not worth arguing about.

Wayne licked his lips and swallowed. She saw his Adams apple bob. He had something more to say. What was so hard toget out?

He spoke, "It was fear again--my fear for your safety that made me such a hard-ass. Make me talk smack about you wanting to be in law enforcement. Then I realized that if you're not scared--or if you are but you're dealing with it--I have no right to insert my ownfear."

Sage looked away. When she turned back to him her face had softened. "That sounds like something my dad would have said." She cleared her throat. In a softer voice she said, "So--have you found someone, too?Some gal willing to give you benefits?"

"No one. But I'm okay with it."

"Well, like you said, Taylor may be a stand-up guy but didn't you think, at least once time, *why him but notme?*"

"Yeah. For maybe ten seconds. But everyone has a right to choose. Anyone who's smart is cautious, particular about it. So maybe some couples' pheromones can't get that tango step. They move on until they find someone to dance with."

Sage realized the knot in her gut had eased. "Right. One more thing. Tell me how you found time to stalk me. Don't youwork at your dad's car dealership?"

"He promoted me to maintenance supervisor. I'm the boss of the department. I take time off if I need to."

Sage felt the muscles in her shoulders soften. She shook her head at him. Finally, she sank down on the top step of the porch. "I believe you. You are hard-headed and relentless enough to do all that."

"Yes ma'am."

They sat in silence for minutes until she said, "I don't feel so mad at you any more. I don't like the way we ended it either. Okay, sure, we can be friends. But don't expect me to give you one of my kidneys if yours fail. Or, be godmother to your firstborn brat. Or even bake you a cake on your birthday."

He offered a handshake. She took his hand with an expression that clearly said, I hope this isn't a mistake.

He smiled and shook his head. "About calling you a cupcake…."

"Yeah. I didn't appreciate being compared to baked goods."

"Actually, you're the least cupcake of any woman I know, even though you might look it."

She leaned back against the balustrade. "Ah. That might have been a compliment. Maybe I should thank you. So, even if I can't scare them with a hand grenade, you have my back now?"

"Yeah."

"I won't need a hand grenade, you know. Police aren't supposed to arrest people with brute force or kill someone based on sheer suspicion. Something as small as a stare can work wonders."

Humor sparkled in Wayne's eyes. He raised one eyebrow. "Hell, I'm as mean and almost as stupid as any gang-banger and you scared the crap out of me."

"What?"

"Earlier, when you tore into me. You've got one hell of a death glare."

"See--it's what I said. But stop the phony modesty. You're not mean *or* stupid."

"Then we're good?"

She nodded.

His eyebrow again. And a sly smile. "Ah, then once you're in uniform, you will take care of all my traffic tickets, right?"

#

## Chapter Ten

Sage drove home wondering why she hadn't told Wayne about the two people who tried to kidnap her. Maybe because their restored friendship was too new. Memories of the assault still owned a part of her mind, the part that understood shock, fear, violence, and release.

She wouldn't tell Taylor. It simply didn't fit in with what they had together. She hadn't told her mother. Laura shouldnever hear a word about it, so new was her owntrauma and she certainly wouldn't call to talk with any of the friends who had effectively deserted her. Unshared, the experience lingered in memory, unprocessed and raw.

Suddenly the name Susan Barkin came to her. Susan was a young woman she had met the summer before on the beach in Destin, the town of Destin, a favorite playground for tourists and students on spring-break. Sage was there only because the local shore where she usually swam was closed while workers refurbished itwith newer, whiter sand.

Sage found that Susan was neither a student nor a real tourist. She told Sage she worked as a waitress in Georgia and hadcome to Florida for a change of scenery and for the superior beaches.

Susan had a way of looking down instead of straight-on while she talked. Normally it would have seemed off-putting, but Sage knew it was because she was shy; she hid her beautiful face behindher hair or by looking away. The sound of her voice and her ways were soft and gentle. Respecting Susan'sreticence made it easier to connect with her. Between dips in the ocean and walks on the sand they discovered commonalities and they talked.

They met on the beach for several days untilSusan said she had to return to her job in Georgia. Sage asked if they could call now and then to maintain the friendship. Susan revealed she didn't have a phone. Sage didn't say what she was thinking: "What!"

Susan was very different from Sage and her other friends. Why did they get along so well? They emailed for about a month. Then the messaging dwindled in frequency and eased to a close.

Now Sage remembered her with pleasant anticipation. Could she connect with Susan again to rekindle the friendship? She went to her computer where she quickly emailed a note to Susan's old address. Within seconds the message came: Undeliverable. She did a search for Susan's name on the internet but nothing at all came up. It was as if she had disappeared. Perhaps she had never existed on social media.

Sage pulled open the top drawer of her desk and found her police report with the case number. She called the non-emergency number it held, gave her name and asked to speak with the officer assigned to her case.

Instead, a woman voice came on, asking "What case did you say?"

Sage gave her the number. "It was a kidnapping. Attempted kidnapping."

She was put on hold again. She put the phone on speaker and did paper work, busy work while she waited. Her phone showed it was a full sixteen minutes later when a man's voice demanded, "What can I do for you, Miss?"

"Information. I want to know if you've found out anything about the people who tried to kidnap me."

"Let's see, July five. About ten days ago. Have you seen them again, these two people? Any sign of the van?"

"No. Have you?"

"Look, Miss! No one saw this alleged kidnapping attempt but you. No witnesses."

"Alleged?"

"You weren't able to give the officer on the scene any actionable information at all. The van you described could have vanished into thin air--or never existed."

"You're implying I made it up, that it didn't happen?"

"No such thing. I'm saying we have no information to proceed with."

Sage leaned back in her chair, wondering if this detective was someone she might have contact with when she entered the local police force. She said, "Well, then, that answers my question. Thank you, detective."

"Welcome."

She ended the call before he could. So that was it.If she continued insisting they pursue it because she hadn't imagined it or made it up, it would get her nowhere. It might even cast a shadow on her name with police at the academy before she even entered.

She sighed. Time to forget the kidnapping, put the need for a heart-to-heart talk about it in the round file with the police report.

The Academy start date was a few weeks away. What should she be doing? It wasn't as if she needed to prepare by studying. Classroom hours would be limited; besides, she didn't have the curriculum and materials yet. Much of the training would be physical.The best thing she could do was maintain her physicalconditioning.

She called her *Taikwando* partner. "Hey, Taylor, can you come over to practice a little with me? I needto keep in shape."

"You're in great shape, Baby."

"You know what I mean."

"Alright, in a few."

He arrived an hour later. He stepped inside, grabbed and spun her around in a dance. She gave him a reluctant grin. "Cut the comedy, Handsome. Let's do this." She rubbed her palms against her shorts and pulled down the hem of her t-shirt.

He walked to the center of the room, stood with mock seriousness and bowed. She took her place in front of him and bowed. He looked down her shirt, grinned, and reached. "Oh, Baby."

She slapped his hand away, with a look.

"Okay, okay!" he said.

The first move was hers, a cautious move since neither wore protective gear. He counter-moved with a kick to her thigh, which became a caress with his foot. She spun, striking his chest with her fist. He grabbed her wrist and pulled her to him. Heat, the heat of his body against hers. The physical sensations were stronger than her irritation. They swelled to desire.

Half an hour later, she walked him to the door. "It was a bust, wasn't it?" He looked down her shirt. "Damn, Taylor. It wasn't a pun."

Several days later, before their scheduled, bi-monthly lesson, she met Taylor in the *dojang* parking lot and entered with him. Their instructor near the door saw them. He approached. "This is fortunate. I have you two scheduled to spar again today. Last match was satisfactory only. I must see if there is more."

Taylor spoke. "Spar? Together?"

Mr. Kim was not a patient man. "Together!"

They glanced at each other, uncomfortable, sideways glances. The instructor looked from Sage to Taylor and back to Sage, who determined she would not be embarrassed by his inspection.

Their silence told him more than words could have. His eyes widened. He laughed, a loud exclamation of mirth that drew other students' attention. Waving away their attention with one sweep of his arm, he turned back to the couple. His face eased into seriousness again. He bowed to them both at the same time to acknowledge them as a couple. With a tilt of his head he said, "I don't recommend it. Yet who could have prevented it? I will rework my schedule. Today you will study and practice for your black belt exams--alone or with a different partner, as you wish. That will be enough."

Dismissed. As they walked toward the dressing room side by side, Sage gave Taylor a wide-eyed glance instead of the whispered comment of surprise she intended. In return, he pursed his lips in a silent smooch. The hour of prescribed mental and physical exertion that followed didn't fazeeither one and they left together.

As Taylor walkedto her car with her he asked, "By the way, what did you find out about your grandmother at the college?"

"I found it. I have the article. There's enough microfiche in the library to circle the globe, but I found it. Can we can go over it together?"

"Not today, Gorgeous. In to work early. They need me to unload a shipment of pine."

"Well then, let me show it to you, quick." She opened her car to retrieve the article and handed him the smudged paper with wavy lines. "It's messy but for a microfiche copy, not bad."

He read only the headline and byline before he turned to her. "William *Jones*. You have to be kidding! Do you believe you can find this particular reporter named Bill Jones?"

She felt her lips tighten in frustration. Why was he so negative about this? She said, "Just read the article."

When he looked up from the page she asked, "What do you think?"

"Seat belts. Did they even exist back in nineteen seventy-eight?"

"I did some research. In nineteen sixty-eight, Congress passed a law. Manufacturers had to include them. They were available but most people didn't use them."

"It raises some questions, doesn't it?"

"We need to find the man who wrote this. I've been on the computer for hours. No luck. I figure if we each take some time every day to search for the name in different areas, we're bound to find him eventually."

"How old do you figure he'd be by now? Maybe we need to look in retirement homes or in cemeteries."

"Well, if he was in his twenties or early thirties when he wrote it, he'd be in his sixties or early seventies. Probably retired by now."

"Or dead."

Sage put a hand on his shoulder. "Are you going to work with me or not?"

"All I can, Babycakes. I'll start with Georgia; you stick to Florida. We'll hope he didn't move to Timbuktu."

#

**Chapter Eleven**


Sage determined to think only of the mystery around Holly's death in the remaining weeks before her world became the Academy. She looked up the name Jones and William Jones in the white pages online. Only four in Oak Bayou. Four phone calls produced four different responses, none positive. She took out her map of the area, found the dot indicating her town. She consulted the map's scale then drew a circle with a one-hundred-mile circumference. Then she scanned the maps for all populated locations within the circle. Those locations added eight more William or Bill Jones's.

She reached for the land line. It felt wrong, stepping into people's private lives with questions. Well, police work would eventually require calls, interviews, questions, violating physical boundaries as well.

She started with the first number on her list with her most pleasant but matter-of-fact voice. In an hour of searching for reporter William Jones she eliminated all but three names, those whose phones didn't answer or asked her to leave a message.

She rose, stretched her arms and went out to the deck, where she took in the smell of damp earth, green growth and pine needles. She sat to watch squirrels scamper and spar in the tulip tree. An unbelievably fast, agile one stopped suddenly. He twitched his tail, rotating it in a circle to sass his opponent. She laughed out loud.

Before long she felt her cotton shirt clinging to her back from the gathering humidity; time to go inside.

What now? The newspaper again. The receptionist hadn't been able to tell them anything. In this call, she asked to speak with the person in charge. After frustrating discussions in which she denied her interest in personal ads, subscriptions or obituaries, she convinced the receptionist to transfer her to the editor-in-chief.

"I'm sorry I can't help you," he said. "It was a long time ago, years before I started with the paper. Even if those records existed, I couldn't give them to you. We never disclose information concerning a reporter-- except his name and e-mail address. That much hasn't changed. People can get upset over the more disturbing facts we have to print. They often blame the people who write the stories."

"I understand. I looked on my own. I searched the name on the computer in Oak Bayou then within a hundred miles around. I made twelve calls to different Joneses, with no luck."

"Too bad. I'd be shocked if you found him so easily. Reporters come and go in a small-town paper like ours, unless they have family in the area and no ambition. Most of my people don't stay long. They move around, try to work their way up to the big time, win those Journalism prizes, maybe even the Pulitzer."

\* \* \*

One early morning after her fruitless talk with the newspaper editor, Sage came into the house from her front porch where she had watched the sun rise, a glorious production in gold and scarlet, extravagant beauty rivaled only by Florida sunsets. In the bedroom brushing her hair, she suddenly dropped the brush on the dresser and went to Taylor, folding her arms around him. "Come to the beach with me."

"The beach? All that water?" He made an exaggerated grimace. "You know what fish do in water?"

She laughed. "Everything, wise guy."

"No, I'm not fond of the beach." He slipped his foot into the other shoe. "Sand gets into the worst places."

She squeezed his shoulder. He was funny, made her feel desired and...and the way a normal woman felt. She sensed Taylor's complete acceptance while Wayne's objections to her joining the police force had made her question her wisdom--even her femininity. The beach, she remembered. She said, "Well then, I won't go. It's too hot, anyway. I need to stay and look for our William Jones."

"Found anything yet, anything at all?"

"I started with the United States Census; I figured they had exactly what I was looking for. I learned there were exactly one million, four hundred twenty-five thousand, four hundred and seventy William Joneses in Florida in twenty-ten. However, there was no contact info for them." She described her other search efforts. "No luck there either."

"Sounds like a lost cause."

"Actually, it occurred that I might get information from a college. Most reporters have a degree in Journalism. I checked, learned which colleges in Florida offered a Journalism program back then. I figured our Mr. Jones entered college at around age nineteen or twenty, so I estimated the probable year of his graduation. I called the University of Central Florida in Orlando and University of Florida in Gainesville to find men who graduated between those estimated years. The registrars were wonderful about it. My list has only thirty-six names. How are you doing?

"With...with the search? I haven't found much in Georgia."

"What data base are you using?"

"Same as you. White pages from the internet. I found dozens of Bill Joneses. Common as cockroaches. My calls were all no-go. And a lot of those Joneses are damned rude.

Hung up on me like I was a telemarketer or a scammer. I think we can rule out Georgia."

"Well. Then I refuse to be disappointed; it's one more possibility eliminated. I can give you a few pages of this list to work with me."

"Regrets, sexy gal. I couldn't stand the excitement. You're stimulating enough." He grabbed and held her.

\* \* \*

On the day doctors released Laura from the rehab facility, Sage and Wayne threw a party for her. Sage invited Laura's friends from work, from her exercise class and of course several neighbors. After those invitations were in the mail, she thought of the two friends who had effectively abandoned her months before. Now her mother was well and Sage was back to her usual sociable self they might renew their friendships. She sent the last email invitation with a flourished keystroke. She hadn't been this genuinely happy and at peace since before her mother's accident. Taylor couldn't come to the party because of his work schedule but Wayne came early to help her prepare and then host the event. They had been talking or texting every day recently. Today they started by wrapping the front door with a huge welcome sign, then moved on to prepare refreshments. Wayne's mother had come with him; she helped in the kitchen. All Laura's friends and coworkers Sage had invited showed up.

Sage had told her mother about the party, thinking a surprise might overwhelm her. It was Lee Pendfield who drove Laura home. Sage watched them come up the walk together. Laura burst into tears at the 'Welcome Home' sign above the door. A room full of guests greeted her. She wiped away her tears, smiled and hugged--or was hugged by--each one. When the flurry of greetings slowed, Sage took her arm to lead her into her bedroom. "Mom, I'm sorry. This was too much."

"It was. But it was wonderful. It feels right." "You haven't even seen the rest of the house yet,
your house."

Laura didn't answer while she looked around slowly. Then, "I'm seeing my bedroom," she said, "and it's perfect— the way you arranged my antiques."

"Do you want to lie down now? I can deal with the guests."

"Nonsense. Let's go out and mingle. And have some of that food that looks so scrumptious."

They returned to the party and found Ben had left already but the others were there and beginning to gravitate toward party fare laid out on a sideboard in the dining room, buffet-style. Although it was only ten o'clock, options for drink included Bloody Mary's, Screwdrivers, iced coffee with rum, and a concoction with orange juice that Wayne called a Fuzzy Navel.

Finally, everyone had served themselves and were busy eating. Sage went to stand by her mother and Lee. Laura held up a glass filled with orange juice and vodka. "I haven't had a drop of alcohol in months--not this kind, anyway--to drink." She sipped and smiled. Lee grasped her upper arm. "Now, Laura, you need to go easy with that." He nodded toward the living room and she allowed herself to be led there to sit on the sofa beside him. Sage watched and wondered. When and how had Lee become so controlling? More to the point, what else was it about Lee that puzzled her? He had apologized for snapping at her over the *Perfect* photo, yet never explained what provoked him. The picture of Holly had made his hand shake and the tone of his voice rise. Had he known Holly? She would be around his age now, if she were alive. If he knew her, or anything about her, surely he would have told them. Her questioning mind allowed one fleeting suspicion to enter then depart before she was fully aware of it.

About an hour into the celebration the door bell rang. Sage looked toward the door in surprise; most of their friends were here already. It was a florist's delivery man with a huge arrangement of hydrangeas,pink roses and blue irises. The tiny envelope attached bore Laura's name. Sage placed the vase on the end table next to Laura and handed her the envelope. "Youhave an admirer."

"Not that I'm aware of." Laura opened the tiny note then turned to Sage. "Do you know someone named Otto?"

"A friend, a business man from Georgia. I've been showing him around the area."

"A close enough friend to send your mother flowers?"

"Probably not. He said he would be here a week, but it's been almost two. He comes into the coffee shop."

"Did you tell him about me?"

"Not much. In fact, I don't remember telling him they were releasing you from rehab today. I'm sure I didn't give him our address."

"He must know more than you believe he does.

Well, they're beautiful and they smell lovely."

Sage recalled the roses he had sent her. "Flowers must be his thing."

Lee was listening. "What's this man's last name?"

Sage turned to him, trying not to glare. Why was he intruding in the conversation? She said, "His name is Wagner. Why?"

"I might know him. Is he an old friend?"

"No. Didn't you hear what I said?" Lee shrugged. She said, "He's easy-going, generous and pleasant to be around," then wondered why she sounded like she was defending him--or herself.

Laura must have sensed the exchange should endthere. She said, "Well, I feel like I've had as much fun as I can

91

tolerate for my first day home." She stood. Sage went with her to her bedroom, then retrieved the vase of flowers to place on her mother's night table.

Laura sat down on the bed with a sigh then lay back. Sage removed the orthopedic boot, then the shoe from the other foot. She drew back the bedcovers and held them while Laura eased herself under, her head onto the pillow. She smiled, gave Sage a small dismissive gesture with her hand and blew her daughter a kiss when Sage walked out.

In the hallway, Sage stopped, leaned back against the wall and closed her eyes, smiling. A voice startled her. It was one of her friends, Carolyn. "This is a nice party," she said, touching Sage's arm. "But I had no idea your mom was so badly injured." Sage didn't answer. Carolyn said, "Can we talk for a minute? Sort of private?"

They went out the back door to the deck and sat down in the wooden Adirondack chairs complete with gently arched leg and foot rests which turned them into lounge chairs. Carolyn pushed the foot rest aside to sit down, remaining upright. Sage thought she looked uncomfortable. Eager to have it over with, she asked, "So what do we need to discuss?"

"Taylor."

"Oh?"

"You're aware he's from Gator Bay, down south?" "He told me that, yes."

"Sage, I hope you understand why I'm telling you this. I value your friendship so much. I want you to understand I won't ever take it for granted or back away again if you're in a crisis."

"I can say the same thing to you, Carolyn. This-- whatever it is you have to tell me must be serious."

"Well, I know some people down there, where Taylor's from. They tell me Taylor has quite the reputation."

"Really?"

"As, uh, as a lady's man, they call it if they're trying to be polite. Sort of a love-em-and-leave-em guy. He's been engaged more than once." Carolyn was silent then as if trying to gauge Sage's reaction.

Sage pulled her long hair over one shoulder and smoothed it down with both hands. "I'm not as shocked or dismayed as you probably expect. I can see that in him. Don't worry about it, Carolyn."

"You're not mad at me then?"

"I'd never kill the messenger, even if the news was worse."

Carolyn reached down to pat Sage's shoulder, a gesture that felt sympathetic but condescending to Sage. Then the woman smiled and walked away.

Minutes later while Sage still thought about Taylor, Wayne came to sit beside her. "Thanks for letting me help with the party. It was fun." Sage nodded. He said, "Not every woman would forgive a man who acted like I did a few weeks ago."

"Not every man would admit he acted like a stupid ass and ask to be a friend." Then aware she was changing the subject, she asked, "Hey, why were you there the day we met in the hospital? Visiting someone?"

"Yup. My neighbor's kid. He fell off a trampoline and broke his leg, a nasty fracture. He had surgery. After, he was going stir crazy in there. Even his phone didn't keep him busy. I went to keep him company. Why?"

"It didn't occur to me at the time to ask. I was too worried for my mom."

#

## Chapter Twelve


Sage shooed away the few party guests who offered to stay and help clean up then sat to have coffee before tackling it herself. She took a few sips of the steaming brew then placed the cup on a coaster, leaned back, relaxed tense muscles and closed her eyes. Taylor materialized behind her closed eyelids. Instantly a frisson of desire shot through her. She smiled to herself. Was that all he was to her, a sex object? Oh. Maybe. She certainly was that to him.

She rubbed her eyes. There was more to it, of course. In his embrace, her sexuality was resurrected, her awareness of her own personal power restored. Would she let what Carolyn told her change her feelings about him. She ruminated for half an hour but couldn't resolve it or let it go. He would be home by now. She picked up her phone. "Hey, Taylor. I didn't wake you, did I?"

"I'm getting into my uniform for tonight. What's up, Gorgeous?"

"We didn't get to talk much the last few days because of the party. There was so much going on."

"Yep. Sorry I couldn't come. Oh, about the name search, our Mr. Jones. I don't have much time for it since I do a lot of overtime at the lumber yard."

"I gave Wayne a few pages. He promised to make calls. That's not why we need to talk. You know, even when we're alone we don't talk much about serious things."

"Serious things? How serious?"

Did he think she was asking for a commitment? No, I mean our ambitions for the future, our past, things like that."

"Right now, I don't have any ambitions for the future. I tried the entrepreneur thing and it didn't work out. Your future, my love, will be fine. This is amazing! I'll have a po-po all my own."

"Taylor, please don't use slang for police. It's disrespectful."

He continued as if he hadn't heard. "Can't wait to see you in uniform. Can't wait to take it off." He chuckled. "Ummm. We can play with your handcuffs"

"Taylor! I've told you a lot about my family, things I'm not especially proud of."

"You're changing the subject. And I don't know what you mean."

"Well, the fact that my mother doesn't know who her father is. You haven't said much about your family or your past."

"My past. I get a sense you're not referring to my first car or the sports I played in high school. Sure, I have a past. Past loves, baggage from past lovers. I'm considerably older than you. Naturally I have more baggage than you."

"That's not  "

"I will not open those bags and take out each piece of old crap to discuss it with you. You need to keep yours on the down-low, too. Because I'm not going there."

She didn't answer. A single tear slid down her cheek in disappointment. More than disappointed, she felt devalued. She cleared her throat. "Well, now we've established some rules."

"Listen, Gorgeous, you know I adore you. Let's not make things more complicated than they have to be." She didn't reply, Taylor's voice came again, low and soothing, "My love, you are the juice in a ripe peach, the melody in a love song, the color in a rose."

"Really? Shakespeare?""Uh, maybe. Probably."

"Good enough. I'll let you go now, Taylor. I've got some clean-up to do." She plunked the land-line receiver back in the charger and scrubbed at her face with her palms. Taylor had initially been supportive of her law enforcement plans. Now he joked about it--in terms referring to himself and his own pleasure. Whereas Wayne, his objections to her plan came from his concern for her. If she placed them beside each other in her mind, Taylor and his charm were empty, devoid of respect. Wayne's image stood forth with substance and strength of character.

While she picked up and cleaned, she refused to admit Taylor into her mind again. Questions about Otto took his place. Otto was an enigma even after she had checked his background, talked with him, been around him several times. She couldn't forget they way they had met. He appeared out of nowhere--well, out of the ocean actually--and quickly became her companion and benefactor. Why the concerned tone in Lee's voice when he asked about Otto?

She put the vacuum cleaner away, stowed the glass cleaner in a cabinet and went out onto the deck. She didn't sit down in one of the sun-warmed chairs. Instead, she took a deep breath of the pine-scented air, turned her face to the sun for a moment, then strolled back and forth on the pinewood planks.

"What are you doing out here, Sweetie?"

"Uh, nothing, Mom. Just lollygagging."

Laura limped forward. She reached to smooth Sage's forehead with her hand. "I didn't mean to surprise you. Is that a tiny wrinkle on your forehead? What are you worried about, for heaven's sake?"

"Nothing, Mom."

"What do you mean, nothing? I can tell you're upset about something."

"Mom! I said it's nothing." Sage instantly regretted her tone, reminiscent of teen-age rebellion. She gave her mother a quick hug. "I'll get started on dinner." Laura nodded; she wasn't up to cooking yet.

In the kitchen Sage thought she would probably burn the meat, undercook the vegetables or createsome other disaster. Why hadn't she listened to her mother, Laura's urging her to learn to cook?

While she prepared the breaded chicken breasts and vegetables, it came to her. Her relationship with her mother was changing--to what it had been when Mom was nurturer, planner and head of household. Change was in the air, it seemed. What if her whole life's trajectory was in flux, a flurry of change? Seeming chaos was an illusion, recent theories said; then what unrecognized pattern in her life directed herfate and might reveal itself tomorrow?

* * *

After dinner, they watched TV for a few hours before they went to bed. Sage was usually a sound sleeper, but this night unanswered questions whirled in her mind. Her dreams were often as lucid andlogical as waking speech or waking activities. Tonight,her unrest produced confounding dreams filled with strange characters engaged in activities she neither recognized nor named.

Around three a.m., a clear image thrust her from sleep. She lay on her back, staring at the ceiling wide eyed, replaying the dream that started with the same Holly-with-stars-in-her-eyes photo from the attic. Holly was again the main character who enjoyed the same luxurious setting. At the table with her, the same man, the same mumbled word 'nubile.' The man stood, as before in her daydream in the attic, but instead of walking away, the man turned toward Sage. In her dream tonight, she turned away, unwilling to see his face yet his eyes pursued her, caught her. Down-turnedat the outer corners, they were dark and dense as the oily smoke from a funeral pyre. Otto's eyes.

97

She woke and sat up. Her heart was pounding at the incomprehensible fusion of dream-fantasy and reality. She shivered, realizing she felt icy cold. She went to adjust the air conditioner, found a heavier robe in the closet to wrap tight around her while she went to the kitchen.

Next day she determined last night's crazy dream wouldn't put her off. She would find out more about Otto, uncover some covert intention or motive of his or else put her doubts to rest.

At the coffee shop, during a lull in the morning rush, she came from behind the counter and went to the corner table where Otto sat alone drinking his latte. "Otto, thank you so much for the flowers you sent my mom."

"*De nada*, Sage."

"She would like to send you a thank you note, but you and I always meet someplace when we go adventuring together. I don't know your address."

"My lovely friend, I fear any letter sent today would not find me. My company needs me back in Dwightsburg." He shrugged, as if in resignation. "Ah, but I have a few more days. There is something important I'd like to discuss with you before I go. Can we meet?"

Sage looked toward the work station where Kaylee was juggling new orders. She rushed to say, "I have plans for tonight and tomorrow. Day after tomorrow at my place would be okay. In the morning. I don't have to be here until noon."

"Oh, I wouldn't want to interfere with your friend's visit."

"Can you be at my house by eight-thirty day after tomorrow?"

He nodded. "Certainly." She tried to smile at him before she rushed back to a new crowd of customers.

Driving home she remembered his words, "your friend's visit." What did he mean? No, she didn't have to question it; she knew. More to the point, how did he know about her morning trysts with Taylor? And he had agreed to come to her house but didn't ask for the address. How would he find her? He must know that too--the flowers he sent to her mother's homecoming. Then she remembered the dream. His knowing eyes in the dream.

#

## Chapter Thirteen

The day of Otto's visit dawned sunny and humid, as usual in July but by the time she finished her morning coffee on the deck, clouds had begun to gather while distant rumbles of thunder announced a rare morning thunderstorm. Afternoon thunderstorms were an almost daily occurrence during the summer in parts of Florida.

She waited for him, looking through the narrow window panel on the door. He arrived in his Lexus sedan and ran up the walk without the protection of an umbrella. She was ready with a paper towel to wipe the rain from his face. "Hi, Otto."

"Hello my fine friend." He wiped his feet on the inside door mat. A blinding flash followed almost instantly by a crashing boom startled them. Lightening had struck very close by. They stood frozen. Silence. The overhead light fixture blinked off. She said, "Well, the power will probably go on again soon. We don't need a whole lot of light to sit and talk. Let's go to the dining room. It has the most natural light."

"That will work. I am not afraid of thunder and lightening and it seems you are not either."

After they were seated, she asked, "Did you have trouble finding my place?"

"Not at all, my friend." He looked perfectly at ease sitting with one leg over the other knee, impeccably dressed in linen slacks and his signature untucked shirt. Both looked a little damp. Apparently, he didn't notice.

She excused herself and went to the kitchen to get coffee. She placed the mugs on the table. "It finished brewing before the electricity went out. It's still hot."

He sipped his then licked his lips with a hint of displeasure. "I miss the coffee of my country, I must admit. It is so much richer than any I have had here, even at your excellent cafe. If you ever come to Argentina, you must be the guest of my family, the ones who remain there. We would honor your visit with the greatest hospitality possible. And the best coffee," he added with a smile.

"Thank you, Otto. That would be nice," she said, mentally dismissing the possibility of a trip to Argentina. She noticed Otto looked different in the dim lighting. Shadows filled the hollows beneath his eyes and cheeks. His face seemed to echo the dark silence of the house.

Lightening strikes and resulting thunder had moved some distance away but the electricity was still off. The rain persisted. The sound of soft drops on the leaves of many trees, spatter sounds from hard surfaces enveloped them in a muting cloak, a feeling usually soporific to Sage. Now the dim quiet felt ominous.

Otto cleared his throat. "Sage, I must now ask of you a great favor. I haven't explained to you my hobby. No, hobby is not the right word. It is my passion. To be of assistance to poor or unfortunate children."

"In South America?"

"My dear, there are poor children in every country in this poor world. Even in the United States. In Dwightsburg, not far from where I work, there is a group home for children born with some great defect. Most are from poor families."

He instantly backtracked, "I use the wrong word again. These children have some disability, a mental problem or a physical problem so the poor parents are unable to care for them. Most of these parents gave up their parental rights so the children could be cared for at the Haven. Few of the youngsters are fortunate enough to be adopted."

"That's so sad."

"Yes. Over the four years I have been on the Board, only a few went to foster homes. Several of those returned to us because they required too much care. The Haven is the only home some of them will have until they are eighteen years. Then most will go to a group home for adults."

"You're helping them?" she asked, instantly regretting the doubt in her tone.

"Certainly."

You're a benefactor to these children. How kind of you, Otto."

"I am on the board of directors. I contribute whatsmall amounts I can spare from my personal funds. I assist in fund raising, to find other contributors. Isometimes go to play with the children."

"I'd like to contribute something, too. I don't havemuch disposable income but..."

"Oh, no. I would not ask you for a financial commitment." He reached into his shirt pocket. "Here, I brought a recent newspaper article to show you." Thearticle, dated six weeks earlier, was from a Savannah newspaper. He said, "Dwightsburg is a small town south of Savannah, near the coast."

Sage read the article and looked at the picture of the facility he called the Haven. It was a large, two- story brick home set on a wide swath of lawn. The house featured four round white columns supporting the gabled roof with four windows on each side and anarched, fanlight window above the front door. A broadset of twelve shallow brick steps led to a wide front porch. A one-story addition on the side of the originalstructure featured a long, wheel-chair accessible ramp.Sage looked up at him. "It's beautiful. You have only a dozen or so children there?"

"Twelve is our capacity. As for you, I admire so much your skills in swimming and in martial arts. I wish you would come to our campus to share those skills with our children."

Sage sat back into the sofa. That's what this is about!

She said, "Well, I'm flattered you would ask me, but I've never taught swimming or *Taikwando* and I've never worked with special needs children."

"For many years we try to find physical activities they can learn and enjoy. When you come...ah...if you come, it would be to find out if they enjoy these activities. We do not have unreal expectations for them. You must play with them, show them these things. If your teaching stimulates their enthusiasm to participate, we will find professional teachers to continue."

"How old are the children?"

"Ages from two through seventeen. Our activities director and the doctor say most of the children ages eight through eleven will be able to participate. You would have a class of five or six in number." He added quickly, "At all times, there will be an attendant or even two with you. They are familiar with all the children. They will be your right-hand girls."

Sage tilted her head and suppressed a smile. It might be fun, a unique opportunity to share her favorite activities. She tried out a new picture of herself, teaching children.

Otto must have known he had piqued her interest. "We ask only a few days from you. A week maybe, ten days at most of your time and skills. The Haven's foundation will pay for your travel plus any lost wages."

Sage took her cup from the table and sipped slowly before she answered. "Otto, I'm flattered you've asked me. Actually, I would love to teach the children. When would I do this?"

"As soon as possible."

"I have another commitment starting August first. This is July thirteenth...ten days would be the twenty-third...travel...yes, I could do it if I left in the next few days."

He spread his arms in a triumphant gesture whichmade her laugh. "Say you will do it!"

She held her palm over his forearm until he took the hint and lowered his arms. She said, "I will do it ifI can find someone to fill in for me at work and someone to look after my mom while I'm gone."

"I understand. You must take care of your family as well as your personal life. So, if all goes well, will you be ready to leave soon?"

"If things work out, by next Tuesday." "Wonderful. I return also on Tuesday. You can

accompany me in my car. Now let me give you a brochure with the web site and other information that may interest you."

Unaware of the gesture, Sage rubbed her hands together at the prospect of a new challenge. She had never been around children much or done much babysitting. But someday she might have children of her own. This would be a chance to learn how to playwith and teach them, help them by sharing a bit of herself. She turned to Otto, the brochure still in her hand."Wait. Where would I stay while I'm there? Are therehotels?"

"I would offer you the guest room in my house, but it would not be appropriate, would it? No. There are two hotels within walking distance. With your permission, I will reserve a room at the best of them. Again, the Haven will take care of all the charges."

She nodded. It was obvious to her that Otto had accomplished what he had come for. He was pleased. The thunderstorm had abated when she saw him to thedoor, the rain was now a gentle mist. He declined her offer of an umbrella.

Sage went to living room, which was even darker than the dining room since the electricity had not come on. Soon she began to question herself about the unreality of this development, this new Otto he had revealed. Otto of the sad eyes and many compliments, Otto the clumsy swimmer, Otto as the young man in her dream who uttered the word *nubile*. Now Otto the philanthropist, champion of disabled children offering her a new adventure.

The house sprang to life with a sudden glare of electric lights and sounds of awakened appliances. For Sage, shadows of unease about Otto and this new development lingered. To shrug them off she put dishes in the dishwasher, tidied the living room then went to her bedroom to get ready for work. The routine didn't lull her. How did Otto acquire the knowledge of her home's address, of Taylor's morning visits and the date her mother would come home from rehab? Had he spied on her? Her neighbor Ben had described a black Cadillac SUV surveilling her house. That didn't fit with Otto's black Lexus sedan. The white van, the attempted kidnapping swirled in the maelstrom of questions. None of it meshed; the pieces wouldn't form a picture. The trip with Otto. She would arrange for a professional care-giver to help her mother with her routine in the mornings and again at night. She would be fine. It would be therapeutic for them to step back from each other for a week or so, reset their relationship in its normal mode. At the Cafe, the woman who normally filled in for absent baristas would love more work.

Oh. What about Taylor? She called. He was home from work. She gave him the briefest account of her plan. He said, "I can't take more than a week or so without you, Gorgeous. Don't stay longer."

"I think we'll both survive, Taylor. Bye." She threw the phone in her bag and left.

Otto Wagner drove away from his latest encounter with Sage smiling to himself--at last. He had never before worked so hard to acquire a donator. The two idiots he sent for her had failed, requiring this rare, personal effort. Soon he would have the reward: not only the money but the satisfaction. This one, this Sage, was special. She was worth it.

#

## Chapter Fourteen

Driving away from his meeting with Sage, Otto settled back into his seat, reflecting on his success. Then he compared this small victory to the culmination of his father's and grandfather's ambitions. Otto's grandfather, his *Opa,* escaped the end of the *Reichstag* along with the relentless process of apprehending and punishing perpetrators. His grandfather could not abandon the *Revolution der Gesinnung,* the Nazi's desire to build a superior race of men--men with strong bodies, pale eyes, but more importantly, with extraordinary minds and spirits!

His *Opa* sparked the continuation of the plan in his adopted country, pushed it forward with every clever means or brutal application of force he had learned as a General. During his very early years, Otto heard his grandfather utter the word *Rassenhygien* many times. It meant racial hygiene, a euphemism for genocide. His son's cohort grudgingly learned to apply a new set of skills--persuasion.

During the last of grandfather's days on earth, transplants of human organs, kidneys and livers became medical routine. In 1967, less than ten years before Otto was born, the first heart transplant became world-wide news.

As Otto grew up, a few among the neo-Nazi coterie tired of the extended, subtle means for eventual world domination set by his *Opa.* It was a goal they themselves would never see. They lusted instead for the instant gratification of money in hand. For a reason and by a means forever a mystery, they chose to profit from organ selling. They had no compunction about kidnapping then killing the most vulnerable people they could find.

107

It was he, Otto Wagner, who turned the practice from random brutality with modest profit to refined search and acquisition, which yielded immensely greater financial reward. His early process was crude. He would spot a man or woman he deemed superior in some way. By careful negotiations with people already in the business, he had them 'taken care of.' Their bodies allowed him to offer sick or dying recipients a much better product than the kidney of some homeless drunk or the liver of a street prostitute--at a much higher profit.

The massive science project of mapping the human genome was completed when Otto was twenty-seven years old. The advance in genetic science sparked the rise of commercial companies which offered DNA analysis to the millions. Some of the data lay in plain view, for public access.

Otto was by then a graduate of an equally new branch of knowledge, cyber security. Considering the need for blood typing and tissue matching in transplants, Otto developed an algorithm to select the best prospects for a particular transplant. He and his business partners quickly became boutique suppliers in the growing market for organs.

A new but perhaps related need cropped up a few years later. The wife of one of Otto's closest associates was unable to bear children. She yearned for a male baby with blue eyes in contrast to his dark hair. By then, Otto's expertise in computer hacking in addition to knowledge of genetics allowed him access to several databases.

Out of almost a thousand profiles he reviewed, he identified a woman whose DNA might assure those features. His associate promptly kidnapped her to hold her captive. The obstetrician he paid manipulated her hormone production so the likelihood of conceiving a male was extremely high. Another accomplice with the desired physical features was happy to impregnate the kidnapped woman. Nine months later, *voila!* a boybaby with blue eyes and dark hair. Otto knew if he could accomplish this rather complicated feat for a friend, he could do it again for a better reason--for more money.

\* \* \*

The day after Otto's visit, Sage went back to her list of elusive William Joneses. She narrowed down the list of journalism graduates to five. As she picked up the page, one name stood out. William *Z*. Jones. It was unusual; what did the Z stand for? Then she remembered children from elementary school with the last name Zess. As an adult, idle gossip told her some women with the last name passed it along as a middle name for their children, family pride in action. Okay. This might be it. She searched another data base where she came up with a telephone number for William Z. Jones. It was the same area code as hers. The other numbers suggested the home was located in Twainville Crossing, not too far away. This had to be it! She picked up her phone. Hesitated. Wayne had been dedicated to the search, while Taylor gave up on it. If it was a victory, she wanted to share it with Wayne.

She pressed his number. She didn't wait for hello. "I found him! Our elusive newspaper reporter. I'm almost certain it's him."

"How? Where is he? Did you talk to him?"

"Not yet. If it's him, I want you in on it."

"Great. When are you calling him?"

Again, she hesitated. "Well, I…."

"Sage. You're making a short story long."

"If he agrees to see me, I'd like you to go with me."

"I will. But I can't leave right now. I'm in the middle of changing the oil in my car. My hands are covered in grease."

"Then I'll come there." She had to remind herself not to speed on the way to his house. She found him sitting in a folding chair inside the open door of his two-car garage. She noticed his scrubbed-clean hands and the closed hood of his pickup truck.

He rose to greet her with a smile. "Ah, here she is, the plain-clothes detective! Graduated from patrol, she is now locating missing persons and solving crimes."

"And visiting my cohort in his man cave."

He gestured toward a back corner where a desk held a closed laptop. He asked, "Would you like a beer?"

"No thanks. Let's get to it."

He pulled out another canvas folding chair and opened it for her to sit. She took out the list with one name and number circled in red. She handed it to him. "Read it to me." She entered the number as he gave it then put her phone on speaker. She held her breath while it rang.

"Yeah?"

"Mr. Jones, my name is Sage Stevens."

A dial tone.

She pressed Redial. He answered. She quickly said, "I'm a real person, not a telemarketer."

"Real my ass. Phony as the next one, I reckon."

A dial tone.

On her third try, she raised her voice over his curse words. "Mr. Jones, my mother's maiden name was Wallace. Her mother was Holly Wallace. I live in Oak Bayou, Mr. Jones."

The cursing stopped. She heard a throat-clearing gurgle. Then, "What do you want? Shit, never mind. I know what you want."

"Please, Mr. Jones, let me come talk to you."

"Who put you up to this? You got a reporter with you?"

"No, no. Only my friend Wayne Kelly--you know, from Kelly Auto Sales. He helped me look for your telephone number."

"Skip the bio. I'm familiar with the name and the dealership. I'm not impressed. And I'm surely not afraid."

Sage looked at Wayne with startled eyes. "Mr. Jones, nothing I say or do should frighten you. I'm looking for information. I promise you nothing you say will become public. I really need to find out about my grandmother."

"She's...she would've been your grandmother?"

"Not would have been. She was. So, please."

"Come on then. Tomorrow. Around ten." Another dial tone, the final one.

She keyed off with a shaking hand. Would this meeting lead to solving the mystery about Holly? Would she learn the rumors were true, that Holly was murdered? A seemingly random thought intruded: was there a connection here to the people who tried to kidnap her? Unlikely as it might be, the notion stuck.

Wayne put his hands on her knees and leaned toward her. "Hey, this is freaking you out, isn't it?"

She couldn't answer. He touched her cheeks with his palms then his thumbs smoothed the swell of her cheek bones. His hands slid down her neck to her shoulders. He massaged the tense muscles then probed the back of her neck with gentle fingertips. Finally, she looked up and smiled at him.

At nine-thirty the next morning Wayne drove to her house in his truck. They found the road to Twainville Crossing was similar to many other backroads in the Panhandle. It was flat and straight, a tunnel carved through a wall of pine trees of many kinds: slash pines, pond pines, scrub pines, sand pines and long leaf pines. The endangered long leaf pines of course bore no leaves; their long "brooms" were composed of three needles while other pine tree brooms held only two.

In fifteen minutes, they drove over a rise where they saw a wide body of water flowing into the Bay and from there to the Gulf. The bridge held a sign: Four Mile Creek. As they crossed it, Wayne said, "Anywhere else in the world, they'd call this a river." Indeed, the creek widened here into a wide expanse of at least a quarter mile. Pleasure boats were moored randomly about. A two hundred feet long barge laden with who knew what, floated motionless on the glassy surface.

Sage said, "God, I love the South."

"All of it? Alligators, hurricanes and all?"

"We don't have to worry about hurricanes between November and June, do we?"

"Not until global warming set in."

She shook her head. "I never think about alligators. Well, only if the fresh water I'm standing or swimming in is larger than a mud puddle."

"Yeah, the South does have its charms, to quote several million people."

Miles later he turned the pickup truck onto a long dirt driveway lined with ancient, spreading oaks. Their branches, big as the trunks of most trees, dripped Spanish moss. He turned off the air conditioner and rolled down the window. The atmosphere was thicker here, amid unrestrained semi-tropical growth.

A small frame house sat at the end of the drive surrounded by native plants and trees. The house bore peeling white paint with dirt-grey windows. Two wooden steps below a narrow stoop led to the door. Before Wayne could set the brake and turn off the motor, the door opened. The man who stood looking at them was tall and thin. He wore khaki pants and a long-sleeved flannel shirt, in spite of the cloying heat and humidity. The man jerked his head toward the interior. "Get in here before the neighbors strain their eyes."

Sage looked around. There were no other homes in sight, none that might harbor nosy neighbors. Inside the door, a small wiggle-tailed dog greeted them, capering around their ankles. Sage said to the man, "Mr. Jones, thanks so much for letting us come. I'm...."

The man turned away to scoop up the dog. "You already told me who you are. You sure as hell know who I am." He motioned them toward a sofa. He sank down into a worn leather recliner, settling the dog on his lap. Only then he said, "Now tell me what you want from me."

They sat. Sage stopped looking around the small room; her focus narrowed, intense. She saw the man's face and heard the sound of his words but she lost the smells of dog and cigarette smoke. Finally, she was here. Now she would find answers. She pulled a page from the leather binder on her lap. "This article you wrote. I have questions "

He grasped the arm of his chair with one hand. "I expected them. Millions of words I wrote in my career. You choose that to talk about? An accident from decades ago?"

"Mr. Jones, was my grandmother murdered?"

His other hand stopped fussing with the dog's ears. He spoke in the softest voice yet. "You'd have to ask those who were there."

The implication stunned Sage. "Who? Who was there besides her?"

He leaned toward her, anger in his face. "Whoever drove a nail through the seat belt holder so the belt wouldn't pull down, for one. And the driver of the truck that forced her off the road. Her little tin bucket-

-they called it a sports car--didn't have a chance. Oh, yeah, for certain at least one Highway Patrolman was there-
-eventually."

She was momentarily speechless. Then she said, "I tried to track down the accident report. It should have been archived under the Freedom of Information Act if nothing else. They said the record wasn't available, didn't exist. I showed them your article from the newspaper. That's when they claimed the accident report was lost in a fire around sixteen years ago."

He said, "Not surprised. Wouldn't have done anything for you, anyway."

"Why?"

"Because it didn't say shit, that's why."

Sage clenched her hands until her knuckles turned white. "Why was it fatal? Why did she die? Even without the seat belt…."

"Speed limit was only sixty back then, but at night on back roads they always did seventy or eighty. It's a wonder she was still in one piece. Car wasn't. Total loss, a pile of crap."

Sage felt stricken, a picture of the accident now forming in her mind. She was at a loss.

Wayne must have noticed the look on her face. He jumped in to ask, "Mr. Jones, who was the reliable informant you referred to in the newspaper article? And how do you know a truck forced her off the road?"

"Highway Patrol officer caught the case. I read his accident report the day after. Never mentioned a ruined seatbelt or a truck. He's dead now. Might have been natural causes. I heard news of the truck from a witness."

Sage inhaled sharply. "Who?"

"Old boy knew me since I was in diapers. After he read the paper, he called. He said my reporting wasn't worth a plug nickel. He saw the whole thing, the truck that ran her off the road, then high-tailed it away. Made the old boy stop his pickup. He run to her car fast as he could, see if someone was still inside. Saw the seat belt holder was ruined, but she wasn't in there. Found her body yards away, pretty-near wrapped around a tree. He got out of there faster than he got in. Knew it was a made-up job. Knew he might have an accident himself if it got out he was a witness. Threatened to kill me if I told anyone, 'specially law enforcement. He didn't trust a soul, probably not his own grandma."

Sage asked, "This man...."

Jones interrupted as if he knew the question. "He's long gone, too. Old as Methuselah even back then."

Sage was lost in this tale of malevolent tragedy. Her mind revved, an engine unable to catch and start, unable to function. Then she sniffed and blinked. "Mr. Jones, I do appreciate this--this information. I mean to keep my promise not to go public with any of it." He looked at her, expecting more. She added, "It appears there's no way to find out who was behind it. The officer is gone, the witness is gone. The car is probably gone, too."

Jones nodded. "You're right. I checked. Highway Patrol said it was an accident, owner was deceased. Her little convertible sure wasn't salvageable, so it went right to the junk yard." He abruptly put the dog off his lap and stood.

Sage knew he had dismissed them. She didn't move. "What else can you tell me, Mr. Jones? What else?"

His face turned flatter, his eyes colder. It looked as if he might command them to go. Instead, he said, " Is one more thing. A man came to see me a few days after. A young man. Don't recall his last name but the first was Lee. That's all I've got."

"Please, Mr. Jones."

"Well, he was a nervy cuss. Said he went to the Highway Patrol and the coroner before he came to me. Asked a bunch of questions no one knew answers to. Or weren't about to tell him, more likely. Said he was looking for a necklace she wore, a gold necklace with the word 'perfect' on it. Said he knew she was wearing it, had to know who took it. Weirdest thing I ever did hear. Guy might have been nuts." For the second time he said, "That's all I've got."

Sage stood and thanked him. With eyes fixed straight ahead she walked out, hesitated at the steps and almost stumbled on the second one down. She turned to see Wayne still in the house. He shook hands with the man, rubbed the dog's head and patted its wiggling butt before he followed her.

She stood motionless in front of the truck's passenger side door. Wayne opened the door for her. They got in. Wayne turned the truck around, swerving down the track to avoid mud-filled pot holes in the driveway. The motion made Sage feel even more off-balance. Her fists clinched in her lap until her knuckles ached. Wayne turned to her. "Hey, your face is white. Was it so hard for you to hear all that?"

Her palm went to her chest. "It's not that. It's Lee. This person 'Lee' he mentioned. I might know who it is."

"Why do you look so scared?"

"I ...I can't explain right now. I have to check it out-- find out if what I believe could be true."

Wayne pulled the truck onto the shoulder and stopped. He turned and took her hands. "Your hands are cold. I'm sorry this was so hard for you. Do you regret coming here?"

All she could do was shake her head.

He said, "Lee. There was a Lee at the party for your mom. Not that guy?"

"Yes, that guy. Right now, he might be with her. What is he doing here in Oak Bayou? What the hell does he want?"

"Hey, come here, come here." He held out his arms. She turned and leaned into them, putting her head on his chest. He pulled her closer and rubbed her upper arms with his hands until she stopped trembling. She pulled away slowly. He looked into her eyes, brushed her face with finger tips strong and rough, yet she felt their tenderness. She felt safe and comfortable again, but also something more. Perhaps it was only an understandable affection for a good friend. Perhaps more.

#

## Chapter Fifteen

After the visit with Jones, Sage eased into the seat of the truck and leaned her head back. Silent, eyes closed. They stayed closed for the rest of the trip. Wayne didn't say a word, probably thinking she was asleep.

She knew by familiar sounds when they pulled up in front of her house. She opened her eyes Wayne glanced over at her and smiled, reaching for his door handle. She grabbed his arm. "There's something I have to check out before we go in. Can I use your iPad?"

"Sure." He reached into the back for it. "Here, I'll log you in." He keyed in a few strokes then put the device on her lap.

"I didn't do this part earlier," she said, "the family tree thing, because it's expensive. I should have. It's important who Holly's partner was, my grandfather. Or is, if he's still alive." Minutes later, her head jerked up. She looked at Wayne with her features hardened into a grimace. "It's him. It's Lee Pendfield. That's his car beside mine in the driveway."

Wayne shook his head. "Your mother's friend, Lee? But...?

She said, "You don't understand why I'm angry do you?"

"No."

"You will after I confront him."

He searched her face before responding, "Well, if he needs a talking to, let's do it together." They got out. In front of the truck, she took his hand. He put his arm around her waist.

Laura opened the door for them. Lee watched from his seat on the sofa; he smiled and nodded as they entered. Laura looked at Sage, then at Wayne and back to her daughter. "Sage, what's wrong?"

"Ask him", she said, lifting her chin toward Lee. He rose from the sofa. "What?"

Wayne's arm still held Sage's waist. He said to Lee, "Sage has some questions to ask you."

Laura took Sage's arm as if to pull her toward the sofa. Wayne intervened. "Maybe the table would work better. Can we go in there, Miss Laura?" He used the polite address of a younger southerner to an older one. He motioned toward the dining room.

"Well...why not?" Seated at the dining room table, Laura was first to speak, turning to Wayne. "Questions. I have some, too. What happened? Why is my daughter so upset?"

Sage spoke for herself, "Mom, it's about Grandma Holly. It's about your mother."

"That's not--how could it be...?"

"Mom, listen. You understand, I've been wondering about her since I went through those things in the attic and found her picture."

"Well, you called me but    "

"Mom, I had to find out how she died. Why she died, after you told me about the rumors. I found the newspaper article written at the time of the accident. Then I found the man who wrote the article. It's very clear...." She turned to Wayne, who nodded at her. "We're both convinced she was murdered."

"Oh!" Laura gasped and shook her head. She turned to glance at Lee before she turned back to Sage.

"Well, it's all family business. What does this have to do with Lee? Really, this is unnecessary."

Lee had lowered his head. He stared at the table top. Then he looked up. "No, Laura. It has everything to do with me." He turned to Sage. "Exactly what did you find out?"

"That you knew her. You asked about her after her accident. You looked for her necklace, a gold necklace with the word Perfect. It was in the picture that shocked you so much--back when you and Mom were still in rehab. For all I know, you're the one who had her killed."

"Sage!" Laura shouted.

Lee was quick to respond. "No, Laura, let it go. This needs to come out. Sage, I didn't kill her. I loved her. She was my wife." Laura turned to stare at him, shocked stiffness in the lines of her body and face. She leaned toward him, an arm outstretched, and almost fell off the chair. Lee grabbed her shoulder while she steadied herself. Tension crackled in the silence.

Wayne finally spoke. "Lee, you were married to Miss Laura's mother. You're her father?"

Lee nodded.

Sage turned to her mother. "If he was too cowardly to admit it, I have proof. Proof from the DNA web site. He's your father, my grandfather."

He nodded again. Sage surged from her chair to stand over him. She exploded, "You coward! Why didn't you tell her? What were you doing, sneaking around here pretending to be someone else? What the hell is wrong with you? Where in hell have you been all her life?"

His mouth flattened into a grim line. He lowered his head. Silence. The sound of a large clock on the wall, unheard until then, sounded unbearably loud. He finally looked up and turned to Laura. "They did kill Holly. Then they tried to kill me." He paused and Sage saw the paleness of her mother's face. Renewed contempt for the man rose in her.

Without words, Lee unbuttoned two top buttons on his shirt to reveal a round, puckered scar on the left side of his chest below his collar bone then held up his arm to show two similar scars on the inside of one forearm. "They couldn't

120

risk their scheme being exposed. We had no idea how dangerous they were until "

Sage looked at the scars. "They tried to kill you?"

Laura began to cry. "This is too much. I don't want to hear it." Sage stepped behind Laura's chair and bent down to hug her mother, cheek to cheek, but her eyes still held Lee's.

Laura caught her breath and stilled her sobs long enough to say, "Wait." She rose slowly, still cautious of the boot on her wounded foot, and left the room. She returned a few minutes later holding a box of tissues. She wiped her eyes with one and put the box in the middle of the dining room table. She turned her chair away from Lee toward Sage and sat down. "Go on."

Although Laura would not look at him, Lee spoke to her only. "I longed to come back for you, Laura. God, you were my baby, my tiny sweet baby, but I knew you were safer with Holly and her parents than you would be with me. Because I knew about their plan--the plan to create a master race. Before I left, a few friends in town assured me they would watch out for you and Holly's parents."

"Who in this town cared so much about us?"

"I can't risk betraying them if the threat is still out there. I believe it is. Through a few good friends I kept track of you. When you turned eighteen, I figured you were old enough to handle this kind of revelation. Then your grandparents died. Before I could get here, you had joined the Army. I thought the Army was a very good choice. By the time basic training was over, you would feel like you belonged again. With people you could identify with. You'd have a job, a way to support yourself. I wasn't so worried about you then."

"What about when I left the Army?"

"I didn't find out right away, not until you married Steve. I felt some reassurance he was taking take care of you. Then Sage was born. I wanted to come back. I dreamed of coming back. But there was always a risk-

-to both of us. With Steve and your new baby, you were happy and safe."

"Years went by," Laura said. "So many years I was happy. I wouldn't have been if I knew you were alive and avoiding us. Then Steve died."

"I didn't know it until the day I learned about your accident. So serious. I knew I had to come."

She turned to look at him. "So that's why you showed up at the nursing home. There was nothing you could do for me while I lay in a hospital bed."

"I was there."

"Well, what about the other times I needed a father, needed someone to care for me, support me."

"There was never a time I knew you would welcome me if I came knocking on your door. But then the accident-- I knew you might not survive. I might never see my own daughter again." He rubbed his eyes and blinked while he stared at nothing, as if trying to focus on a mirage. "During all those years I was doing work I hoped would deliver justice to Holly's killers. I lived it. It kept me sane." He crumpled, face in his palms. Laura pushed the box of tissues toward him.

Sage would not let him escape into his grief. "You keep saying they. They shot you, they killed Holly. Who, Lee? Who are they?"

He looked up, wiped his face and nose. "You learned in school about the Nazis during the Second World War-- their obsession with a master race?"

Sage and Laura looked at each other and shook their heads; both had drawn a blank. Up to then, through the family's personal revelations, Wayne had been silent. Now he said, "Wait, you're talking history now. You can't lie, cover over the facts."

"I'm not trying to."

"What do those facts have to do with you and Holly in nineteen seventy-eight? The Nazis lost the war in the nineteen-forties. Their delusions about a master race evaporated."

Lee shook his head. "I'm not lying, Wayne. You have to understand--the survivors, the ones who escaped, hadn't surrendered. They never gave up their fantasy of a superior race. They merely moved it to another continent. To South America."

"Sounds stupid but probably harmless," Wayne said.

"They never relinquished their lust for power."

Wayne shook his head. "I can't believe they were that arrogant. We thrashed them to hell, bombed parts of Germany into dust. I saw pictures of Dresden on TV, what it looked like after the war."

"You and Sage--you have innocent hearts, hearts oblivious to true evil."

"So, a few Nazis who escaped to South America wanted to start a hereditary line of superior people. So what?"

"During the War, German officers learned a lot about aggression and resistance They learned overt attack wasn't always a winning strategy. It wasn't then, much less after the war with their small, scattered numbers. They adopted a game plan used by the European resistance fighters, brave men and women inall the occupied countries."

"What, smuggling people, blowing up trains?"

"Escaped Nazis formed a network of covert operatives who engaged in their own kind of guerilla warfare."

Wayne said, "It sounds like some whackadoo conspiracy theory. Cut to the chase, Lee."

"Nazis planned for some of their especially gifted operatives to gain political office. Others were supposed to specialize in international affairs. As seemingly innocent citizens in those positions, they could use propaganda to accomplish their goals."

Sage interrupted, "Who were they? Why did they kill Holly and try to kill you?"

"A key part of the plan was to build their numbers, starting with brain washing then aggressive reproduction. They believed their followers, if not they, themselves, would achieve world domination."

Sage still stood behind her mother's chair. She remembered the word *nubile* from her dreams. She leaned toward Lee. "Aggressive reproduction? Are you saying they forced Holly into...into...?"

Laura looked into Lee's face shaking her head. "The thought of it makes me sick. I'm afraid of what you're going to say next."

"No, no. One of their operatives did find Holly and tried to recruit her. She was a stewardess--now they call them 'flight attendants'--anyway, she flew with Pan American Airlines. It was international, including locations in South American. It's where and how they found her. They told her it was only a loose-knit group of people, sort of a dating group or matchmaker's clientele. They could identify each other by a gold Perfect necklace for women and a silver bracelet for men with the same word. They pledged to date only their own.

When these two Perfects married, they would receive a guaranteed income and be pressured to have children. The operatives' assumptions were if the parents couldn't embrace the whole scheme, their children would be taken and brain washed until they were thoroughly indoctrinated."

Sage was still angry. "Are you telling us Holly fell for it?"

"Well, maybe before she understood. I met Holly a few years before they found her. Not long after, Holly confided in me. Together we did some investigating. We didn't find the group was doing anything illegal but we both knew it wasn't right. I wanted her out. She wanted out. She spoke to the man who recruited her but he wouldn't let her go."

"I can't believe this." Sage said.

Lee's voice softened to barely above a whisper. "I loved her very much. We married in secret. No witnesses but the court clerk. I still have our marriage certificate. It's in a folder wrapped in velvet in my safety deposit box at the bank." He gulped, his Adams apple bobbing. Silent tears began to stream down his face.

Sage thought a man in tears should inspire a person's sympathy. She couldn't summon a whit of compassion for him. She paced in a half-circle around the table as if to skirt the angry wall his revelations had built around her. She stopped. "Okay, it's time for a break. I suggest we all take a walk or get a drink of water. Whatever. Alone.

#

## Chapter Sixteen


Lee remained at the table, motionless, silent. Laura stood. "I'm going to my bedroom to lie down." Wayne went to sit in his truck. Sage went to the kitchen, trying not to remember what she had just heard. Unexpected, like a punch to the head during a Taikwando match, facts jolted together in her mind. They killed Holly because she refused to join them. They thought she and Lee knew about the whole perverted plan, and might reveal it.

Yes, Germany and South America; it made sense. Otto Wagner, from Argentina with German heritage. A man old enough to be a son or maybe a grandson of a German Nazi. Otto, striking up a friendship with her, the granddaughter of a "Perfect."

Perhaps she herself was considered a Perfect because of her DNA of disease-resistance and longevity -- one in a hundred thousand people.

She made a cup of coffee which she set aside. She poured ice water into a glass, drank and put the glass in the dishwasher. She filled another glass, paused to wipe the sink, dry the counter and putter around before she finally went back to the dining room, carrying the glass and cup.

Lee had stopped crying. His eyes looked red. His hair now strayed over his forehead. She extended the cup and glass at the same time. He took the coffee. "Black. Nice. Thank you Sage."

Sage went to her mother's room. Laura looked up from the bed with eyes dulled by confusion. She shook her head and lay back down on the pillow. She had had enough. Sage went to pat her mother's arm, but comforting words would not emerge from behind her anger. She gritted her teeth, walked to the front door and lifted her hand toward where Wayne sat in the truck. He came quickly, returned to the table with her.

Lee sipped his coffee. Silence, filled only by the now-ominous sound of the ticking clock. Sage looked at Wayne. How had Lee's revelations affected him? He raised both eyebrows at her. Finally trusting herself to speak she said to Lee, "Some things are making more sense. You were married in secret and Holly got pregnant."

"We kept the marriage a secret until she was around four months along and she started to show. The airline would fire her if they knew she was pregnant. The Nazis were still monitoring her. If they saw she was pregnant, they would know it wasn't by another Perfect. We weren't sure what they might do to her, so I took her to upstate New York. We managed to sneak across the border to Canada. A friend of mine there took her in until she gave birth. Until she had Laura." "That's why mom was born in Quebec City. We always wondered about that and why she relinquished her citizenship there."

He nodded. "When the baby--when Laura was two months old, Holly decided she couldn't hide forever. She didn't want to keep the baby from her parents. That's why she came back. She kept wearing the damned necklace, hoping it would fool them, keep them at bay." He closed his eyes. "But they killed her anyway. They must have taken the necklace right off her the night of the so-called accident. I wanted to find it because the one who had it was also behind her murder. I wanted to destroy it. It was as if the necklace--everything it represented--killed her."

Sage's mind scrambled to assimilate newly- revealed facts knitted together, where before there were only random, frayed strands. Holly was murdered and Lee had been a fugitive from assassination for forty years. The murder had been deemed an accident, whether from an honest mistake,or through some manipulation by the Nazis. No one had held them accountable.

Lee began to speak but she didn't hear. "What? I'msorry. Say it again, please."

"So, I came back after Laura's accident. I planned tell her about Holly and me, but her head injury compromised her too much. At the hospital I sat by herbed at times you weren't there. She must have noticed me even though she was barely conscious most of the time. I couldn't say, 'Happy to meet you, I'm your father.' I kept waiting for the right time to do it. I...I was her friend Lee Pendfield. It was so good, to be herfriend."

Sage studied his face. She guessed at what he wanted to say but wouldn't, "I don't know anything about being a father. I was afraid."

He spoke. "It's such a relief now. I'll answeranything she asks." He looked up at her. "First I have to say I'm sorry. To you as well as to Laura. For the shock. But mostly, for not being here all those years." Sage gave him nothing but a nod. She and Wayne rose at the same instant, going into the living room to sit on the sofa. Lee also rose but went to the front door.

He paused to turn and look at them, then left without another word. Wayne took her hand. "Glad he's gone. How are you feeling?"

Looking into his eyes, she managed a smile. "Notsure. It was a bomb-shell, wasn't it?"

He raised his eyebrows quickly three times. "Bam-chick-a-wow-wow."

She laughed. "My sentiments exactly." She looked down at his hand so naturally cupping her own,the size and strength of it, the warmth. She smiled at him. "I must be okay. You made me laugh. You know,I had an inkling all along. He looks similar to mom insome ways. There was something about him, but I couldn't make my mind go there. Not until William Jones said his name."

"That's why you needed my iPad. You checked the DNA site."

"There was such a small chance he would have done the DNA thing and it would be with that particular company. But when I got into the screen with relatives' names, his was the first that popped up. The only reason I was able to keep myself together was so I could confront him."

"You did."

Sage withdrew her hand from his, smoothed her hair back from her forehead, bringing her pony tail onto her chest to stroke it a few times before she turned anxious eyes to his. "Did I tell you about my trip to Georgia?"

"Georgia? No."

"This might sound a bit paranoid but I think you'll understand." She told him about Otto and the Haven. When she finished, he shook his head. "Sounds like a damned cam-shafter to me."

"A what?"

"Cam-shafter. Mechanic's slang for a bad situation. Don't go."

"I told Mom. She was okay with it. Then I did a few more computer searches and made some calls. I didn't do an in-depth investigation, but the Haven is a real place. He's known there. Besides, Otto might have information about Holly and how she died. If he goes back to Georgia alone, I'll never find out if he's connected and if so, how."

He didn't answer right away, apparently mulling it over. Finally, he said, "It's been a long time since the start of the Nazi conspiracy Lee described with no hint of it in the history books or the news. I won't try to talk you out of it but we need to keep you safe up there. How can we eliminate the chance it will turn bad?"

"I'll call or text every day. To Mom and Taylor, too. And I'm taking my gun."

"Good. Remember you can count on me if it does turn bad.

She told him the day she planned to leave. He asked, "Isn't that date too close to when you start the police academy?"

"The ten days I committed to ends two days before the Academy. Being busy up there will keep me from having nerves about it."

* * *

The next morning, Taylor came for his usual early morning tryst with Sage. They lay in bed after their love-making, Taylor's eyes level with hers on the same pillow. She closed her lids and replayed their conversation from the night before, after she shared what Lee revealed about himself, his role in her family.

Taylor said, "Well, if he had told you a month earlier, he could have scored for Father's Day." A sinking feeling in her gut erased any reply. Remembering it now, she sighed and closed her eyes.

He asked, "How long did you say you'll be gone?"

She rolled away and got out of bed. "Ten days."

"Playing with a bunch of retarded kids? Wouldn't you rather stay here and play with me?"

"Calling the kids retarded doesn't go an inch toward convincing me to stay. I'm excited for the opportunity to teach them. It might be the biggest responsibility, the biggest challenge, I've ever taken on."

"Are you getting snippy with me--and after what I just did for you?"

"What we did for each other. I enjoyed what we did together. Maybe too much. I'm hitting the shower."She went into the bathroom.

After a few minutes, she heard him yawn and stretch. He opened the bathroom door and raised his voice over the noise of the shower, "Hey, if that guy Otto tries it with you, you tell me, okay?"

"Yeah, sure." As she dried, she heard him move around, getting dressed. Then he yelled, "Later, Babe," and was gone. She wrapped a towel around her and went to the window. Yes, there. He was gone. She asked herself if Laura would be relieved. She probably knew whenever he arrived and when he left, although her bedroom window faced the side yard instead of the front. What did Laura think about the relationship? She stood blinking, her hair dripping onto the towel. What did *she* think about the relationship? That she didn't feel the same about him any longer. She wanted it over.

* * *

It was eight o'clock on a Wednesday morning. Otto pulled up in front of the house and came inside to carry her bags to the car. She got in beside him, her mind racing. He turned to smile at her then started the car. The car pulled away. She fought the urge to look back at the house. Instead, she faced forward. Her heartbeat was as rapid as if she entered a sparring match. What was the real purpose of this trip, if not what he had described to her? The urge to turn, examine his profile flashed thought her mind; she instantly suppressed it.

Otto remained silent. After a while she was able to notice the car's smooth ride and quiet interior.

He asked, "A little music?" Without waiting for a reply, he turned on the CD player. The music was classical, vaguely familiar. It relieved her of the effort to initiate conversation while she tried to decide when and how she would question Otto. She had to determine if he was connected to the group that murdered Holly. Somehow, she must get him to reveal himself.

They drove across the state line into Georgia. Otto pulled the car over at a roadside rest stop. He said, "It's not quite time for lunch but I prepared a little treat to welcome you to my state." He got out, took a large basket from the trunk and placed it on the bench of the picnic table. He brought out a white linen table cloth to place over the dirty, worn wooden table. Out of the basket came a bottle of champagne wrapped in a cloth folded around dry ice, and a silver dish mounded with ripe strawberries. She didn't comment on the extravagant display of luxury while he uncorked the bottle and poured the champagne. He held up his champagne flute. "A toast to your visit."

They finished the elegant snack without conversation until Sage said, "It was so nice of you to arrange this, Otto. Thank you."

"You are certainly worth it, my dear. You are one in a hundred thousand."

Her smile vanished; her lips went numb while her mind scrambled for clarity. One in a hundred thousand? My DNA. It isn't a silly compliment. It's another thing he knows about me that he shouldn't! Her thoughts leaped; memories connected. Otto could be with the people who tried to kidnap me. Coming with him was probably a deadly mistake.

She stood abruptly. She smoothed down her shirt, rubbed her palms together to help her compose herself enough to ease out the next words. "Otto, maybe I shouldn't have accepted your offer to teach the children. I'm not trained for it. I'm having second thoughts. I know it's late to back out but...."

"My Dear! Sage! You must not back out on me now. The children are expecting you. This self doubt is most unnecessary and most unlike you."

"You are a gentleman Otto, and if I want to return home...."

"Wait! I...I must show you something." He turned and went to the car. She couldn't see what he was doing, but his hands worked at something on the driver's side door or maybe on the floorboard. What, a gun? No, Otto would not!

He walked back to her with something in his hands, something wrapped in red velvet. He said, "Here, this will dispel your self-doubts. I want you to wear it, and to believe it." His right hand slowly unwrapped what he held cupped in the left. A necklace of gold shaped in the word "Perfect."

He said to her now-deaf ears, "Here, I will fasten it for you." She felt his hands on the back of her neck, cold metal on her skin. Her heart stopped. "So, no more doubts. We will stop at the Beach Club for a late lunch before we reach the Haven."

\* \* \*

That same morning in Oak Bayou, Wayne struggled to keep his mind on business at the car dealership while he checked people in at the repair division. The shop opened at seven a.m. on weekdays. By six forty-five a line of cars had

133

already pulled up at the entrance to the service bay, motors running, drivers trying to look patient. He usually enjoyed saying good morning and overseeing their maintenance requests. Today Sage's trip to Georgia preoccupied him.

With morning check-ins finally completed, he went inside to the customer service desk where a few moments of idleness allowed him to ponder over the man Sage was about to spend ten days with. Well, not with, exactly, but around.

Ten days was a long time. She would text Taylor as well as her mother, probably call, too. Why hadn't he asked Sage to call him? He could call her, of course, but He should talk to Taylor, exchange information, coordinate with the guy to make a real safety plan for her. He looked at his watch. Right now, Taylor would be getting ready to leave his twelve-hour watchman shift at the lumber yard. Wayne asked his assistant to take over, now that the first cars in line were being serviced.

Wayne reached the lot to see Taylor start to get into his car. Wayne approached while Taylor scowled at him. Neither man reached to shake hands. "Hey, Taylor, remember me? Wayne, Sage's friend. She introduced us a week or so ago."

"Yeah. What's up?"

"I'm thinking that since she'll be up there in Georgia for over a week maybe you made arrangements to go up there, see how she's doing?"

"Why should I? What's it to you?"

Wayne's baritone voice tightened. "I'm her friend. I need to be sure she's safe."

"Why wouldn't she be safe? She'll call me now and then. Nothing to worry about." Taylor took out his phone and pressed a few keys. "Ah, there she is. They're not even halfway there."

Wayne's gut clenched when he got it. "You have her on GPS tracking. Did she agree to that?"

"Hey, I do it with all...."

...all his women! Without conscious intent, Wayne's fist shot toward Taylor's face but quick as a thought, his fist popped open. His palm landed on Taylor's cheek with a loud whap! Taylor's head jerked sideways. The phone dropped from his hand. His martial arts training took over. He spun sideway, lashing a powerful kick at Wayne's knee.

Wayne dodged, lunged forward to grab the smaller man's arm, pulled him around and held him backwards in a modified choke hold. He growled into the back of Taylor's ear, "Your nose would be squashed all over your face, Tinkerbell, but I don't want Sage to have to look at the ugly mess. She is *not* one of your bimbos. You treat her with respect or you'll be the sorriest dip-shit on crutches. You're not the only one who knows how to sweep a knee."

He released his hold with a push away, grabbed Taylor's phone from the ground and walked to his truck. Taylor hurried to his own vehicle without looking back and pulled away.

Wayne brushed dirt from Taylor's phone to look at the GPS map. The little dot was stationary at a place north of the Florida/Georgia border. Why did they stop? While he wondered and watched, the dot slowly began to move again, North. He took a deep breath, settling back against the seat. That little dot represented Sage. There she was and she was moving in the expected direction. His face softened into a smile. He dropped the phone into a cup holder and headed back to the dealership.

On the way, he turned on the radio. He switched stations once, then again. Music worked for only a few minutes to forestall his guilt over taking another man's phone. Greater guilt was the fact he desired to do exactly

135

what the other man did, monitor Sage. His reason for wanting the information was different, he told himself, not prompted by jealousy or a need to control her. He would give the phone back to Taylor later today after he left the dealership. Let the little creep spy on her; his jealousy and desire to control hermight also work to help keep her safe.

Rock music suddenly gave way to the hourlynews. A man's voice droned on about local politics. Wayne reached to turn it off. A word caught hisattention, Jones. Then, ".... William Jones. The man and his dog were found dead in the home early this morning. Police have launched an investigation. A source close to the case said man and dog were shot todeath."

Wayne felt his foot twitch with the urge to jam on the brake. *Their* William Jones. An investigation is under way. Another story followed; he wasn't listening. He turned off the radio. Jones murdered? The few homicides in this backwater area were usually the result of drug deals or domestic violence. Jones was a recluse, a harmless old man.

Wayne pulled up at a stop light, clenched his hands into fists and pounded his thighs. Jones died because he knew the whole story behind Holly's murder. Someone knew he and Sage visited Williams. That someone suspected Williams might have revealed damning facts to them. Who would suspect that? Who was still harboring guilt and seeking to protect themselves after all these years? He followed the facts to a terrifying conclusion. Whoever they were, he and Sage might be their next targets.

#

## PART TWO

### Chapter Seventeen

On the Tuesday morning before Sage and Otto headed for Georgia, Susan Barkin drove from her home in Dwightsburg, where she lived, toward her waitress job at the Beach Club Restaurant. The small town of Dwightsburg, some distance from Savannah, was known if at all, for the facility called The Haven. As she drove across the bay bridge that sunny morning, Susan's thoughts of death surfaced again, surfaced like a casual thought about how busy it would be at the restaurant today. For Susan Barkin, the thought of death was an integral, ever-present part of her consciousness. Now she wondered if she swerved and accelerated, would the low concrete barrier give way, let her car tumble to the water far below? Probably. Especially if she was already going fast then stomped the accelerator to the floor. She had considered it before, but today she decided it was a real option. Not that she enjoyed the idea of a violent, painful death, but the other methods weren't sure-fire; she had learned those lessons early.

In the ninth grade, at one of the high schools she went to that year, she made her first attempt after she saw it in the movies. A woman took a lot of sleeping pills then slept to death. She thought about it. It would be such an easy thing to do. Trouble was, she didn't want her mother, Eva, to find her body. Something like that could send Eva into another chaotic, psychotic, manic episode. It might involve crisis workers or police. It might end with Eva in a psych ward again or maybe even jail - again. No, she needed to protect Eva.

Susan went to the drug store, bought a large bottle of over-the-counter sleep aids. Next day she took them to school with her. She would have to swallow the whole bottleful to be sure it worked. She stood at the water fountain in the school's outer hallway to take them. It was not an easy thing to do.

At first, she took one pill at a time, washing it down with a sip from the fountain. It was taking a lot longer than she expected. She crammed handfuls into her mouth and slurped water. The taste of dissolving pills made her shudder. She continued until the bottle was empty. There. She had done it. Should she feel satisfied now? Maybe she should be afraid, afraid of death. Strangely, she felt nothing, unaware that normal emotions were no longer available to her. They had become weak and fuzzy, wrapped in the protective gauze of depression.

In class she began to feel drowsy. She almost fellout of her chair. The teacher sent her to the nurse's office. She tried not to stumble on the way down the hall. Someone watching might think she was drunk. The nurse asked what was wrong. Susan said she was just tired. The nurse took her temperature, reported it was normal, then led her to a far corner of the room to a cot with clean white sheets. Susan looked down at it with blurry eyes, her mind telling her it was good enough to die on. She lay down. She slept.

The dismissal bell rang at three-thirty. It didn't waken her. The nurse called her name and shook her shoulder until she opened her eyes. Damn, I'm not dead, she thought. Why was this taking so long? Nowshe was awake again, would she be able to walk home? The next thing she remembered, her mother was shaking her awake. Awake in her own bed. "What's wrong with you?" Eva asked.

"Dying...took...sleeping pills."

"No, you're not dying. Get up."

Strange, her mother sounded almost normal. "Get up." Eva took her daughter's arm and helped her out of bed. What was this? Eva never touched her.

Down the stairs and into the car. Then, where was this? Not a doctor's office or a hospital. They were in a movie theater, watching a movie. A movie? She didn't understand it, couldn't follow it. She closed her eyes. Eva nudged her. This happened several times. She slept with her eyes open. It was all she remembered until the following day, when she got up and went to school again.

She waited--a day, two days--to find out what her mother would say or do after her suicide attempt. Her mother never mentioned it or referred to it in any way. Susan wasn't sure how to feel. Relieved? Maybe. Disappointed? Maybe. She didn't have the energy to decide.

A few months later, Susan's home room teacher, an older man with greying hair, called Eva to come to the school. Eva turned a surprised face to Susan. "You must have done something really bad. I guess you shocked both of us. Now you have to go with me to face the music."

In the classroom, her teacher began talking with Eva while Susan stood back, almost behind her mother, frightened and embarrassed. What was this about?

The man exchanged a few pleasantries with Eva while he searched her face, as if looking for something he couldn't find. Then he asked, "Do you know your daughter is *very* depressed?" Eva didn't answer. She turned, grabbed Susan's wrist and walked out. The subject never came up again with Eva. No questions asked, therefore none answered was typical of Eva's relationship with her daughter.

Driving toward the restaurant where she worked, Susan remembered, thinking What a stupid girl I was! Suicide by over-the-counter sleep aids. Ha! The human body is so much tougher to kill, much tougher than people realize. A

139

person with a serious illness or injury rejoices after learning that fact; a depressed person rages or cries--or sleeps with their eyes open.

Susan reached the Beach Club, a seafood and Southern cuisine establishment with a deck overlooking the bay. No more memories now, she scolded herself. Time to listen, remember what people say, what they order. Act the waitress. Pay attention. Smile.

The restaurant's decorator had held true to the stereotype. Ocean-turquoise paint colored the walls, sandy beige colored floors and accent details of sea shells and fishnets completed the cliché. The lay-out was utilitarian, one large area for tables and booths. There was a horizontal aperture in the kitchen wall that looked into the dining area to provide visual communication between cooks, servers and diners. Most of the business here was lunch during the week and lunch or dinner on weekends.

Susan suspected Ray Henry, manager/owner of the restaurant had hired her as a server, inexperienced as she was, because she was beautiful. He hoped she would attract male customers and keep established ones coming back.

After setting up for lunch, she went to the back room. She wiped her hands on the apron over her uniform dress then picked up a paperback novel. She sat down to read in a worn easy chair the manager had brought from his home.

Her skirt, short as was required, hiked above her bony knees.

Thus occupied, she didn't see Ray come out of his office. Some hyper-awareness caused her to look up. He stood in the doorway staring at her. Her breath caught in her throat. He nodded, turned and went back to his office.

Ray seldom spoke to her but when he did it resurrected memories of their one-night stand. Those recollections haunted the part of her consciousness that still held hopes and maybe even dreams, the very small part of her not dead enough to forget the vagaries of life.

From the first, she admired his refined face, his fine, straight brown hair and light blue eyes. He was handsome but far too controlled in the way he walked and spoke, too pale in this land of suntanned bodies to attract most women. Susan warmed to him immediately.

Her romantic fantasies began in the first week of her hire. Alone in her small apartment listening to music or at night on the edge of sleep, she dreamed they would both remain at the restaurant some evening after clean-up and find themselves in deep conversation. They would mention amusing details of the day's events. Some restaurant-lore joke would make them laugh together. After a while they would reveal their personal selves to each other in cautious, conversational vignettes.

Her fantasies moved to the day he would take her to a night club. They would dance, bodies close, heated. In the small hours of the new morning, their bodies would slow and harmonize, soft and close. They would stroll on the beach, watch the rising sun spread molten gold over the ocean's tranquil surface then walk home together to make love.

When her dreams progressed to a bodily encounter, it was always some scenario seen in a film or read about in a romance novel. It was the romance, the sweet imaginings she cherished, not the sex.

She roused herself from the start of a new fantasy and closed the book. Ray was the second man to have sex with her, not the first. The first happened when she was fifteen, during one of Eva's manic phases. At those times she was-- what her psychiatrists called--hyper- sexual. She would tell Susan to go to bed, put on a revealing dress with high heels and go out. An hour or so later she usually returned with a man in tow. Once in a while he was still there in the morning. Susan knew to keep out of their way. She retreated into her MP3 player with earphones on.

Since Eva and her man-du-jour occupied the only bedroom, Susan slept on the couch. One night she curled up on the small rug in front of the refrigerator. When her mother leaned over her to grab something from the refrigerator, the light woke her. Eva saw Susan's eyelids flutter. She whispered, "Go back to sleep." She took two bottles of beer from the refrigerator and went back to the bedroom.

On the day she lost her virginity, Susan was in the bathroom brushing her teeth. The door opened. A naked man walked in. She jumped, startled and wide-eyed. The man flashed a quick grin at her. "Hey, Gorgeous, what's your name?"

At first she couldn't speak. Then, "Su--Susan." Not listening, he spoke over her name. "Ummm. Dessert." He moved toward her.

She dropped her toothbrush into the sink and darted around him toward the door.

He blocking her way out of the tiny room with hisbody, his naked, hairy body. The curly matt on his chest tapered, arrowing down to a thatch around the erection he aimed at her.

One second she was reaching for the doorknob. The next, he yanked down her pajama pants, grabbed her bottom and lifted her up with her thighs apart to impale her. She cried out in pain. Shock and pain immobilized her. Then, screaming, she punched and pummeled his face, his shoulders, his grinning face. Undeterred, he turned his face from side to side to avoid her blows while he humped her. The heel of herhand shot out to push his chin away from her face. The thickly muscled column of his neck didn't yield. Alcohol breath enveloped her. His hard thrusts shoved her back against the door painfully, again and again.

Quickly, then, he gave an open-mouthed grunt of satisfaction and stopped. She struggled, pushed against his shoulders until he backed up and dropped her. Her feet touched the floor then tangled in the discarded pajama pants. Her knees gave way. She knelt on all fours, gasping, crying.

He turned away, grabbed a tissue to wipe himself then threw back the toilet lid and shuffled forward to send a yellow stream splashing into the bowl. He shook off the last drop and turned to look at her with the self-satisfied smile of a man just finished with a hearty steak dinner. A shadow of concern flickered across his face then disappear as quickly. He blurted, "You were too damned tight in there, Pretty Girl. Got me off too fast." He unlocked the door then was gone.

Susan used both hands against the wall, struggling to stand while she shuddered in pain. Her whole body shook. Then her tears stopped. She looked down at herself, uncomprehending. She went into the shower. She didn't feel the steaming hot water. Soon her skin turned bright pink but she didn't see it. She didn't return to her body until the hot water ran out and cold struck her awake.

Careful, she thought. He might still be here. She dried, put her pajamas back on and ventured into the open doorway, listening. Nothing. She crept to the bedroom door. It was open. She saw her mother in bed alone, asleep, snoring softly. The man had gone.

That day and the next she waited. To see if her mother knew. Eva did not. Susan waited for a week. To see if he would come back, attack her again. He did not. She waited for almost a month. To see if she was pregnant. She was not. His hair. Susan still remembered the hair, all the hair on his body, even now. Thankfully, in her nightmares he remained faceless.

Dismissing the memory, she stood and dropped the book on a table. Why did Ray come stand in the doorway to stare at her like that? Maybe there was still something here, something between them that could grow beyond their one coupling.

After her initial romantic fantasies about him, she was surprised to realize he wanted her, too. Then it happened, when and where he chose for it to happen. He took her to his apartment then directly to his bed. It took longer than she expected but wasn't as painful as she expected, either. She kept her eyes closed to diminish the uneasy physical sensations as well as her embarrassment. She wasn't experienced enough to pretend she was enjoying it.

After he finished, he rolled off the bed and quickly started to dress with his back to her. Then she knew something was wrong. What did she do wrong? He slipped on his shoes then turned to look at her lying face up under the sheet, stiff and wide-eyed. "I'm sorry, kid. It never should have happened. It won't happen again. You've still got your job if you want it. No hard feelings. It never did happen as far as I'm concerned. Let's leave it at that, okay? Nothing happened. Agreed?"

"Okay." Feeling somehow relieved, she pulled the top sheet off the bed, wrapped it around her and went to the bathroom. She sat on the toilet, thinking, it's messy and awkward. People get so wound up over it. It got Eva into trouble, for sure. But I'm not like her. Not at all. Making love, as some people called it, hadn't touched the vise-like grip of her nothingness.

That Tuesday, lunch and dinner services were busy. At four o'clock, another server came on to serve the early bird diners, the slow-moving, weathered- looking retirees. The part-time server's many years of experience in restaurants had toughened her. She appeared almost as mature as the retirees but not nearly as genial. She grumbled constantly because of the small tips they left. "They should stay at the bingoparlor and leave us alone," she'd say. "Unless it's a single guy. But even most of them don't get it. Theyleave too much for a tip but not enough for a blow job." Susan could only raise her eyebrows and try to smile. The other server liked the late-coming diners because they were generous with themselves. They ordered higher-priced entrees with margaritas, mojitos or beer leveraging up their bills and therefore, the tips.

That Tuesday, the other woman left on the heels of the last customer to count her tips in the car before driving away. Ray locked the doors and turned on the Closed sign. The bus boy/dishwasher did the last of his chores, then a quick mop-up in the kitchen before he said good night. Ray tallied the receipts and bagged them for deposit while Susan took care of the mundane details: cleaning, refilling salt and pepper shakers, preparing for the next day. In the evenings she would linger over trifles, hoping to walk out with Ray, perhaps talk a little in the dark privacy of the parking lot. Tonight, he stood at the door waiting and watching as she grabbed her purse and walked toward him, smiling.

"Christ!" he said, startling her. "Why don't you eat something? You're starting to look like a damned scarecrow. Go take some left-overs from the refrigerator."

She stopped dead still, silent.

"Oh, for God's sake, I didn't mean to sound that way. You should sit down and have a big dinner before we start evening service--or after it, maybe. If you'd fill out a little and you'd look spectacular."

She lifted her chin. "Watching customers slobber down steak and seafood makes me sick. Raw meat, stinking fish and grits swimming in butter." She shuddered. It was a natural and deeply felt reaction rather than a feigned display.

He shook his head. "You're a gorgeous girl, Susan. With your face and that long, honey-colored hair, you could land any guy you wanted."

She lowered her head so he didn't see her mouth. "I don't want any guy."

"And that's the problem." He tilted his head back toward the dining area. "While you're on the floor, pretend you do." He opened the door for her. They reached their cars at the same time. He sat to wait until she started her car and pulled away.

She headed home, feeling numb except for a sodden lump in her chest. For a second she thought she might cry but she didn't. Couldn't. Her childhood had robbed her of tears. She wasn't aware that in a normal childhood, a petri dish of nurturing love feeds the youngster's physical development as well as their developing emotions, energies and passions. She didn't understand it but sensed her own development was stunted. Something crucial was lacking in her.

Her drive took her toward the bridge over the Bay. Similar to many bridges in this area, it rose from water level to a high arc in less than a quarter mile, constructed to allow large boats easy passage under it. She drove upward toward a western horizon holding the dregs of sunset, bruises on the edge of a darkening world. With the apex of the arc ahead, she saw only sky, nothing but sky. Elation caught her, quickened her breath. She would do it, drive right into the sky. She pressed the accelerator hard. A sensation, a feeling of exultation filled her.

Damn! She lifted her foot. She couldn't do it. Not now. She couldn't exit life without leaving a single trace of her existence behind. There were things to do at home. The apartment to leave clean and decent. A note to say Buddy, her half-brother from her mother's first marriage, her only close relative, would get her little yellow Mercedes convertible. The low-mileage, well-maintained convertible sat safely in the one-car garage attached to her apartment. She was driving an older model sedan with more than a hundred thousand miles on the odometer. She would never drive the convertible off the bridge. It didn't belong down there, drowned in forty feet of salt water. Buddy would love the little car and take care of it.

Eva had surprised her with the convertible on her birthday one year--the one year Eva landed more than one or two acting roles in Hollywood and was on her meds for bipolar disorder. They had food and shelter that year.

Two years afterward, the aspiring actress and mother of two drove her own convertible off a cliff on Mulholland Drive. The coroner ruled it an accident.

Susan neared home with resignation. The thrilling new sensation of exultation was gone but seductively lingered in her mind. It will come again, she thought. In the seconds she let go of this life, its years of deprivation and grieving, anger and confusion. She anticipated, no, she *knew* she would feel overwhelming relief as she drove her old car over the concrete bridge abutment, into the sky.

#

## Chapter Eighteen

On Wednesday in Oak Bayou, Wayne pulled directly into the customer parking lot adjacent to the showroom instead of the employee lot in back. He left the motor running, absorbing the news he had heard. If some evil descendant of the group that had murdered Holly had just now murdered Jones, he and Sage might also be in their sights.

Without leaving the truck he called her. No answer. He drummed his fingers against his thigh. He tried again. It went to voice mail. He left a message telling her to call him--now. Then a connection flared in his memory, an image of Lee's wounds, courtesy of the master race group. Lee might have key information he hadn't shared with them. Talk to Lee.

He didn't have Lee's number but he did have the land line number at Laura and Sage's house. Laura answered on the second ring. He made an effort to be polite, to chat for a few minutes before he asked about her father.

"I've been trying to reach Lee myself. We're talking now I've gotten over the shock...of...of I still
call him Lee."

"When did you talk to him last?" "Yesterday. I'll text you his number."

"Can you give me his address, too? I'll pay him a quick visit. While I'm there I'll ask him to call you."

"Great. Good idea."

The address she gave was in a neighborhood of manufactured homes set on a dozen small cul-de-sacs with an access road that curved and doubled back on itself. The neighborhood was a maze. He drove around for at least ten anxious minutes.

Finally, there on the side of a double-wide mobile home he saw the address he looked for. Around the home there was no real landscaping. No vehicle in sight. Blinds covered the front windows.

He left the truck with the motor still running, went to the door and knocked--hard. No answer. After the third round of knocks, he walked around back. No outdoor furniture, no barbeque grill or other signs of recent occupancy. He looked in a back window. Dark inside.

He felt the emptiness of the place. He pulled out his phone. His call to Lee's number produced a message saying the number was no longer in service. Damn! Enough of this. If he could talk to Sage, he'd be able to find her. Where was she now? Back in the truck, he pressed the start button on Taylor's phone. It now required the security code he didn't know. His one small, tenuous connection with Sage was gone.

He pulled up a map on his own phone to determine the way he would drive to reach the Haven. Then it occurred that they might deviate from the logical route up the Interstate to take more scenic back roads. Without the GPS to track her, it would be a long shot to reach her while they were in route. He stared at his phone, wondering whether to call and leave another message.

It rang, making him start. Sage's ringtone. "Wayne. I can't talk long. I'm in the restroom. Otto knows about me."

"Knows what?"

"I can't explain but I'm not safe with him. I'm going to leave, get away from him. I might need your help. I'll call you."

"Wait! Don't hang up. Where are you? Is this because you heard about Jones?"

"Jones? No! I don't know what you're talking about. I'm at a restaurant on the Interstate, north of Novanda, Georgia. I have to get away from him."

"Where would you go, what would you do? Don't leave. I'm coming for you!"

She hung up.

Wayne's jaw clenched until his teeth hurt. Sage had just verified his suspicions. He had to find her, get her back. Now he knew the route they were on but they had almost two hours' head start. Even if he left soon and ignored the speed limit, he might not catch up with them before they reached the Haven. If that was even where he was taking her. The idea of a more sinister destination stabbed at him. He put the truck in gear. Taylor's phone rang. Answering would activate it so he could get back on GPS tracking. He picked up.

It was Taylor's voice, thick with anger, "I want my phone back! Give it to me now or I'll have you arrested."

"I need it. I'm going to get Sage and it can tell me exactly where she is."

"What the hell? She's on a little detour in her life, doing what she wants to do. Leave her alone."

Wayne kept his voice calm. "Listen to me. She's in danger. If you believe the guy she's with is okay, you're wrong. Give me your security code. I might need it."

"Code your ass. You need a swift kick to the head, Bozo."

"Listen to me! If you care for Sage as much as I do.... I'm not going to do a thing with your phone except find her. When we get back, I'll bring the phone to you. You have my word." Taylor's pause was long. Wayne waited. He expected the other man to hang up. Instead, Taylor said one word. The security code.

Wayne lifted his shoe from the brake and peeled out. At the dealership, he pulled around to the back lot near the fence. A friend of his father's had left his police cruiser there while he took a week's vacation, claiming it was safer here than in his driveway at home or parked at the police department lot.

Wayne scanned the row of cars. There. He drove back to the entrance and raced in to retrieve the key. He ignored the startled looks of other employees and barged into his father's office long enough to say, "Dad, I'm taking Delaney's cruiser. Can't tell you why right now. Later."

In minutes he was on the Interstate, police siren blaring, rushing north at a hundred and ten miles an hour.

Almost two hours into his pursuit, Wayne's own phone rang. Answer it? Not if it was his father. No, it was Laura's land line number. He put it on speaker.

Breathless, Laura said, "Wayne, a second ago I got a call from Lee. He's certain the people who killed Holly and tried to kill him are after him again."

"Did he say anything about William Jones?" "Who? No. He said something I didn't understand. He said 'It's not what I thought. It's worse'."

Wayne raised his eyebrows. What could be worse than murder? He said, "Then I don't understand either."

"I can hardly hear you with that noise going on.

What is it? A police siren?"

"Miss Laura, Sage needs to come back home. I'm on my way to get her."

"I'd love to have her back. But why, for heaven's sake?"

His mind scrambled for a believable answer. "We-- Sage and I--don't favor the idea of her being away from home. She has to enter the Academy in about a week." Her silence gave him time to say, "Miss Laura, I went to Lee's house. Now I understand why he wasn't there and why I couldn't get him on the phone. Do you have a new number for him?"

"No, and the old one doesn't work. The number he called me from didn't show on my caller ID. He said it was a

151

burner phone. A burner phone--like some gangster in a movie!"

"If he calls again, give him my number." Wary of more questions, he blurted a goodbye then ended the call. It was rude. He didn't enjoy being rude. The adrenalin of an hour ago might have worn away except for Sage's call. She said she wasn't safe.

He shook his head. Whatever. Committed to this plan, he would work it to the end. He glanced down at Taylor's phone, touching it to light up the screen. The dot was stationary again. They had probably stopped for lunch. The place looked to be less than half an hour ahead of him. Grateful the road was flat, straight and uncrowded, he pushed the cruiser to a hundred and fifteen.

#

**Chapter Nineteen**

That same morning, Wednesday, while she got ready for work, Susan looked into the mirror, combing her hair. She didn't understand men--mostly boys--who had called her pretty or beautiful, who asked to go out with her. All she saw in the mirror was the face of a pale wraith resembling her mother, a ghost lacking the spark of viability. No matter. Someone who was barely alive wouldn't suffer by killing herself? Being dead would feel a lot like this.

At work, a first couple drifted into the Beach Club for an early lunch. Susan took their order. She was able to smile at the cranky, sour faced woman, only vaguely aware something inside her had shifted. It was the realization her suffering would soon be over. She had made the firm decision to kill herself. Anticipation of exquisite relief filled her.

She went to place the order. Through the window into the kitchen, the cook winked at her. Normally, she would turn her back, simply walk away. Instead, she shook her finger at him as she would at a naughty child. It surprised them both.

Susan seldom saw her customers or thought about them in any context other than their food preferences and how they interacted with her. Today, the next couple coming in made her curious. The man had been here many times. She remembered his name from his credit card, *Otto*. It reminded her of a cartoon character's name.

The girl with him looked familiar but she couldn't say why. At first they appeared to be father and daughter; but no, Otto's appearance was strikingly unlike the young woman's. Maybe lovers? No, that wasn't it, either. Otto was considerably older. Their body language appeared cordial rather than intimate.

Susan went to take their orders. Otto was excessively polite as usual. The girl looked up at her. "Susan? Susan Barkin!"

She suddenly recognized Sage. She opened her mouth to respond when panic hit her, illogical, unreasoning panic. Her plan! Something new like this might threaten her plan. A flurry of emotions rose to congeal in her throat. She gulped them down. "Uh, no. You must be thinking of someone else." She saw Sage looking at the name tag pinned on her uniform. She said, "Lots of Susan's in the world. Now, what can I get for you?"

Sage ordered, trying not to wonder why Susan denied her, denied they even knew each other. Merely another aberrant event in this very strange day? She opened her napkin and slapped it onto her lap. There was something much more important on her mind to feel annoyed with this hiccup. How could she get away from Otto--far enough and quick enough away so he couldn't follow and catch her? Or should she wait? Was Wayne coming for her, as he said?

Their orders came. She looked at her plate instead of at Susan, the server who delivered it. She picked at her shrimp salad longer than she should have. In order to get away from Otto she had to appear normal, unsuspecting.

After what she thought was a reasonable time she excused herself and went to the restroom to call Wayne again. What had he said about William Jones? She didn't remember but nothing concerning Jones could be good news. She closed the stall door and took out her phone, holding her breath. The call to Wayne went straight to voice mail. She exhaled disappointment. She walked slowly back to the table to rejoined Otto, who was talking with the beautiful, waif-thin waitress Sage was sure was Susan Barkin.

Susan was saying, "Why, how wonderful, Mr. Wagner. I didn't know you were involved with the Haven. That's...uh...that's...well, bless you for doing it," and she turned away as if uncomfortable with her own words.

Otto looked at Susan's retreating form. The wrinkle between his eyes deepened. Sage slid into the booth across from him. She put her purse on the seat beside her, her phone on the table and tilted her head toward Susan with questioning eyes. Otto smiled. "The poor thing appears to be painfully shy, or maybe depressed...or something." He looked directly into Sage's eyes. "So, my friend, are you ready for the last leg of our trip?"

She hesitated too long, her idea of what might lie ahead cloudy and tinged with fear. But this was not the time or place to get away. She rose. Then stopped. Distant sounds, first heard moments ago, a barely audible whine, was growing louder. A siren.

In the doorway marked Manager, a man in pressed slacks and a white shirt appeared to stand listening. Two faces with wide eyes appeared in the opening to the kitchen. Three other diners looked up from their plates. The sound escalated to a shriek. Then stopped.

Sage leaned out of the booth and looked through the window. The door of a police car swung open. Wayne! He strode up, came through the door. Their eyes found each other. She, and it appeared everyone else, watched him come to her. She slid out of the booth, ready to go to him, but Otto reacted instantly, too. He scrambled from the booth to step in front of her.

Wayne gave him an up-and-down glance, then stepped around him. He held out his hand to Sage, "Let's go. Come back with me."

"Wayne! I...uh...I didn't expect this."

Otto turned to her. "I should hope not." Then to Wayne, "What is this? Who the hell are you and why this dramatic display?"

Wayne's deep voice emerged in a growl. "I don't owe you an explanation, Wagner. And neither does Sage." He turned to her again. "Do you trust me?"

"Yes."

"Then let's go."

She reached back to grab the handle of her purse. Then her other reached and held Wayne's solid grasp. Her scalp prickled; she felt Otto's eyes boring into their backs.

Outside, she ran to the cruiser and climbed in while Wayne kept one eye on the Beach Club's door and another on the entrance to the parking lot, wary of interference.

No one coming after them. He got in. Sage grabbed the seat belt, jerked it down and clicked it in. Still too shocked to speak, she watched Wayne at the wheel pull away, gravel spraying behind from the rear wheels. A minute later at the on-ramp to the Interstate, he accelerated hard. Her back pressed harder against the seat.

He turned to glance at her. "Sorry. I'm overdoing it. No one's chasing us. I've got you."

Sage shook her head at him. "I've never been so glad to see someone in my entire life! How did you find me? And since when do you drive a police cruiser? "

"Kind of a long story."

"One I need to hear!"

"Okay. Simple. I appropriated the cruiser after I knew you were in danger. I couldn't let you strike out on your own in the middle of nowhere. But I'll let Taylor explain how I knew where you were."

"Taylor? What does he have to...?" She stopped. There on the dashboard was Taylor's phone; she recognized it but refused to entertain the thought of how it answered her question. She said, "No matter. You managed it. I'm glad."

He turned to take a longer look at her, nodding.

She said, "Wagner was lying about why he wanted me to come to the Haven. I have to tell you something that might be connected, although I don't know how." She gathered her memories then told him about the couple who attempted to kidnap her weeks ago.

Wayne turned to her. "Damn! Now I'm sure I needed to come get you. Lee was right. Some sort of weird plot, some conspiracy is circling around us--around you."

"I think it started with my Grandmother Holly. Oh!" Both hands closed around the 'Perfect!' necklace. She had forgotten it in her anxiety to escape from Otto. She said, "It's a long story. Wagner tipped me off when he gave me this necklace; it's connected to my grandmother." Wayne turned to look at her with quizzical eyes but she couldn't slow her scattered thoughts enough to explain. She said, "You mentioned something about William Jones when we talked on the phone."

He reached to take her hand before he answered. "Jones was murdered yesterday. Lee took off. On the run again. People after him."

She shook her head and half-closed her eyes as if in pain. "A harmless old man murdered and Lee gone again. How is Mom taking that? How is Mom?"

"I... haven't talked to her since she told me about Lee-- a while ago."

"It's too real. It's like the plot of a book or a movie, but way too confusing. I need to call her." She reached into her purse for her phone. She felt for it, rummaging. Then she looked into the purse while she continued to search. "My phone. It's gone! My contacts and emails. All my pictures." Her hands clenched into fists atop the purse. "At the restaurant. I must have pushed it off the table when I looked out the window. It's still there."

Wayne uttered a string of mumbled words she suspected were curses. "We can't go back for it."

"I know." Then, "I could call it with your phone. If someone answers they might give it back."

"Would it be safe, considering the situation? With Wagner and the stir we caused back there?"

"No. It wouldn't. We can't do anything about it now. But once we get home, I'll get a new android. I can probably retrieve all my data and photos because I synched the phone with my computer." A second later she said, "Oh, damn! My suitcase. In the trunk of Otto's car."

"Is there anything in it you can't replace?"

"I could replace it all in one shoppingtrip. No problem." Minutes passed while she remained silent. Then, "I can't figure out Wagner. It has something to do with my DNA. He's aware my profile is one in a hundred-thousand. Otto's profession is cyber security. He must have hacked the data. But why?"

Wayne tilted his head in an I-don't-know-gesture. She said, "Maybe he was planning for me to be a *Perfect* in the master-race scheme. If it still exists. What I can't figure out is how the Haven fits into any of it. Why is Otto involved with a bunch of special-needs children?"

"Maybe it doesn't matter. Do you really buy the master race thing Lee told us about--that it's still operating?"

"It doesn't seem believable, does it?"

"Not to me. When Lee was on the phone withyour mom, he said, 'It's worse than that'."

#

## Chapter Twenty

At the Beach Club Restaurant, Otto Wagner remained seated, attempting to cool the intensity of his anger. He recognized his own confusion as well but would not betray himself to the others, onlookers who devoured him with their eyes, with their avid curiosity. How many minutes before the damned voyeurs stopped staring-- minded their own business?

Minutes later he sensed a lessening of attention. He threw a twenty-dollar bill on the table for Susan's tip and went to pay the check at the register. He walked out the door to the black Lexus, his refuge on wheels, feeling it was a shamefaced retreat.

A short drive took him to a place out of sight of the restaurant, away from traffic. He stopped the car, and sat back trying to collect himself. What just happened? It was a damned scene that didn't make sense. The guy who took her, 'Wayne,' she called him, wasn't wearing a uniform but the car was a Florida police vehicle. The state of Florida had no jurisdiction in Georgia. Ah, but the FBI had in every state. They investigated kidnappings of children and those that crossed state lines. Had Sage claimed he kidnapped her? If so, the FBI certainly would intervene; he had driven across a state line with her. Fear joined his confusion. The FBI had vast resources. Their involvement might reach enough to expose Dr. A, the Center, destroy their whole setup.

He inhaled deeply to ease the knot in his chest. No, the FBI would have arrested him on the spot if they were involved; then all he had to deal with was a guy name Wayne? And what had tipped him off that Sage was never meant to return home to Florida?

The screw-up by those idiots Jack and Jill, the failed attempt to kidnap her in Oak Bayou. That had probably spooked Sage, made her suspicious. After he staged their accident in the Bay and befriended her, she somehow became aware he knew more about her than he should, that the 'friendship' he worked so hard to establish held a hidden agenda.

Jack and Jill--was their mother a joker or had the siblings earned their nicknames? Dr. A had hired the local criminals with the minds of baboons over his objections. Now he would have to explain to Dr. A just how they lost an exceptional DNA prize. Another thought joined his bitter reflections. What if Sage or that Wayne person had learned about the Center somehow? If Doctor A even suspected it A mental image of the woman in one of her rages frazzled his thoughts.

He got out of the car, walked around it twice, trying to calm himself. He had to make calls. Back in the car, the first was to the Haven. The secretary picked up immediately. He lowered his voice, trying to sound normal. "Hey, Julia, I've got bad news. Our new recreation teacher backed out. She's not with me and she won't reconsider. You need to tell the Director and the doctor." His eyes closed while he listened to her brief response. "Yeah. I'll probably be in tomorrow."

Now Jack and Jill. Jack answered. Wagner said, "It's off. Don't ask me why." He waited. "Because it's off! That's all you need from me. It's your fault, because you screwed-up in Florida." Then, "You get nothing! I don't give a damn for your time and planning." He stopped to listen, aware his anger had made him sputter. "If it was up to me, I'd kick your sorry asses down the hill. However, no matter how stupid you are, A wants to use you. Since she does, I may have another job for you soon. I'll call."

He wiped his spit from the phone, aware he was saving what he despised for last. Doctor A would still be at the Center today, getting ready for her next patient. Why did she bother calling them patients? Bodies would be more accurate, since it was the only thing she dealt with. The Center was her chop-shop, simply a place to dismantle and distribute parts.

His mood didn't improve as he drove the dirt road, then the narrow track leading to the well-camouflaged underground shelter. He parked on the concrete pad above it and got out of the car. He stepped toward the switch to lower the car into the Center's two-car underground garage. He hesitated. Was this the time it would refuse to work? Or leave him suspended in the vehicle half way down?

The mental images poured curse words in Spanish from his mouth. He turned toward the alternate entry, a vertical shaft holding a metal ladder. It hadn't been used since the first time they explored this accursed hole. Three strides took him to it. With anger-knotted muscles, he yanked two metal latches on the cover of the hatch then pulled the handle. The metal screeched, squeaked and groaned, sending a shower of rust particles down the shaft. He turned and descended the metal ladder into darkness.

He emerged into the airlock, his palms slick and rust-red. The metal flakes clung to his shoulders and coated his hair. He clapped his hands together, swiped them against his slacks, heedless of stains, then bent to brush particles from his hair. She was waiting for him in the exam room.

"Wagner. What are you doing here today? Why the hell did you come down the hatch? What if someone sees the car up there?"

She never wasted time on pleasantries. He was as quick and as blunt. "Forget it. I came to tell you we lost the Hundred-thousand. She's not coming."

She didn't screech in surprise as he expected. Instead, her eyes narrowed seconds before she turned and walked away from him. She turned back before reaching the opposite door. "How much did we calculate we would net from her? Let's say at least three infants at--I estimate a million each. Then more than half a million for her heart."

"And three or four more years in this mole-hole? It's not worth it, A."

"So you say."

"I was okay with selling organs. It was simple. I picked them for you and brought them to you. You carved them up and cremated the remains within a day. By the following day, the organs were half a world away. We've tried the baby manufacturing. As far as I'm concerned, it's not worth it. We can pull in half a million for a heart without nine months of waiting."

"I'm telling you, we can push our profits to the max with your ability to do phenotyping. We can guarantee the parents the eye and hair color they want, the shape of the face, half-dozen other features. No one else offering male-parent newborns can match us."

"I'm not convinced."

"We have only one breeder now, that's the problem. We need to expand, find a facility that can accommodate six at a time instead of one or two."

"Your mind is focused solely on the money. Whatabout the risk involved in bringing the men in toimpregnate them?"

"We could collect the sperm and inseminate them ourselves. Or take the patients to the men."

"The patients; you mean the victims. The men; you mean the sperm donors, the baby-buyers. Even if that part went off successfully, without a leak, a betrayal, an arrest-- we'd still have six pregnant womenin the same facility at the same time. A damned maternity ward! I won't partner with you on that kind of circus."

Wagner wanted to walking away, tired of looking at her face. Instead, he turned his palms up to look at the red stains. "How did you get into this, A? How did you go from doctoring a sick old billionaire to this?"

"None of your business. Why are you asking?" "You found this facility while you were taking

care of the billionaire in his mansion. Then when he died and the mansion burned down you approached me to join the cartel. Why?"

Her face twisted into a sneer. "Not because I wanted to rule the world. I'll leave that to you and your Nazi friends."

He leaned toward her. "That word doesn't offend me as much as you wish. The Nazis were deluded to believe they were superior--potential creators of a master race. Their War forced good, strong men to fight and die by the hundred-thousands and sturdy women to reproduce like cattle. It didn't make them rulers of the world. It got them defeated. Afterward they tried to continue the scheme. It was sheer stupidity."

"Not all of them died for their stupidity, and aren't you glad."

"My generation knows how to identify real human superiority. IQ tests and DNA tell all. No bullshit, no lies."

"Then why don't the brilliant people in this country fill all the political offices and why don't the physically gifted fill the armies?"

"The brilliant ones command the media. The physically gifted ones make millions playing their sport. The power to rule is in the money and the media."

The doctor cocked her head.

"Media to convince them and money to buy them. Certain people whose names we know accomplished it while my parents were still tagging their followers with gold necklaces and silver bracelets. Those power wielders and their followers are entrenched now, in control of the economy and the military through politics. My generation couldn't begin to compete with them. We did the next best thing--we went for the money."

"Then why can't we...?"

"No! I'm not even going to discuss it. Yes, we lost the best one I've ever found, but there's another one I've had my eye on for a couple months. Not nearly as perfect, but you can have her in a day or two, as soon as I arrange delivery."

The doctor crossed her arms under the small, pointed peaks of her breasts. "And what am I supposed to do with this new patient?"

"How to process her is for you to decide. You have the list. There's nothing unusual in her DNA profile but she's O-negative with a gorgeous face and long blondish hair."

"So, another surrogate who could produce a light-skinned baby for one of our filthy-rich, Middle- Eastern potentates. They're our best customers for body parts. We haven't begun to fill their desire for lighter-skinned babies."

"This one--I don't believe she could survive it. Susan, her name is. She's too small and thin, too physically fragile for pregnancy or even a lot of organstuff. She'd die on you."

The doctor clenched her fists and took a step toward him. "Then why should I bother with her? Why bring me someone I can't use?"

"No one will come after her, that's why. She has no close relatives, lives alone, has no friends I can find. There won't be a troublesome amount of police involvement like there would have been with the Hundred-thousand."

"This person is local? None of our organ donors have been local for obvious reasons."

"She's different. I'll get her to you tomorrow or day after tomorrow." He turned and left. At the top of the ladder, he punched open the hatch to climb down. Squinting in the sunlight, he climbed into his car and accelerated hard off the concrete. The car fishtailed in the sandy soil; he cared nothing about the deep wounds he carved in its surface.

He reached ingress to the paved rural road, but instead of turning onto it he stopped, letting his hands fall into his lap. This was not the way he had planned it. He moved to this tiny backwater town expecting somehow to inhabit a normal life. How stupid! He could never forget his heritage. The intelligence, the bravery, the determination of his grandparents and their Nazi-inspired idealism was part of him.

When he was a child, his grandfather's steely blue eyes, commanding voice and iron-bound determination made him tremble and cower. The personality of his primary role model had imprinted on him, mind and soul.

So, the cartel. Did he believe he could resign or retire? Blood in/blood out, the gang members' motto was the cartel's philosophy as well. A member who wasn't all-in could not be trusted; therefore, he could not be allowed to live.

Well, at least...at least what? He had lost Sage. After spending weeks in the little town, grooming her for the Haven and the Center. At least what? But yes, he still had the necklaces. He had acted prudently by placing one in the car--in case Sage was difficult, in case he had to ply her with gifts to get her to Georgia. Even that had not worked.

He reached under his seat to the compartment welded in place. He brushed it with his hand for reassurance. It was a secure and easily-accessible safe for ten thousand in cash, several passports with different names and another little Sig Sauer--in case. His safe at home held half a dozen necklaces identical to the one Sage now wore. They were from his grandfather. His memories of the man, the true Nazi, were few. Among those was a guttural phrase, *gut mannlich,* good boy, and a heavy hand like the claw of a predator grasping his shoulder. The necklaces were more than gold trinkets; they were symbols of the past, his inheritance from a man who planned to rule the world.

#

## Chapter Twenty-One

By quitting time at the restaurant, Susan forgot the strange episode of the patrol car and the bear-like man who took Sage away from Wagner. She still felt bad for pretending not to recognize Sage but it was necessary. She would not lose focus or let anyone or anything weaken her intent to carry out her plan.

Now as soon as she finished wiping down the tables and took out the trash she could go home. At the apartment she would write a note about the Mercedes convertible then put everything in order.

Her hand with the dish cloth stopped in its arc. She stood upright. It had been a long time since she drove the Mercedes. The battery might be dead. Probably was. Another thing to check out before she did it-- before she checked out. Wouldn't be okay to leave a non-functioning vehicle for her only heir.

She reached the table where she had served Mr. Wagner and the girl. She put her hand in her pocket to touch her tip money. Why had he left a twenty-dollar bill? It must have been a mistake. She swiped the bench seats for crumbs and bits of food. Oh, a phone. On the seat where Sage had sat. Susan picked it up and dropped it into her pocket. Things left by customers included sunglasses or paperback books, occasionally a wallet or purse. She always turned them in to the manager for his lost-and-found box. She never kept valuables. Her life simply didn't include luxury items; she never won things or acquired things she hadn't earned. With the possible exception of the convertible. Had she earned that by fitting into her mother's strange lifestyle, by never rebelling as a normal teenager would?

Once, another server who loved to gamble invitedher to go with, to the casino located on a ship in off- shore waters. Because she was reluctant, the woman drove her to the dock to see the ship. It was lit up as gaudily as a Christmas tree. She heard faint sounds ofup-tempo music and trills of laughter, the voices of Sirens floating across the water, promising pleasure and riches. She finally agreed to go. There, she foundthe noise, the cigarette smoke, the strange machines were alien. They lured her into pointless activities ending in disappointment and loss.

She returned to her apartment feeling emptier than usual, although she didn't recognize the feeling. She couldn't have described it that way. When a co- worker later asked if she had enjoyed her first casino experience, she said, "I never win anything. I'm not lucky."

Today, an unpleasant awareness brought her out of her fugue. She spent much of her time, as she had just now, in memories of the past or inwardly musing in a kind of daydream. She told herself to say present while she went to the area in back of the kitchen to retrieve her purse and put on her other shoes. She always wore her uniform dress and apron home. Tonight, she would be sure to wash and iron them so they'd be fresh and clean. She wondered if they wouldfit whoever took her place. Probably not.

She walked to the parking lot. Her hand went to the phone in her pocket. She climbed into the car, sat down, put the key in the ignition but didn't turn it. Whyam I keeping the phone? she wondered. She didn't owna cell phone herself, but it was no excuse. The thing couldn't be of any use to her in the day or maybe two days she had left.

* * *

Otto pulled into the four-car garage of his multi-million-dollar beach-front house. He sat behind the wheel while the garage door closed behind him. Overhead, interior lights went on automatically and the door to the hallway unlocked. Yeah, things might seem normal but the working parts of his plan had gone wrong so fast. What else might come at him without warning?

He got out and went back to the trunk to retrieve his suitcase. Damn. There was Sage's red suitcase beside his. Another errand to take care of. He returned from the Goodwill store an hour later, thinking it was a wasted day. No, he corrected himself, it had been a thoroughly disastrous day.

He carried his garment bag and suitcase into the master suite to unpack. The room held mahogany furniture with dark green textiles, subdued and masculine in character. He began to unpack but couldn't concentrate enough to begin the usual routine, his mind roiling with memory of the scene at the BeachClub. The loss of a DNA superstar. It had taken weeks to befriend her, weeks away from the Haven. Now it had come to nothing. The Center. Damn the Center!

He went to the den, poured a glass of premium scotch neat, took a cigar from the humidor and sat in the leather chair cleverly designed to hug his back like the arms of an ardent lover. The Center. Dr. A's three hatchet men were professionals with skills the local brother and sister criminals would never achieve. She called the three the 'Neutralizers.' They had reported former threats were reemerging. Her murderous troika would gladly take care of them, eliminate the human threats, one by one.

The muscle-bound Wayne who kidnapped Sage was certainly a threat and maybe Sage herself. What a pity if the Neutralizers destroyed her. The plan for her had been solid. Dr. A had already informed recipients on the list about the superior quality of the organs they would get. For products from Sage, she had upped the usual price by thirty percent, which the recipients accepted, eager to pay more for the best.

He had arranged for Sage's hotel room to be located on the ground floor wing opening onto the rear parking lot. After she had worked with the children at the Haven for a few days, Jack and Jill would do their thing. Well after midnight, the two would use the duplicate key card to enter her hotel room. The injection would subdue her instantly. Then, the part he suspected they enjoyed, Jill would wound her with a knife, enough to leave half a pint of blood or as much as a pint. Doctor A had given instructions on exactly where and how to cut her. Thus effectively neutralized but leaving a false clue as to her fate, she would arrive at the Center in less than an hour for Dr. A.

He drained the last of the scotch, put out the ridiculously expensive cigar and threw it in the trash, not bothering to save most of it. The clock said it was dinner time. He went to the kitchen, grabbed a frozen entree from the freezer and put it in the microwave. When the liver and onions were hot, he sat down at the counter to eat, rather than in the breakfast nook or dining room.

While he ate, his thoughts went back to Sage, to his plan for her. When she disappeared, leaving behind only traces of blood, police would initiate a high- profile investigation. There would be weeks, maybe months, of publicity with a huge cast of searchers combing the area, candlelight vigils, pathetic pleas from her mother. So much drama. Finally, the case would go cold. They would conclude someone had kidnapped and murdered her.

Memorial tributes would follow. By that time, Sage's perfect organs would be.... His fork stopped mid-way to his mouth then clattered back onto the plate. Damn! Hadn't he dealt with his ridiculous squeamishness? It was absurd; it wasn't him, not in his DNA.

He loaded the dishwasher then went to his computer. The screen saver was a picture of Sport, his favorite kid at the Haven. He picked up his phone. After giving instructions, he was able to reach the kid. "Hi, Sport. How are you?"

"Mister Otto!" The voice was slurred, thick-tongued. Sport was a Downs Syndrome child. "I miss you Mister Otto. When you coming back?"

"I miss you too, Sport. I'm back. I'll come see you and the other kids tomorrow."

"Right now! Today."

"Tomorrow for sure."

"Yay. Will you play ball with me? I play...I play before."

"Yesterday? Yeah? You pitched good?" He talked with Sport for five or six minutes more, until the twelve-year-old began to stutter and hesitate. Otto recognized it as a sign the child was tired. He ended the call.

Damn! He was not a bit reassured. Sport had recently received a diagnosis of kidney failure. It was severe; his pediatrician had put him on dialysis three times a week.

Sport could not understand the procedure, and certainly not the reason for it. He often became impatient in the chair; once he tried to pull out the dialysis port. His kidney failure was a death sentence the dialysis would only delay-- without a transplant. Otto had tried, but there was no way he could get the kid on a transplant list. They had declined to consider Sport, given his short life expectancy as a Downs child. It was as if the kid was on Death Row.

#

## Chapter Twenty-Two

The next morning, Thursday, at the Beach Club, Susan greeted Wagner by pulling a twenty-dollar bill from her pocket and putting it on the table. "I figured this was a mistake."

"No, it is not. Put it back in your pocket!"

She started at the sharpness of his command, then surreptitiously watched him finish his breakfast so quickly he couldn't have been tasting it. Was he waiting for her to mention the scene yesterday? She came to take his plate and leave the check. He stopped her. "Susan, yesterday we talked about you visiting The Haven. Have you ever been there?"

She shook her head.

"Wouldn't you like to meet the children?" She nodded. "Well then, why don't we fix it? I can arrange a tour. I'll show you around myself tomorrow."

"Okay. Thank you." She silently wondered why she agreed. Last night she tried to start the Mercedes but it wouldn't turn over once. A man was coming later today to service it. With the convertible fixed, tomorrow would be her last day--ever.

Wagner took her hand to pat it. "Susan, the kids love visitors. After you meet them, you'll forget their issues and see what nice youngsters they are. It will be a treat for them."

"I hope I won't have to cancel."

"So tomorrow after your shift is over... Oh, let me reconsider. The road there was torn up by all the rain lately. Some of the ruts are still flooded. Let me pick you up in my Jeep. Can you meet me after your shift, in the parking lot of the old factory?"

"But I'm not working tomorrow. I... I have a dayoff."

"Then how about bright and early? Nine a.m.?"

"I guess so."

"Never guess at things, Susan," he said with asmile. She smiled back at him. "That would be nice, Mr. Wagner."

"Otto."

"Okay, Otto. Thank you." She retreated to the kitchen with his plate, her eyes wide with curiosity.

Wagner watched her go, having not the slightest doubt. Most women would tell someone about his invitation, maybe one of the kitchen staff; Susan would not tell anyone.

He walked out to the parking lot to call Jack and Jill. "Tomorrow morning, at nine. Usual place to pickup; usual transfer spot. She's thin and fragile. Go easy with her. I'll have the usual payment for you." He ended the call. They weren't bright, but he could count on them. Doctor A had initiated them by convincing them they were her employees for life--if not by their choice, then by hers. They had never been granted knowledge of or access to the Center--and never would.

Most of their donors, his and Dr. A's, arrived by plane. They hadn't the vaguest idea of what awaited them. Instead, they harbored some dream, some expectation of exorbitant reward carefully crafted and implanted in their minds by Otto or one of his procurers. Jack and Jill would meet the victims at the airport. Without a single stop they would transport the donors to a hidden turn-out on the county road, where they would meet Wagner.

Even so, the duo's curiosity was stronger than their caution. One day after the usual handoff of a victim to Wagner, they left the secluded spot to follow him to a mysterious destination he called the Center. They

173

demonstrated their poor judgment and zero skills in covert tailing while driving the white van.

Wagner pulled his Mercedes into the concealing pines and heavy undergrowth to wait for them. The van came close. He stepped in front of it. It stopped. They didn't move. He waited, a staring contest. He won. They slowly got out to stand in front of him. He pulled the nine-millimeter Sig Sauer P365 from his back holster and pointed it at one then the other. "Try it again, and it's the last thing you'll ever do." The shock on their faces was laughable. He was sure their own mental pictures of Otto, previously painted in pastel colors, suddenly went dark. He still smiled when he remembered it.

\* \* \*

Later that Thursday in Dwightsburg, Susan cleaned and tidied her apartment then sat at the kitchenette table to write out her will. Since she owned little of value except for the convertible, it was easy. The road service guy came in late afternoon. He was prompt and efficient. He was also young and attractive with a self-aware confidence. The convertible hood was so close to the far wall, he told Susan, he would have to bring equipment into the garage to start it. When it was purring again, he asked her, "How long has it been since you drove it?"

"A few months. I'm glad you fixed it so quick. Thank you."

"Here, I'll show you how to put the top down." Without waiting to know if she wanted it down, he completed the task and said, "You need to drive it around for a while, speed limit the thing, juice it. Make sure everything works okay." He didn't leave. He smiled a slow deliberate smile, revealing a dimple in his cheek. He said, "I'm fine with all kinds of cars but this one's cracker rich.

Matter of fact, I should come with you to be sure it doesn't die on you. I don't want you to get stuck out there somewhere." He put an oil-stained, yellow nailed hand on her shoulder. "Then I'dhave to come save you."

She shrugged his hand away. "No. I don't need company to drive it around." She got into the car and backed it out of the garage, so close to him he had to suck in his gut and press his back against the wall.

She waited, the car idling while he closed the garage door, climbed into his truck and left. Then ontothe Interstate to charge the convertible's battery more. Driving, she remembered the night before hearing a muffled ringing sound repeated many times. It had barely registered. Then it did. She was only mildly curious. Her worldly concerns were fading in as the time drew near for her to leave the world.

At that moment the phone, still in her jacket pocket, rang again. She let it. It didn't bother her; it didn't matter. Visiting the Haven didn't matter either; she wondered why she had agreed to it. Sure, once she had an idea of volunteering there. Poor kids. She felt akin to them in a way she couldn't identify. They probably didn't know of her plan to visit so they wouldn't know it if she chose not to go; they wouldn't know and therefore wouldn't feel bad. She could decide to skip it and go--go now--to the bridge.

#

## Chapter Twenty-Three

On Friday morning, the day Susan was to visit the Haven, Taylor in Oak Bayou winced at the pain in his shoulder. In the mirror he saw a purple bruise left by the hand of the Neanderthal named Wayne. Night before last, Wednesday night, the guy came to the lumber yard where Taylor worked to return Taylor's phone. He had claimed he would bring Sage with him but she wasn't in the truck. Wayne had tossed the phone at him and drove away without a word. Now Taylor had his phone back, for all the good it did him. Sage hadn't answered his calls Wednesday night. Thursday, he forgot it completely. He would call her again today, before he slept.

Back at his apartment at eight-thirty, he pulled off his uniform, walking around naked while he grabbed something to eat. He was sleepy but never went to bed before he ate, before ten o'clock.

He took a bite of the microwaved sausage and cheese sandwich. He wondered why Sage hadn't answered his calls Wednesday night or called him on Thursday. Maybe she was too tired from the ride to and from Georgia the same day. Or maybe she was dumping him--for the Neanderthal. The thought bothered him more than he imagined it could. There was something different in this one. He'd try to phone her again soon. Before he took the last bite of the sandwich, his memory strayed to an alternative— other--women. There was always Mandy.

* * *

Susan left the house early Friday morning dressed in blue jeans, a short-sleeved shirt and her light jacket for the morning chill. She turned her car in the opposite direction from the bridge, toward the Haven instead. Backing out of the visit, betraying Otto and the disabled children would not happen.

She arrived a little before nine at the prescribed meeting place, off the secondary road leading to the Haven. She looked around, thinking it was a strange place to meet someone. The asphalt parking lot had buckled over sprouting weeds. The decaying factory was a skeleton, exposed bars of rusty metal with crumbled masonry showing faint remnants of graffiti.

Comfortable with her decision, she lowered her seat back to recline whileshe waited for Otto. The sound of a car approaching made rise to peek out the window. It wasn't Otto's Jeep. And it wasn't Otto! It was a white van. It pulled up within inches of her car. A man and a woman jumped out. The man jerked open her door. His grasping hands reached for her.

"No!" she screamed. She struggled, trying to jerk away but the awkward reclined position kept her down. The man grabbed at her arms and held her. Another face appeared next to him, a woman's. Something sharp stabbed into her. Pain in her arm. It was thelast thing she remembered.

Susan woke. Consciousness stole away her oblivion, rather than breaking over her like a wave. Just as old poets described, like the dawn it stealthily devoured her star-studded darkness inch by inch,ever upward with the sun of awareness in tow. A visceral instinct kept her motionless, her eyesclosed while her alertness grew. Hearing is the last of a dying person's senses to depart. It was the first of hers to awaken. She heard a man say, "Look at her back there, sleeping like a little kid with her pretty hairall spread out."

A stab of panic. She tried to open her eyes but something pressed against them. A blindfold. She felther wrists bound together in front of her. She heard andfelt that they were moving. She was lying on her side in the back seat of a car—no, it must be the white van. Her upper arm stung. She felt a stickiness around the pain. She smelled it and knew it was blood.

The same voice, "I'd love to go back there and pet her like a dog."

The woman's voice, "Grammar, Stupid. Would you pet her the way a dog would pet her, or you would pet her as if she were a dog? You're not going to do either."

"Ha-ha. You have to keep twisting my words around, don't you?"

"I know what you're thinking. You want to rape the kid but you can't. It would be the last straw for Wagner. He'd plug you as casually as if you were a tin can at target practice. Wagner gets her undamaged, the way he expects all of them, even the men."

"Well, speak of the German Turd, there's his car. One little squeeze before we turn her over."

Instantly, Susan felt a hand grope between her legs. Shock exploded in her head but fear paralyzed her, stopped her from flinching, kept her still as a corpse.

The vehicle stopped. The door opened. Rough hands pulled her out. Two people lifted her, began to carry her. She opened her mouth against the gag, trying to scream. A noise stopped her--a ring tone. The phone! It was still in the pocket of her jacket. With bound hands, she reached for it, grabbed it. The man carrying her yanked it from her hand. Dropped it. He bent to pick it up, unbalancing their hold on her. She slipped to the ground, her face inches from the phone. Her captor had keyed it on by accident. A man's voice, *hello, hello!* Rough hands reached for her again. She screamed, "No! You're hurting me. Stop! Stop!"

In his apartment in Oak Bayou, Taylor jumped. The phone nearly slipped from his greasy hand. Oh God! The shrieks were pure terror. He stared at the phone for a split second, then keyed on the map to give its location. "Sage!" he yelled into it. The call dropped. He pressed the key to get her back. It rang. Then nothing. He tried again. Nothing, not even voice mail. He threw his own phone on the sofa, watched it bounce onto the floor.

Echoes of the cries sounded in his ears, noises he hadn't imagined she could make. Behind the terrified words, he heard a man's voice, maybe two voices. Men hurting her? What the Hell! Where was she? Sage hadn't been in the truck when Wayne returned the phone. The map on the phone showed she was still in Georgia. He didn't remember the name of the town or the group home where she was going to volunteer, much less the name of her hotel. But Sage's mother would know.

He grabbed his car keys, went to the door, opened it. Warm air caressed his naked genitals. He had forgotten he was nude. He slammed the door. Inside, he jerked on jeans and a shirt. He jumped into his truck and made it to the Stevens house fast. He ran up the sidewalk and tried the door without knocking first. It was locked. He pounded. "Laura! Open the damned door! I need to talk to you."

Ben appeared at the fence. "Hey! You over there. What the hell? Stand down."

Taylor shot him a finger insult.

"I said stand down, Jerk, or I'll come over and deck you."

At the same instant, Sage opened the door. "Taylor. What's wrong?" She glanced back over her shoulder at her mother, who was limping toward the door mumbling the same question. Taylor gaped at Sage. He stepped inside and closed the door to neutralize the threat from Ben. Both women waited for him to say something. A knock on the door. His arm moved to keep it shut. Sage pushed his arm away and quickly opened it. Ben stood there, frowning. He glared at Taylor. Turning to Laura, he asked, "Is this guy bothering you, Mrs. Stevens?"

"No, Ben. He...he's surprised or excited over something. Thank you. It's kind of you to check on us. Isn't it, Taylor?" Taylor gulped and nodded. With a parting glance of warning at Taylor, Ben left.

The three stood looking at each other. A moment passed before Taylor demanded of Sage, "Was that you on the phone?"

"When?"

"A few minutes ago, damn it. Maybe six or seven minutes."

"On *my* phone? Calling you? No. It's up there where I left it. By accident."

"In Georgia? Then who was screaming?"

"Screaming?"

He managed to give what little he knew for an explanation. After listening, Sage and Laura asked questions he couldn't answer. He said, "It had to be someone up there. While she was telling them to stop, I could see the map. It was only a few seconds but...." He stopped, thinking Sage didn't know he had installed a GPS tracker on her phone. He said, "Quiet. I have to think." He walked into the living room and sat down on the sofa. "If I concentrate, I can remember what I saw. Get me a pencil and paper."

Working on a clip board, he drew an oblong; inside it he sketched a map, mumbling while he drew, "Yellow lines—two intersecting highways here and here. A bullseye kind of symbol for a town, there. A tiny blue area—maybe a lake there. Green must be the woods. Okay, here." He stabbed the pencil point into the paper then carefully marked the indentation with a small x. "That's what I saw. That's where she was."

Sage took the clipboard, looking at the map. "It was a woman? You didn't recognize her voice?"

"I thought it was you."

"Oh! Maybe I know who it was."

"Who?"

"A woman I met once, Susan Barkin. She waited on us at the restaurant. It seems logical she would have found my phone. But whoever. We have to help her. This map you drew is the area around Dwightsburg and the Haven." She went into the office. Laura and Taylor followed. She rifled through a basket holding maps. She unfolded the one of Georgia, placed Taylor's hand-drawn map beside the Dwightsburg area using her finger to compare landmarks. She turned to Taylor, "The place you marked would be here." She pointed to a spot. He shrugged.

"There's a different way to find out." She started the computer, accessed the internet and brought up a mapping program. She compared the program map to the hand-drawn one then clicked on what appeared to be the identical location. The longitude and latitude appeared at the top of the screen. "There. You can't get any more precise than those coordinates."

Laura and Taylor looked over her shoulders to study the map. Laura said, "There's nothing there. The town's at least ten or fifteen miles away."

"But this is it. Has to be. We have to call the police. Ask them to go there. Taylor, will you talk to them?"

He cocked his head at her. "Do I have a choice?"

She didn't answer. Using the land line, she called the police department in Dwightsburg, put the phone on speaker then handed it to Taylor. A woman dispatcher answered. Taylor tried to explain. She said, "Okay, let me recap. So—you heard someone on the phone saying men were hurting her. You don't know who it was or what was going on. Somehow, you managed to get the GPS

181

coordinates where this—whatever—happened. It appears to be out in the pinewoods."

"That's right."

"Then it's outside our city limits. Call the County Sheriff with this malarkey." She hung up. The dial tone made Taylor jump.

Sage searched her computer for the number of the Sheriff's Department. "Got it."

Taylor shoved the phone at her. "You can call the damned sheriff. I'm not in the mood for another sarcastic jerk. I'm done." He walked out. The women turned to look at each other. They listened to the sounds of his footsteps; the front door slammed closed.

"It's us two, then," Laura said.

"Not a problem." Sage made the call to the male dispatcher at the Sheriff's Department. He listened carefully before asking, "Exactly what is your interest in this situation, Ms. Stevens? Why are you calling, rather than the person who allegedly heard these screams?"

"He left. He gave the information to the police dispatcher before she told him we had to call you—the county. It was my phone. It *is* my phone. I left it by mistake up there at the Beach Club restaurant. Whoever found it must be the one in trouble. Maybe it's the waitress or one of the waitresses. It involves my phone so it involves me. I feel responsible."

"Uh huh. Can't do a thing about it today. Deputy up in Bragg County died in the line of duty. All of 'em here are going, including the one on his day off. Read those coordinates to me again." Then, "Okay. Maybe this evening or tomorrow. Thank you for calling."

At the dial tone, Sage swung around in her chair. "Damn."

Laura said, "At least they didn't blow you off completely. They probably think it's a hoax."

"Yeah. Well, I'm going to buy a new phone and call them again. I'm not going to drop this. Or the issue I have with Taylor."

At the store, Sage was disappointed at the limited selection of phones. She could buy one with newer features online, but she wouldn't wait, not even a day. Home again, she went into the office to program the phone. Before long she stopped, listening to the silence in the house. At this time of day her mother would usually be limping around trying to help with the housework.

In her bedroom, Laura lay on the bed face up, her forearm across her eyes. Sage sat down on the bed. "Are you okay, Mom?"

Laura lowered her arm and turned her tear-filled eyes to her daughter. "It's such a lot to handle. A lot to take in over the past week or so. I hate it—a woman yelling for people to stop doing—whatever they were doing to her. And I'm worried about Lee's safety."

"I am too, but we have to believe he can take care of himself. All those years he was on the run, he was safe. We have to trust he's safe now, too. Somewhere." Laura didn't answer. Sage sat with her, wondering how ironic it would be, what a travesty it would be if Laura's father had reunited with her only to desert her again—forever.

#

## Chapter Twenty-Four

Susan woke. She lay on her back on a cot in a small room. It was white; everything was white all around. What was this? The high school nurse's room? "Ah, about time." It was a woman's voice. "All in one piece, too."

Susan looked up, blinking until she brought the woman's face into focus. "Who are you?"

"Doctor A."

Susan looked around. A sink in the corner of the room, an examination table with stirrups for pelvic exams, a balance-type scale. Along the side wall, she saw several medical devices she didn't recognize, shelves holding a box of surgical gloves, tongue depressors, and other medical supplies.

"Am I in a hospital?"

"In a manner of speaking. Sit up now."

She used her arms to struggle upright then swung her feet to the floor. Blood made a whooshing sound in her ears. "I feel a little light-headed."

"Nonsense. Stand up." The woman reached for both her upper arms and pulled her to standing. The woman was dressed in grey scrubs with a stethoscope hanging around her neck. She was tall and thin with an angular look. The lines of her collar bone were visible beneath her scrubs. Her sharp elbows protruded from the short sleeves. Her face was large and square with a pronounced jaw line, small brown eyes and thin brown hair.

Susan said, "I remember someone attacked me in my car. Then I was unconscious. They did something to me." Her breath caught at the memory of a man's hand between her legs. She shivered and rubbed her hands together. Her fingers felt icy cold. "Did the police get them?"

"Don't ask questions. Get up on the table so I can examine you." The woman grasped her arm, pulled her across the small room, then made her step up and sit. Her bare bottom touched cold artificial leather. Someone had removed her clothes. She wore only a thin cotton exam robe.

Doctor A said, "Your pulse." She grabbed Susan's wrist and glanced at her watch. Her fingers touched something of interest. She examined the welt of an old scar. Her eyes widened. She grabbed both Susan's hands and bent them back. Thin white lines on both wrists revealed the work of a razor blade. The diagnosis of self-harm could have been reached by a non-medical observer. She flung Susan's wrists from her own hands, her face revealing both surprise and contempt. Then, inexplicably, a smile crept over her features, revealing cigarette-yellowed teeth. "We eventually get everything we ask for, even if we no longer want it."

Susan blinked. What does that mean? This unattractive woman doctor smelled of cigarette smoke and she was not nice. Without more words, the doctor took her pulse, her blood pressure then examined her eyes and ears. While the woman listened to her heart and lungs and tested her reflexes, Susan looked around again with increased curiosity. The room held no natural light, no windows. She saw no photographs, paintings, or other cheery, personal objects.

"Lie back for the pelvic," the woman said.

"What?"

One of the doctor's strong, long-fingered hands landed on her chest to shove her down. "Now scoot back," she demanded. Her hands guided and placed Susan's feet into the stirrups. Her abrupt manner and not-at-all-gentle touch was unlike anything Susan had ever experienced with a doctor or nurse. Her stomach clinched into a knot. Fear

185

again? Wasn't her supply of fear exhausted after the man and woman grabbed her the way they did?

The exam was rough and painful. The doctor said, "Not a virgin but not pregnant. One more thing before we're through. Lie down on your stomach." Susan turned over. Something cold swept over her shoulders, her waist, the backs of her knees. The doctor moved to her other side. Before she knew what was happening, the doctor secured and tightened three straps holding her down to the table. She had no knowledge of the panic that so often follows the feeling of being restrained. She yelled, "What are you doing to me? Letme up."

The doctor stood at Susan's side. "This is going to be unpleasant. Skip the theatrics. They won't get you anywhere."

A tearing pain ripped through her hip joint. Her head raised in protest. Futile. She screamed. She muffled the sound to a grunt, then lowered her cheek to the table. Finally, a horrible pulling sensation. Then relief. The doctor's voice, "Bone marrow sample. We're done now."

Susan expected the woman to remove the restraints. Instead, she took the things in her hand to the counter, inserted them into containers and put away other items, taking time to wipe surfaces. She came back to release the three restraints without a word, turned to a cabinet door, pulled out a wad of clothing and threw it on a chair. "Get some clothes on."

Susan didn't move. Her body wouldn't. Shock waned but the impact of the savagery inflicted on her in the past few hours remained. She felt every bruise, scrape and needle stick along with other wounds and humiliations. She looked at the doctor, still moving purposefully around the room. Anger rose in her chest. Outrage pushed away remnants of fear and pain. She sat up, breathed deep, bared her teeth. She shrieked at the doctor, "Why didn't you just kill me, you nasty bitch!"

Now standing in the doorway, the doctor smiled again. "Later." She pulled the door shut behind her.

Susan stared at the door until her body sank down, slack as a marionette released by the puppeteer. Numbness enveloped her again. Her mind was heavy, soggy from floods of emotion which had engulfed it then ebbed away. As much as she wished to, she couldn't shut it off. This day was supposed to be her last, wasn't it? Was she dead already, lying here?

She experimented by drawing a deep breath, then forced herself to take several more. After a while she was able to summon again her unfamiliar, seldom- used anger. Damn them! She would make this her last day after all. The people who inflicted pain on her today, controlled her, lied to her—she would deny them satisfaction by *her* actions, defeat them and their deviate motives, whatever they were.

She sat up with effort, climbed off the exam table then shuffled to the chair to put on the featureless cotton clothing. Her purpose was to find anything she might use to kill herself. She read once that men who committed suicide chose to be stark naked when they killed themselves. She couldn't bear the idea of anyone finding her body nude.

Once dressed, she went to the door. She tried to open it. Locked, as she expected. She explored one of many cabinets beneath the room's countertops, looking for—a rope, a knife? Preferably, a scalpel. It would be the carotid this time. It had been so stupid, back then, to cut her wrists. She hadn't even bled right. Not enough to die, anyway.

She rummaged through the second cabinet. A man came in, a tall, muscular man with dark brown skin matched by a shiny bald head. He grabbed her upper arm and swung her around toward the door. He mumbled, "She said you might be up to something." He dragged her, feet scuffing the floor, stumbling, through the door into a wide circular area, past a closeddoor then stopped in front of another door. His huge hand encircled her arm while he unlocked the door with the other hand and pushed it open.

He turned her with both hands to look up at him, as if he handled a rag doll. His smile showed even white teeth. Then his voice emerged, deep and throaty but also soothing, "My name is Cranston. I'll be taking care of you. Be calm now, sweet sister." He pushed herinside. The door shut behind her with a deep-soundingthump. She turned to look at it. It was a very large door.

She stood there. She knew nothing, felt nothing but her heart pounding in the shell of her body, so unaware of herself in shock, she didn't realize she was looking around. *Is this a room?* There was nothing here. Walls and floor, a ceiling high above emitting fluorescent light. Grey, greyness without form. She took a step forward. Then back. The floor was not hard. Not soft, either. It was resilient. Rubber or something similar to it. She breathed for a while beforeshe walked to the wall and touched it. Soft, padded. Well. Okay. A padded room. She lay down then on herside, her back pressed firmly against the wall. Pining for oblivion, she slept.

\* \* \*

Susan sensed someone standing over her. A person holding a plastic tray. She smelled the food it held with no interest. Her awareness went to her body.A soggy feel under her buttocks, between her legs. She had wet herself. It occurred to her she hadn't used the bathroom and had nothing to eat since early this morning. If it was still the same accursed day.

The big man, she couldn't remember his name, looked down at the dark stain. In his rich, soothing voice he said, "Here's your dinner." He put the tray down beside her. "Don't worry. I'll get you another pair of scrubs."

"And my shoes."

"You won't need those again." He left.

Later, a different person came in. Susan lay without moving, without looking up. The voice was the doctor's. "You don't have to eat. A few days without won't do you any harm but if this hunger strike lasts longer than two days, we'll tube feed you. Trust me, you won't like it. Here's your change of clothes and a damp towel. Strip."

She didn't move. She wouldn't. Then she admitted to herself the dire knowledge. If she didn't obey, this vicious doctor would rip the clothes off her. They were clammy and smelly, anyway. She stood slowly, stripped naked and sponged herself clean. She picked up the scrub pants and shirt of faded blue cotton, only a size or two too large. No underwear. Cloth slippers instead of shoes. She glanced up at the doctor, whose expression warned Susan not to ask. She dressed in silence. The doctor gathered the soiled items, picked up the untouched tray of food and left.

Susan lay down again on the not too uncomfortable floor. Was it this morning things went totally insane? Friday morning? Nine hours ago, if it actually was dinner time. Her drifting thoughts snagged on the words of the soft-voice Jamaican, "You won't need those again." She would *never* need her shoes again? Ever? Her body curled into a fetal position. She tried not to think.

How long she remained in a self-induced trance she didn't know. Noise came from the doorway. She listened. It didn't shut. She opened her eyes. Blackness. She blinked. Blackness dark as death. Was she Dead? Blind? She sat up. There, she still possessed a body. Was she blindfolded? She

189

put her hands to her eyes. No. She blinked again, turned her head left and right. She saw not a pinprick of light.

She heard something, something besides her own breath. Swoosh, swoosh. A sound made by the floor.

No, something on the floor...feet, shuffling feet coming toward her. Then a sound, a voice, her own panicked whimpers.

A woman's voice answered. "Don't. It's okay. I'm not going to hurt you."

A quiver inside her. "Why is it so dark? Why can't I see you?"

"Okay, I'm sitting down now. I won't come any closer. You can't see me because there's no light. When they leave, they turn it off so it seems like night. It gradually gets light again. It's supposed to be like morning. It will get lighter and lighter. Just wait. Pretty soon."

Susan cried out, "Where? Where is this? Where am I?"

"I'm not sure, but we're probably underground. None of the rooms have windows. It always feels the same temperature in here."

Susan was incapable of processing all she heard, but the woman's voice was soft, her way of speaking matter-of-fact, even kind. "I'm sorry they got you, but it's nice to have someone else to talk to at night. Sometimes I feel like I'll go crazy with loneliness. Maybe I already am—crazy. I sure hope you don't go crazy. That would be the pits." A long pause. "What's your name?"

"Susan." A minute later, able to control her fear, Susan asked, "What's yours?"

"Grace." A pause. "Susan, would it be alright if I come close enough so we can touch? Only our hands. Don't be scared. You have to believe I would never hurt you."

"It's okay if you do. Just kill me! Come over. Put your hands—whatever they are—around my throat. Kill me." The words dissolved into unrestrained sobbing.

A touch on her arm. A warm hand. A small, warm hand. She continued to cry. An arm, sliding down her back to curl around her waist. She held her breath. Another arm around her then. Two arms encircled her body, warm and human. The warmth of another body against hers. The arms, the body, began to move her gently, slowly, rocking her, cradling her, rocking her.

#

## Chapter Twenty-Five

On Saturday morning, Taylor called Sage to ask if he could keep his usual after-work visit. Sage waited for him at her bedroom window. Weeks before, after okaying it with Laura, she had given him a key to the house. Today he didn't rap on her bedroom door before entering. He walked over, embraced and kissed her. She didn't kiss him back. He backed away from her to study her face. "What, your monthly thing?"

"Not that at all. Let's talk over what happened yesterday—what you said yesterday."

"Let's not."

She continued, "You put a GPS tracker on me. On my phone." It was a statement, not a question. "You were keeping track of where I went. Is there a microphone in my purse so you can hear what I say, too?"

Taylor snorted. "Don't be stupid. What's the harm? Don't make a big deal out of it."

"I'm not making it anything, Taylor. It is what it is. Tell me this, when did you do it, and is it what you usually do with girlfriends?"

"Since we're asking questions, why didn't you call me Wednesday night after you got back? Or on Thursday? You could have used the land line. Then I wouldn't have freaked out on Friday morning when I heard the screams on your phone. I thought it was you."

"Taylor, there were things you said—things you did—before I went up there. We need to discuss them."

"If we didn't talk about them before, we don't need to talk about them now. Why do you always do this to me, Sage? Dredge up the past?"

She turned and walked out, out to the deck, telling herself *just breathe!*

Taylor followed, coming up close behind her. "Don't walk away from me."

She turned. "I *will* walk away from you if you're talking crap. And I don't *always...do...anything* to you."

"Now you're splitting hairs. Don't go grammar police on me."

"This conversation is over. You have to go. Don't call me. If you do, I'll get a new number. I'll ask the *sabum* not to schedule us on the same day at the *dojo.* Don't bother coming to the coffee house."

"You can't be serious. Just like that?"

"Very serious."

"Sage. We're too good together. I've made you happy the past month, haven't I?" She didn't answer. He said, "Nobody has ever dropped me like...."

"Don't compare me to the others."

"Is that it? You're jealous of my past girlfriends?"

She was silent. True, she didn't savor the fact she was only the latest in Taylor's long line of lovers. What bothered her was that she had succumbed to Taylor's charisma and her own lust without knowing who he was. Was it an act of rebellion against the childhood teachings of the woman named Bertha?

She said, "I don't believe it's jealousy. For a while, we were great together. We needed each other. What we had was wonderful at the time, but it wasn't enough. Isn't enough."

"Great sex isn't enough for you?"

"Now you're being dense."

"I don't know what you expect from me. We get along fine."

"You must know our reasons for being together were getting pretty thin."

"We have a million reasons for being together." He reached for her again with a smile.

She backed away. "We've been winding down to a parting for weeks."

He looked into her face for a long time. "A parting?"

She saw disbelief in the beautiful blue eyes she had loved. "I've said all I have to say."

His lips tightened into a straight line. His eyes narrowed. Without words, he turned to go. The noise of slamming doors followed. Sage listened without flinching. The sounds marked the end of their relationship. She started to go inside—and almost ran into her mother. Laura stepped back to avoid the collision, splashing hot coffee on the deck. "Oh. Sorry, Dear. I wanted to have my coffee out here but then I heard you two. He sounded angry. He looked angry when he went past me."

"I'm not surprised."

"Did you break up with him?"

"Yes."

"For good?"

"Mom, have you ever known me to end something, then reverse and backtrack? It's for good. Let's clean up this mess. I'll have a second cup with you. By then, the Sheriff in Georgia should have something to tell me. I'm anxious to hear what they found."

\* \* \*

The Sheriff proved to be a man of few words, all of them delivered in a slow southern drawl that made Sage impatient. "First light this morning, my deputy and me went to the place—the coordinates you gave us. Wasn't a lake nearby, it was a swampy area. I'm pleased to tell you there

194

was no lady in distress out there, not lying on the ground nor showing herself anywhere near-bouts."

"But you searched?"

"I said we searched. I expect someone might-a-been playing a trick on you."

"My friend Taylor was sure she was in trouble. She was screaming for help. It might be one of the waitresses at the restaurant or someone else who found my phone."

"Maybe you're ponderin' it too much, Ms. Stevens. I got nothin'. Nothin' more for you." With an abrupt, "Bye-now," he ended the call.

Sage gripped the phone hard, making an effort to put it down gently. She was not a resident of his state or his county; from the sheriff's point of view, she was only a concerned citizen from Florida.

* * *

The Sheriff hadn't taken the trouble to tell Sage about Susan Barkin. But because Sage mentioned the Beach Club and its waitresses the day before, he ordered his best deputy to go check it out. The restaurant manager told the deputy his little waitress, Susan, didn't show up for work and hadn't called. The manager added information the gal was from California, had no relatives nearby and no friends he knew of. He was getting ready to go out to her place, find out if she was sick or something.

The deputy drove him in the patrol car. There, instead of a young waitress they found a suicide note. Had she really killed herself? If so, where was the body?

It was the Sheriff's duty then to start a search. He sent deputies and volunteers to search the water's edges; they checked the ground beneath the hundred- and-thirty-feet-tall water tower, went out to the big old oak tree where many, many years before, some hangings had taken place.

They searching most of yesterday, with no luck. One volunteer was still at it today. The Sheriff doubtedhe would find her. The body would turn up of its own accord—some day.

#

## Chapter Twenty-Six

The Sheriff's word 'nothing' didn't satisfy Sage at all. She would not drop it. Instead, she would call to talk it over with Wayne.

"Hey, Sage, come on over. I'll put some fresh shrimp on the barbecue. We'll have collard greens and cheese grits to go with."

"I almost forgot you like to cook." She hesitated. An idea came, about getting some answers. She said, "I can't right now. There's something I need to check out first. This evening?"

As a garish sunset lit the west, he greeted her at the door, handing her a beer, then led her to the patio. Charcoal in the grill was beginning to glow. He motioned her to a canvas lawn chair, and sat down beside her. "Let's have it."

"First, what happened with the patrol car you borrowed to come rescue me?"

He gulped his beer. "Turned out okay. After I dropped you off at your house and returned the phone to Taylor, I gassed it up and ran it through a car wash. I drove back to the dealership, parked it where I found it and went home. Next morning, I texted the officer about it. He wasn't real understanding about it. Didn't even ask why I took it. Finally said to forget it—but never do it again."

"I'm glad you didn't get in trouble. So, the phone I left up there...." Sage related the story of Taylor hearing a woman screaming for help. Wayne put down the cooking tool in his hand while he listened. They agreed they would talk it over more afterward. After he cooked. After they put food on the patio table. After the barbecued jumbo shrimp became a bowl full of discarded tails. She scraped the last bit of cheese grits from her plate while she finished the story. "It bothersme. I can't let it go."

"You believe the Sheriff isn't telling you the whole story?"

"Right. He blew me off." Carrying dishes inside, Sage said, "After we talked early today, I decided to investigate Otto Wagner a little more in depth. I called one of my former instructors in criminal justice. He put me on to a skip tracer, a guy who's expert at finding people—and things people don't want to be found."

She shook her head. "Within a few hours he informed me Wagner owns a small Leer jet. He operates a company called Ardently Imports. When I first met him, Wagner said he works for Denham Communications, their computer security expert. My guy checked it out. Wagner did work there for a few years but they fired him. The woman at the personnel office wouldn't give a date of separation or the reason."

"He sounds like a collection of lies, lies walking." She put the dishes and silverware in the dishwasher, started it then leaned against it while she continued. "I tried to get a handle on his ArdentlyImports, but as far as I can tell, it has no physical address and no employees. Wagner lives in a milliondollar home up there on the coast but has no income source my skip-tracer could find."

Wayne said, "It's the profile of a drug smuggler or a distributor. Someone pretty high up on a cartel's food chain."

"It is. But the Haven I was supposed to volunteer at—he's on the board of directors there, the way he claimed. Everything I could find out matches what he told me. The people there love him. He spends time visiting, playing with the kids. There's no hint at all of anything inappropriate. My guy checked their financial report from last year. Another reason they love him is for the money he donates."

"He must be a criminal anyway, with all that unexplained money. I didn't like him from the second I saw him, up there in Georgia."

"We need to go up there—investigate more. Maybe we can figure it out." She put her palms to her face, then swiped them across her forehead as if to wipe away her frown. "More important than poking around, maybe we can find the poor woman who was screaming for help. If it's not too late."

"I agree. But not today and certainly not in Delaney's patrol car. I've had four beers and I have to fix this leak under the sink. Tomorrow, then. Early. I'll pick you up at six-thirty."

At home again, Sage took care of previously neglected household tasks, paid bills and put the office in order until midnight. Finally in bed, she lay awake for what seemed like a long time. When she did sleep, it was without rest or peace.

* * *

She woke at the sound of her name, a stage whisper, muted but urgent. She sat bolt upright and scrambled out of bed. She glared at a dark, shadowy figure, gathering herself to fight.

"It's me, it's Lee. Don't scream. Don't scare Laura."

Rage set her trembling at the sound of Lee's voice. She kept her own voice low. "What are you doing here? You ran away again. Now you come back in the middle of the night? You're lucky I didn't shoot you." "I came to take you to a safe house. You're in danger here. You, your mother and Wayne. We have to go. Now, tonight."

"That's your thing, Lee. You're the one who runs away."

If the sting of her words hurt him, she couldn't tell. He turned on the lamp on her night table. The light made her squint. She recovered quickly to see him fully dressed, all in black. He held a zippered case slightly larger than a sheet of paper. He said, "Now you should go wake your mother and come back in here with her. I came to you first because I didn't wantto scare her. Don't turn on the light in her room. Here'sa flashlight."

She didn't respond. He lifted the case and said, "I brought some things I hope will be of interest, help you understand what's going on."

She still didn't speak or move. He had broken intotheir house in the middle of the night like a thief. Yet there he stood with an earnest look on his face. He wasa few inches taller than she, weighed maybe twenty- five pounds more. Unless he was a black belt, she could take him down in seconds if she needed to. Then she thought, why would I need to do that, for God's sake? He's my grandfather, Mom's father. She refusedto think of him as an enemy.

Finally, she said, "Okay. I'll go get her. It might take a while. I don't want to scare her either."

When they returned, Laura's hair had been brushed and her face was damp from the cold water splashed on it. She shook her head at Lee and demanded, "What is this? In the middle of the night!" She pointed to the bed until he sat, then sat down beside him with her eyes fixed on his face. Sageremained standing.

From the black case, Lee took out a small ID cardwith his picture on it, a picture of him as a younger man. He handed it to Laura. "For almost thirty years, I worked for Interpol. In Paris, then in Lyons where the headquarters is located now. For one year before I retired, in New York City."

Sage and Laura studied it. The picture was, unmistakably, Lee. Laura turned the card over. There was an emblem of the globe surrounded by olive leaves. As Laura titled the card slightly, a holographiceffect revealed a justice scale and a sword superimposed over the globe. Underlining the curve of the globe at the bottom, letters in black spelled *Interpol.*

Sage said, "So you chased criminals across continents, arresting people. What does that have to dowith us?"

"I wanted to arrest them, burned for it, believe me, but Interpol doesn't make arrests. We are--*they* are-- liaisons between law enforcement agencies in every developed country in the world. They still are. Data bases and communications is their *forte.*"

"Every developed nation has its own criminal data bases."

"Sure. Names, fingerprints, mug shots and DNA. Interpol developed a secure international communications network. It enables law enforcementand Interpol to contact each other, share their data. Interpol can analyze criminal trends on a global scale. For a long time, their most important work was identifying and locating war criminals. Now it's tracking terrorists."

Laura handed the ID card back to him. "It's nice to learn something about you--what you did all those years."

Sage said, "Yeah, background info. Now put it in context. What does that have to do with us? Why did you show up here in the middle of the night?"

He sat up straighter and drew a deep breath. "Theykilled Holly and tried to kill me. I went to the FBI. They confirmed what I knew--it was an international organization big enough and vicious enough to kidnap people, kill people. My FBI contacts connected me with Interpol. I was a continuing pain in the collective ass of Interpol until they hired me.

"Here, let me show you something." He pulled several sheets of paper from his folder. Sage noticed one-inch strips of different colors at the tops and bottoms of pages. Lee said, "These are from their public data base. Anyone can access it. They're color coded. Red for wanted criminals, yellow for missing persons."

Sage leafed through them. "Other colors here, too."

"Black for unidentified bodies, blue for witnesses or potential suspects and so forth. Look at this list." He handed her one with yellow borders, meaning it listed missing persons. He said, "Notice how many of these people are from Argentina? The birthplace of the master race cartel. Now look at this name on the blue sheet."

Before her fingers closed on it, Sage saw a name she instantly recognized: Otto Wagner. Blue for witness or suspect. Abruptly she sat down on the bed beside Laura.

Lee said to her, "Most of my contacts at Interpol have retired or moved on by now. When I called Laura yesterday, she told me what little background information you have about Otto Wagner. Then, she explained what happened at the restaurant in Georgia and the incident of the woman speaking on your lost phone."

Both women nodded without correcting him. The woman hadn't spoken; she had *screamed*. He turned again to Sage. "You and Wayne planned to go back up there, right?" She nodded. "You and Wayne are in danger, Sage. I know they tried to kidnap you. The only reason they didn't try it again is you were coming to them. With Wagner. Now you're planning to go there again."

"How could they know that?"

"I can't say for certain your phones are tapped or you're being watched but we have to assume they are, and you are. As I said, I've arranged a safe house. Certain local law enforcement people I'm very indebted to are making it happen. We need to be out of this house before dawn. Ben will drive you and Laura."

Laura frowned at him. "Our neighbor Ben?"

"I talked with him a few days ago then again this morning. Once a Marine, always a Marine. He's a strong, brave man. You'll be much safer with him in his Humvee than driving in your car or Sage's."

"What about you?" Laura asked. "Aren't you coming with us?"

"I'll be along. Wayne should join us, too. He's involved, isn't he? Oh, give me your phones. I'll put them in a safe place for now. I have new ones for you.Untraceable."

Sage said, "I have a bag already packed for what I thought would be a trip up there with Wayne. Mom,let's go grab a few things for you."

Laura left the room. Lee took Sage's elbow to stop her from following. He whispered, "Do you have a weapon?" She nodded. "A nine-millimeter Glock- nineteen with a fifteen-round magazine."

"Bring it."

"In case the safe house isn't safe? Even if it is, howlong can we hide out there?"

"Well, not until you're old and grey like me, for sure."

#

## Chapter Twenty-Seven

The comforting arms surrounding Susan loosened. The woman's voice: "I said it would get light again. See?"

Susan was unwilling to wake into the nightmare again. Her eyes remained shut. The voice said, "Come on, I have to pee. I'll take you with me to the bathroom. The light comes on in there."

Susan sensed movement beside her, heard a soft grunt. The woman stood. Susan's eyes opened. She looked up through the barely penetrable gloom. "Grace? Is Grace your name?"

Grace ignored the question. "Pretty soon it will be light enough for the cameras to come on. You have to be back here with the door closed by then." She reached down to take Susan's hand and helped her up. It was still darker than midnight to Susan. All she saw was a bulky shape slightly denser than the ambient gloom.

As they walked, Susan tried not to step on the heels in front of her. After fifteen or twenty shuffling steps the sound came--a door slamming shut. Light flooded on, blinding her. She gasped, closed her eyes.

"It goes on automatically when you shut the door," Grace said.

Susan blinked to bring her vision into focus. Grace was a rather ordinary-looking young woman with light skin, dark eyes, light brown hair and a bulging midsection. They stood in a small room where three toilets rose from the floor like mutant mushrooms. There was one sink, a shower head on the wall in the far corner of the room with a drain in the floor beneath it. No mirrors anywhere, bare walls, a concrete floor. Grace was seated on of the toilets. "Go ahead," she said. "If you don't you'll be sorry later."

Obedient, Susan used a commode, then washed her hands at the sink. The running water made her aware she was thirsty. She bent down and pressed her cheek against the faucet to drink. Then she let the water run while she splashed it over her face repeatedly, dashing sleep from her eyes, scrubbing tears and snot and drool from her nose, cheeks and neck. Grace's arm reached around her to turn off the tap. "It stops automatically if you use too much."

The warm bulk of the woman's body made Susan look down. Her eyes widened. "You're pregnant!"

"Really? I hadn't noticed." Her sarcasm transformed the woman's face and voice.

"I'm sorry," Susan mumbled.

"I'm six months; almost seven. We have to get back now." She grabbed Susan's hand, switched off the light, waited a second for the last glimmer to die, then opened the door. She slowly drew her companion back into the darkness, back to where Susan had slept in her arms.

Susan sensed Grace was about to leave. "Don't. Don't go. I have to know why I'm here. You have to tell..." Grace was already halfway across the room. "Tonight," she said. "When it's dark again. Not until."

The door slammed, a sound with the power to break Susan's heart. She waited. Unable to sleep, unwilling to reenter the self-willed trance that provided refuge earlier, she waited. Gradually, it did grow lighter as if day was breaking. This false daybreak was devoid of warmth, without the glory of sunshine, without the twitter of birds or voices of people, without the feel of other living beings present in the world with her.

Eventually, the man with the musical voice came in with a breakfast tray. He put it down, called her by her name and told her again his name was Cranston. He led her out the door, into the same restroom she had entered hours before with Grace, and turned his back while she used the toilet.

Back in the padded room, she decided to eat the food. Minutes after it was gone, she couldn't have said what it was. She thought only of Grace, her questions for Grace. Hours later, Cranston came back, smiling, to pick up the breakfast tray. He walked out with it, leaving the door ajar. She rose, walked to stand in thedoorway looking out onto a circular area about twenty feet in diameter. Five closed doors marked equal distances around the circle. Two pieces of outdoor- type furniture near the center suggested the circlemight have once been a living area.

Cranston appeared through the door nearest to herright. She jumped, startled. He took her hand. "DoctorA said you can go to your room. If you continue to eat and behave yourself, you can stay there." He led her out.

Awareness hit her--someone leading her around again as they would a child. Her almost imperceptible jerk of protest didn't escape Cranston. He steered her toward the door to the left and unlocked it with one ofthe keys on a metal ring.

Her quick glance into the room showed her all there was to see: a cot bolted to the wall, a toilet and sink in full view, a wooden chair and a shelf low enough to use as a desk. On the shelf were three books, hardback books bound in dark cloth, old, thick and substantial. The room looked like a prison cell she once saw in a television show. Cranston turned and leftwithout a word.

There was no handle on the inside of the door. She touched it, ran her palm across it. She traced the narrow cracks marking its outline with her fingers. She stepped to the wall on the right. Solid plaster, maybe even concrete, cool to the touch. Same as the other walls, it held no window or any other feature.

Looking up, she saw in the corner of the wall what appeared to be an opening the size of a shoe box covered by a metal grill. *An air vent.* In the middle of the ceiling was what looked like an ordinary florescent tube. She was sure it would modulate light, as the one in the padded room had, to simulate the setting and rising of the sun.

Hum. She felt only mild curiosity. Yesterday her venue was similar to what she imagined a padded room in a mental hospital would be. Now she was in a prison. What a strange game this was.

Well, let's try something, she thought. She yelled. At first they were hoarse, meaningless sounds, then an experimental "help, help!" She screamed two more times before the door popped open. Cranston bolted into the room, slamming the door shut behind him. "We can't hear you, Sister. The rooms are sound proof. But we can see you." She followed the tilt of his head to what appeared to be a tiny bubble in the wall nine feet up. "You're wasting your time and your voice." He left as abruptly as he arrived.

It came to Susan then. Grace is right. Cameras. Cranston and Doctor A and who else can watch us—watch everything?

She sat down on the cot. She looked at the books on the shelf. She wondered what the titles were, who wrote them, who might have read them before, where they came from. Her first idle ponderings in many hours lulled her. She slept, through an artificial twilight and the first hours of night. She woke to the blinding darkness. She rose from the flimsy cot, felt her way along the wall to the closed door, traced its shallow seams with her fingers and waited for Grace to come. She listened for a noise, the merest suggestion of metal on metal or a shift in air flow. The hair on her neck rose; a chill crawled down her back. Someone had opened the door. She backed up. "Grace? Is that you?"

"No... the bogeyman. Who else, my Susan?" The touch of a groping hand made her jump until it settled on her shoulder. "Grace, you have a key. Why do you have a key?"

"You ask too many questions. Aren't you glad to see me again? Let's sit down and talk."

"Are you with them, Grace?"

"With them? You mean with Cranston and the doctor? Christ in a bordello! Bite your tongue."

"But how did you get a key?"

"By doing Cranston some favors, that's how." "Cranston? What kind of favors?"

"What do you think, Lollypop? Sexual favors. It was the only thing I had to bargain with." She hesitated. "Oh. You do look young. How old are you, little one?"

"Twenty. How long have you been here? Have you tried to get out?"

"Of course I've tried. Tell me what it's doing outside. Is it raining? I miss the rain so much."

"Isn't there a door we can find?"

"A door? You mean the exit? Door E, where-ever it is? If I had a key to the exit, wouldn't I be out of here by now?" She didn't wait for an answer. "You were out there day before yesterday. Do you read newspapers or watch news on TV? My name is Grace Williams. Have you ever heard my name? ...missing person? ...picture on a milk carton...anything about me?"

"No. How long have you been here?"

"Let's sit down." Grace shuffled forward, Susan with her, until they both sat on the cot. Grace asked, "What did you eat the day before they got you?"

"I... what does it matter? You're not making sense."

"Yes I am making sense. I haven't eaten anything but pre-packaged crap for...a long time. Does real food even exist anymore? Is there steak, and ice cream, green salads and apples and...." She sighed. "Never mind. Tell me what's on TV these days. What movieshave you seen? Is Brad Pitt still in some of them?"

"Grace, how long have you been here?"

"You won't quit until I tell you, will you?" They listened to their own breathing. Finally, Grace whispered, "You'll be sorry. You'll wish you hadn't asked."

"I won't."

"We'll see. So, when they took me, it was only a week or so before...before the man raped me. I was pregnant for the full nine months then. "

Susan interrupted, "Cranston? Is he the--did he do it?"

"Someone else. I think they gave me some kind of sedative, because I was so woozy, I couldn't really fight. He held me down. It happened--it happened forthree days. Twice a day for three days, he did it. I haven't seen him since.

Well, a week later, the doctor made me give her aurine sample. She said I was pregnant. Then...after I had the baby...it was around two or three monthsbefore they did it again. Not the same guy. I'm pretty sure I'm six months now, so that would make it...eighteen months? More than a year and a half...I guess." Her voice caught.

Susan struggle to grasp it all. A barely audible keening broke the silence. Susan reached for her arm. "Oh, Grace. I'm sorry. I'm so sorry. I didn't mean to make you cry." A memory came of Grace holding andcomforting her through her own storm of emotions. She said, "I just wanted to know why I'm here and how longbefore I get to leave." She grasped Grace's hands but Grace pulled away, still crying a sorrowful, open- throated wail.

It was a long time before Grace was able to stop her private mourning. She sniffed then cleared her throat several times before she said, "I can't say whenyou'll get to leave, my Susan. If ever. Why do you wantto? I mean, last night you didn't even know who I wasand you didn't ask to go. You said 'kill me.' What were you thinking, for heaven's sake?"

Susan took the question literally. "I... for a long time I've wanted to die. But now I think it's only peace I want. I've never felt it  peacefulness. Mother never

did, that's for sure. Maybe I'm like her. The only way I'll come to it is to die. But those people  what they're

doing is terrible. I hate the thought they own me--they control me. I don't want them to kill me."

"Stay long enough and they will." Susan inhaled sharply. "Well, it's not a peaceful place, my Susan." Grace stood. "I'll take you to visit the person who's been here the longest besides me."

She took Susan's hand to lead her through solid darkness, a thing in itself. Susan sensed they were in the open space she saw earlier. She heard what she imagined was Grace patting the wall to their left, trailing her fingers across it to guide her. They came to another door. Grace dropped Susan's hand. She heard the familiar metal on metal sound of a key turning a lock. They stood in the doorway of another room. An evil vapor wafted toward them.

"John, hello. John, it's me, Grace." The stench of excrement, urine, dirt and sweat assaulted them. An inhuman screech pierced their ears, echoed off the walls, followed by sounds of movement. Grace slammed the door shut with one hand while with the other she grabbed at Susan's shirt to jerk her back. Susan's shoulders and head hit the wall. She pressed against it, palms flat on the cold hard surface, panting in fear.

Grace's voice, "You asked for it. There it is." "What? What? I don't understand."

There have been lots of others who came through, in and out again within a day or two. Came and went like ghosts. But this guy, they brought him here about a month after...after I started this pregnancy. They told him he had cancer in his eyes, that this was a hospital. He was so confused from the drugs they gave him, he believed it. They took both his corneas. He was okay for a while afterward. Being blind, he could only hear them, not look into their lying faces. He believed them."

"I hate them! I hate them!"

Grace ignored Susan's screams. "Then they took one of his kidneys. It started then--I could see the fear in his face. He would tremble when he heard footsteps. Even after he knew it was me, he was still afraid. I guess it was a few weeks later, they did another surgery--took something else, maybe part of his liver. It was what you could call the last straw, I guess. I had to stop going to talk with him at night. I check on him now and then, but he's He'll stay crazy until they use him up and throw him away."

The import of what she was hearing finally struck Susan. "Oh God! Oh God!" Still with her back pressed against the wall, her head turned from side to side. Then the motion went forward and back striking the wall, bashing the concrete with her head.

Grace grabbed at her to pull her away. "Stop! That won't do you any good. Don't you go crazy on me." She explored the back of the younger woman's head with her fingers. "No blood. Good, but you're going to have a goose egg. We're going back to your room." She dragged, rather than led Susan back.

They sat on the cot for a long time, holding hands, saying nothing. Grace broke the silence. "People come in and go out again the same day or the next, from the padded room through the third door. The only time I was inside the third room is the day I had the baby. But I don't remember much except the pain. I don't think they gave me anything for the pain. Anyway, my key doesn't fit the third door. I'm pretty sure it's an operating room. It's where the doctor...takes...things from them."

Retching sounds escaped from Susan's mouth. She gasped, retched, gasped again.

Grace remained silent while her hand squeezed Susan's in weak spasms. She said, "When I was in high school the science teacher taught us chemicals in a human body are worth about one dollar--to maybe as much as five hundred dollars. What baloney. I'll bet they sold my baby for thousands. They wouldn't tell me if it was a girl or a boy. They wouldn'teven let me touch her...or him."

Susan felt a tremor in Grace's hand like a live thing squirming. Grace's whole body shook. Susan reached to embrace the pregnant woman's bulky form. This time Grace was willing to he held and comforted. Then she pulled away and continued as if there had been no pause. "That wasn't all. They took the placenta to use it. They can make medicines, even makeup, outof it. They took the umbilical cord for the cord blood--stem cells can cure cancers. They even pumped my breasts for the colostrum in my first breast milk. It wasdisgusting! By the time they finished with me, I was...well…I felt like an animal; it's how they treated me. Like an animal. I bet they made a million dollars from me, maybe more. Now they're going to do it again."

"Oh Grace. I'm sorry they took your baby. What a sick crime. We can't let them do it again. We can't let them take your baby again. We have to get out of here. We have to find a way. Even if we have to...to beat them up. If that doesn't work we'll kill them. I've had dreams of killing that nasty bitch doctor. Killing someone beside myself, for a change. We have to findaway."

#

212

## Chapter Twenty-Eight

Sage sat beside her mother in the back seat of Ben's Humvee looking out the window. They had left behind the few intersections in town to head northeast. For the past half hour they had seen no hint of street lights. Above the dark horizon, a watery- looking half-moon hung perilously on its backdrop, a sprinkling of tiny stars in a colorless sky.

With her eyes closed, she pictured a map of the area and matched the few turns they made to the roadsshe saw in her mind. They were probably in the pine forests of Georgia by now. She wouldn't ask Benwhere they were. He was on a tactical mission this strange night, a mission requiring his bravery, his skill,his discretion. Her respect for him grew by the mile.

More than an hour after they left the house, he turned the wide vehicle down a dark, narrow path hemmed in by trees and undergrowth. The branches produced a chalk-on-blackboard squeak against front fenders and doors. A quarter mile farther, a large square building appeared. Ben stopped a few feet in front of the structure. One of its doors swung up silently. Then they were inside the dimly lit interior. Itlooked big enough for four or five vehicles, more likea warehouse than a garage.

Ben shut the engine shut off. The silence held them in stillness. Then he opened his door and theirs to set them in motion. With bags in hand, they climbedout, mounting steps that led to a wide door.

Ben said, "I won't go in with you but I'll wait hereuntil you're inside." Sage went back to shake his hand.

"Thank you, Ben. You've done so much for us. More than any other nice neighbor would have done."

He appeared startled. "Whatever. You're welcome." He climbed back in the Hummer and tilted his head toward the door they would enter. He watched until they were inside then Sage heard the door of the Hummer slam closed.

Glaring kitchen lights stopped them. A dozen glowing bulbs refracted off aluminum-clad appliances and reflected off rows of gleaming, copper-bottom pots and pans hanging from the ceiling. The room appeared as oversized, as utilitarian, as the garage.

A man stepped through the far doorway. His feet slanted outward as he approached so he appeared to duck-walk. He was grey-haired and of average height. His stomach was a large round organ with an assertive presentation. It protruding over his belt. On the belt was a large gun in a leather holster. They widened his impressive stance.

"Hello, Sage." He extended his hand casually. "And this must be Mrs. Stevens. Pleased to meet you." Laura took his hand with a weak smile. She turned to Sage.

Sage said, "Sergeant Phillips. I'm surprised to see you here. Mom, Sergeant Phillips is an instructor at the college. I was in one of his criminal justice classes."

"Retired Sergeant Phillips now. My name is Tom, just Tom, please. Come in. I'll show you around." He turned for them to follow.

The house was one-story, its architecture reminiscent of a those in other semi-tropical locals. It consisted of two two-story semi-circles which created an interior courtyard with no means of entrance from outside. In the grassy circle of the courtyard, dim lighting revealed benches, a basket swing hanging from the limb of a tree and smaller fruit trees holding colorful but unripe fruit--pomegranates, oranges and limes. Colors glowed like bulbs on a Christmas tree. Their guide Tom doubled back when they reached the door to the opposite wing. The rooms across the courtyard would evidently remain unexplored.

Tom asked, "Would you ladies prefer to room together, or separately?"

Laura reached for Sage's arm with a look. Sage said, "Together, please."

He led them into a large bedroom with what appeared to be custom-made beds, larger than a twin and smaller than the double beds at home. They put their purses and bags down before they returned with him to the great room at the apex of that wing. Sage and Laura went to a seating area. It held a long sofa upholstered in cranberry fabric and two oversized chairs in a matching pattern. Before they could sit he asked, "Are you hungry? Lots of food in the kitchen."

Laura sank down into the sofa with a sigh. "Not at all." Sage shook her head no. She sat beside Laura, pulling one of many plump cushions onto her lap.

The Sergeant sat, feet planted solidly, knees widespread to accommodate his paunch. "As soon as Lee gets here, I'll leave, but before I go, I'll have a little midnight snack." He looked at his watch. "A four-a.m. snack." He levered himself upward. Before he could go, Laura asked, "Have you and Lee known each other long?"

"My brother has. Lee is best friends with his oldest friend from--well, you know how it goes." He left before she could question him further. Laura leaned her head back. With another sigh she closed her eyes.

Minutes later the sound of male voices from the kitchen sent Sage to greet Wayne and Lee. Lee nodded at her then continued into the great room. Wayne reached her and stopped. His strawberry blond hair looked tousled, a bed-head and his clothes were wrinkled. So was his forehead, probably from a struggle to comprehend the reason for this nighttime move. Sage felt a rush of emotion. She embraced him. "I'm glad you came."

Instantly his arms went around her, too. She pressed close with her cheek against his chest. He looked down at her and managed to smile. She didn't let go. When she finally looked up at him, she said, "I didn't know it could feel right to feel small."

Tom had ignored them while he constructed a many-layered sandwich. Sage took Wayne's hand and led him to the great room. Lee was there, sitting beside Laura on the sofa. Sage and Wayne took the two chairs.

Wayne leaned back in the easy chair, propped an ankle on his knee and looked at Lee. "I'm ready to find out what the deal is."

Lee nodded, "Okay. Thank you for coming with me without a long explanation. We didn't talk in the car. Now I hardly know where to start."

"It has to do with Otto Wagner and the group you told us about, right?"

"Yes, but what I have to say is going to be difficult to hear. For all of you. I hope you believe me. If so, you'll understand why this midnight caper, as Laura called it, was necessary."

Sage anticipated at least part of his narrative. Would she at last learn what was going on, what had been going on for...how long? Secrets and lies had given others control over the situation, over her.

She asked, "Wagner tried to kidnap me because of my DNA, didn't he? But I don't think it had anything to do with the master race scheme we talked about a few days ago."

Laura added, "On the phone the other day you said it was worse than that. How could it be?"

Lee held up both palms. "Wayne, I need to tell you how grateful we are you went after Sage and brought her back. Wagner used the Haven as a cover story. You would never have seen her again."

Laura uttered an anguished sound and grabbed her daughter's hand.

Lee continued, "I'll give you some background so you can make sense of it. The plan for a master race started as a shared delusion by men who were ruthless but motivated by a vision for their future, a mostly nonviolent revolution. The last of them grew old and died before they were able to truly inspire their children and grandchildren to make a gradual march toward ruler-ship.

"The third generation had no idealism and little patience. They pursued the same goal, but abandoned subtle methods. They began a program of kidnappings and sometimes murders in South America but also in satellite locations in the States and Europe."

Sage said, "They were here in Florida when Holly was killed, weren't they?"

"They were. They were responsible. At that time, local police didn't have a clue about the reason behind Holly's murder. The conspirators did several kidnappings in the panhandle. Interpol didn't have enough intel either, to connect those crimes to one motive."

Laura asked, "So what happened?"

"DNA testing was fairly new but someone in their network got the idea DNA would be an accurate, scientific method for identifying superior human genomes--markers for health and longevity. Then one or more of the group got the idea to find those people, not to persuade them to join the master race plan, but to sell their organs--the organs of super-healthy people."

Wayne said, "Selling organs from living people is just an urban legend. Like the guy who wakes up in the bathtub with only one kidney?"

Lee shook his head. "I'm afraid not. Well, that particular story is almost certainly an urban legend but organ selling has been going on almost as long as organ transplants. In other words, for decades. But not organ theft, especially not on the scale we found here." Sage looked over at her mother. Laura's hand had clapped over her mouth. Sage said to Lee, "So, transplants. Like heart transplants. Not from cadavers?"

Lee nodded. "The master race cartel learned a human heart can be sold for more than half a million U.S. dollars, while one kidney, which a person can survive without, is worth a hundred and thirty thousand or so."

"That's why they wanted me...they kill people for...." Sage's voice faded.

Laura turned to look at her. Her eyes seemed to grow smaller in her stricken face until she appeared ill. Lee turned to take Laura's hand. He whispered something to her. She said, "I'm okay. Go on."

He hesitated. Then said, "Making money, big money, overtook and replaced the original goal of the master race cartel."

Wayne said, "Wait a minute. I'm an organ donor. It says so on my driver's license. Why would anyone...?"

"There aren't enough people donating. Not enough organs to go around, to put it bluntly. People spend months or years waiting for a heart, a double- lung or a pancreas transplant. They've met the strict criteria for getting on a list in the first place, but many die while they wait."

"Right. There's a list. There's a system for prioritizing and doing transplants."

Lee nodded. "In this country, the legitimate organization managing cadaver transplants is the Organ Procurement and Transplantation Network. They and their parent organization, the United Network for Organ Sharing, control it all. With medical decision making and carefully vetted lists of recipients.

"So, you're asking what people in other countries do, incredibly rich people who've never been on a list in their

218

lives." He paused before saying, "Desperate people are paying three hundred thousand dollars for a pair of lungs. For a liver, around a hundred and fifteen thousand. Many of them realize the organ is taken from a living person but they don't care."

Sage looked at Wayne, who was cursing under his breath. She tried to hear what he was saying. The ankle he had propped on his other knee came down; he planted both feet on the carpet and leaned toward Lee. "I still don't see how it's possible."

"Hacking into medical records and DNA data bases gives the cartel information on a person's national origins, blood type, disease markers or lack of same, even probable physical characteristics. It allows them to match donors closely to recipients. It also allows them to impress the recipient with the superior nature of what he or she will receive. It increases the amount of money they ask for--and get."

Sage shuddered, then tried to shrug it off. She pushed her shoulders back as if to free herself. "Hacking into data bases--that's Otto. He doesn't have to limit himself to one public data base. He's a cyber security expert and it's opposite--a hacker. He selects the people they want."

Wayne was shaking his head. "It can't be that simple. They need a doctor, a surgeon, to remove the organ and another surgeon--a whole team of surgeons--to transplant it. How could they arrange everything without a huge medical center, a whole set-up?"

Lee responded, "You're right. A doctor, not necessarily a surgeon, has to remove the organ. One or two people can accomplish it in a small facility--especially if they don't have to keep the donor alive. They can put the organ in a container with ice and a cool saline solution and fly it to some destination they've arranged. That's where the actual transplant takes place. Believe me, at some facilities they

219

ask no questions. Most of those places--I hope *all* those places--are beyond U.S. borders."

Wayne looked at Sage, "It's why he owns his own jet plane and has a pilot on retainer. To connect with large airports providing international flights."

"You're talking about Wagner?" Lee asked.

"Yes, but I still can't imagine the medical expertise they would need to pull it off."

Lee had the answer, "The unwilling donor's DNA also gives them blood type. If they do a bone marrow analysis for tissue matching, along with medical observation and a quick set of vital signs, they have more data than some transplant hospitals.

"For complicated transplants--lung and heart-- they have to transport the live donor to the transplant location. Half a dozen of those facilities are under investigation by Interpol in South America, Asia and the Near East."

Wayne shook his head. "International human trafficking. It's not the kind we're used to hearing about."

Sage couldn't remain still any longer. She stood, turned to Lee and spread her arms wide in a gesture of impatience. "So, what is Interpol doing? Why haven't they stopped it?"

"Remember, Interpol agents can't arrest criminals. They coordinate with local law enforcement. You can bet Interpol is on it, but in some poor, undeveloped countries, the authorities aren't inclined to regard the activity as a crime. They see it as a legitimate enterprise supporting the local economy."

Her lips settled into a grim line; her face full of pain. "So, let's go back to the beginning. The beginning of all this for me, anyway. I can guess why master race cartel murdered Holly. They couldn't tolerate her leaving. She might warn other young people or even alert authorities. What I want to know is who killed her. If those people are still alive, I want them accountable. I want them to face justice!"

Lee's eyes closed. Seconds elapsed before he answered. "It's what I've wanted all these years." He took a deep breath before swiping at his eyes. "Even after I joined Interpol, I didn't have a starting point to work from. Holly had told me the name of the group's enforcer, the one who monitored her constantly, but it turned out it was the name and identity of a man who had been dead for thirty years. A fake identity." He looked into his granddaughter's face. "When I heard the name Otto Wagner, I researched, going back to...to Holly's time, our time. I'm certain her recruiter, her contact, was a handsome man in his mid-thirties named Gunther Wagner."

Sage's intake of breath was audible. "Relative of Otto Wagner, I'll bet."

"Otto's Grandfather. And your next question is, 'is he still alive?' No. Neither is his son, Otto's father. Both murdered. Evidently early deaths were common while the group transitioned from master race cartel to organ marketing cartel. Pure chaos, the individuals who held the original goal of world dominance against the money-hungry capitalists. You can guess which side won. The cartel warped into the crime against humanity it is today."

Sage drew a deep breath. "I'm glad you were able to find out who killed Holly--who took her from you."

Lee nodded and gulped.

Sage said to him, "I consider most of our family mysteries solved now. Knowing who you are completes it. But without justice, without accountability, it doesn't satisfy me at all."

#

## Chapter Twenty-Nine

The third day in the safe house brought change. Wayne was tired of making up excuses for why he couldn't come to the dealership to fill the important duties his father had entrusted to him. His absences and the previous act of hijacking the police car challenged the trust and confidence his father had in him. He made it worse by telling his father he had no idea when he would be able to return to work. Their compromised relationship deepened his unrest. He asked Sage to come into the courtyard with him for a private talk.

The courtyard's ambiance was tropical this late in July, damp and warm, smelling of citrus and greenery. Around the front perimeter, tall bird of paradise shrubs and beds of rex begonias alternated deep green and purple hues with bright orange. Bordering the rear wing, ivy climbed the brick balustrade while ferns embraced the half-circle.

In the green sanctuary, Wayne and Sage held hands while they strolled a gravel path to several benches placed under the lemon trees. Bits of waxy green leaves and drops of moisture covered the painted iron benches. Wayne took out his handkerchief to clean one before they sat.

Describing his dilemma to Sage he said, "I may be in danger, but I don't know if that's a reason for ruining my relationship with my dad."

"I know he's very important to you, but isn't your personal safety the bottom line? How would your dad feel if he lost you?"

"Somehow I can't picture being knocked off by this invisible cartel."

"I know. It still seems unreal to me too, but I was their intended victim twice. That makes me believe it. The attempted kidnapping right here in Oak Bayou, remember?"

Wayne put his hand on her knee. "I remember. It makes me furious. But my work at the dealership is important to me. I enjoy it and Dad needs me there."

"I still say your safety trumps any considerations about your work. Let someone else do it."

"Yeah, there are a couple of guys there who could do the job. But not as well--not as diligently as I would."

Sage watched his mouth become a severe line. Deep vertical wrinkles appeared between his eyes. Then he turned to her. "I'll officially resign. Let someone else do it. When this is over, I'll explain it all to Dad. I'll have to face the consequences--without objecting or complaining."

She looked into his eyes, put her hand around the back of his head and pulled it down to kiss him on the lips. The kiss didn't stop. It became a long, serious kiss. It ended. In shock, he said, "What was that?"

"What did it feel like?"

He accused her with his expression, with the tone of voice. "It felt like a kiss. Not just a friendly kiss. It felt like a sexy kiss."

"Well, so it was." She looked away, rubbing her palms together. "In the last few weeks, I've been forced to admit to myself how much I care about you. More than for a friend."

Wayne bent his head as if in defeat. He sighed and looked up. "At your request, I tried to eliminate this element from our relationship. Are you saying it's okay now? Oh, before you answer that, what's up with you and Taylor?"

"I broke up with Taylor. We dated for a month before I realized...I admitted to myself I liked the sex and I loved his looks but I didn't like *him* much. Then I stopped even liking the sex. I still care about him in a way--maybe as a friend."

"I thought our relationship was just friends."

"It was. But lately, when I look at you or think about you my feelings grow. It's like they just expand my heart until I think it will--I don't know. What am I saying?"

"God! You described the way I feel about you. I've managed to ignore it, but I'm as in love with you and hot for you as ever. Thing is, this isn't the time or place."

"You're right. We can't; we shouldn't, as much as we might want to. A lot of things are up in the air right now. We'll figure it out."

He took her in his arms in an unsatisfying, sitting embrace. He stroked her hair and lowered his chin to rest atop her head. Then he cupped her face in his hands, looking into her eyes. "I will welcome, always, each precious part of yourself you're willing to share with me. I love you. I've loved you for a very long time."

* * *

Otto Wagner's mind fixed on Sport as he drove toward the Center. The kid clearly was getting worse. This morning Sport grew tired and stopped after he swung the bat three or four times. He would go downhill fast now, unless they did something drastic--like a transplant. Poor kid. He had no idea his dialysis episodes were keeping him alive. With a child's understanding of death as an ending, he hadn't yet connected his illness to the possibility of his own ending.

Wagner's mood down-shifted as the remains of the ancient estate's privacy wall came into view. Only a crumbling three-foot high section of two right- angled brick walls remained. That large corner harbored nothing but weeds and wild flowers. People looking to salvage materials had cleared out most of the debris years ago.

Then came locals who wanted only to view the destruction of a rich man's mansion. Most filled their curiosity within a few months withoutdiscovering the bomb shelter Doctor A learned about from the owner. He was a very sick old man who she attended as his physician during his last days.

Isolated as it was, Wagner doubted the shelter could remain a secret much longer. There were a dozenpeople and a dozen random actions capable of giving it away.

First, the men who designed and built the bomb shelter back in the early nineteen-sixties, near the end of this nation's fearful preoccupation with surviving a nuclear war. By now, most of the men were either dead or doddering seniors but they may have revealed the secret to others, others young enough to come exploring. Most troubling was the traffic to and from the Center. Hadn't curious citizens noticed the comings and goings of the three of them?

When they first occupied this accursed venue, he bought motion-activated cameras, placing them in trees around the site to warn of interlopers. He reviewed the films but they gave him only tedious frame after frame of night roaming deer, coyote and armadillo. He hadn't yet taken the things down. They alone might reveal the Center to some lost hiker or over-zealous real estate agent.

The above-ground entrance to the shelter lay in adense maze of loblolly pine and black tupelo trees. Hedrove onto the camouflaged car elevator, and got out to press the hidden metal knob that activated it. It delayed sixty seconds before deploying to lower the vehicle out of sight. Each time he used it he wonderedwhat they would do when it gave out. Who would repair it or the dozen other deteriorating mechanical devices making the once state-of-the-art bomb shelter useable?

Three generators in separate underground concrete pods supplied power. An underground well supplied water they hand-pumped into a storage tank inside. For years, he periodically made minor repairs, although his mechanical skills were limited.

Recently he cleaned out the air shafts and filters. The filters were NBC devices, capable of neutralizing nuclear, biological and chemical contaminants in the air. These days, they filtered nothing but pollen.

The shelter's underground garage held two vehicles. The first vehicle down must move forward so the second one descending didn't land on it. With great enjoyment he fantasized it: the mechanism malfunctioned; his car landed on top of the doctor's car with her still in it.

At the bottom, fifteen feet underground, he moved his car forward until it cleared the lift, and stopped it behind hers. The lift mechanism rose to the surface and slid back into place. Lights in the underground entry way came on. He approached the blast door, cursing the paranoia of the men who invented, built and installed it, concrete-filled bent steel with four hinges for extra strength. The five-spoke banker's wheel used to open the thing strained his biceps as well as his patience.

He didn't know how A managed it, but then, how did she manage most of the things she did? How did she manage just being her?

After the air whooshed out, telling him the compression lock still provided an airtight seal, the massive door swung open an inch at a time. He entered the decompression room. Similar to the living area, its reinforced concrete walls were three feet thick. A key was required to open it from the inside as well as from outside. In his more sanguine moments, Otto admired the ingenuity and abundance of caution that had produced this place. This was not one of his sanguine moments.

The decompression room led into the doctor's exam room. Whenever she wasn't performing her primary task in the operating room, she lounged there in her domain, smoking and reading medical journals.

Today he found her lying supine on the exam table, waving her cigarette in the air in time with some musical ditty playing in her mind.

Without rising or stopping her phantom conducting, she said, "You show up so seldom these days."

"I come when I'm needed. You may enjoy playing troglodyte, but I hate this hole in the ground. Why do you make it more disgusting by polluting it with your damned cigarettes?"

She turned her head and blew smoke at his face.

He bristled. "Now have the common decency to sit up. We have to talk."

She remained on her back. "Not about that brat of yours at the Haven again?" Her voice conveyed a habitual scorn.

"Sport is a deserving kid. He needs a transplant. Soon. No one else will do it, so you have to."

"I take them out, Wagner, not put them in. We can't spare a kidney. Unless you produce someone else for me."

He jabbed his finger toward the main area. "There are five kidney donors in there."

She sat up and cocked her head at him. "Oh, counting the three of us? Aren't you magnanimous? Let me count the ways. In there, the pregnant one is too fragile, approaching her third trimester. She keeps both kidneys so we can get a few more babies out of her. The little one--Susan--is special. She keeps hers too. Actually, I'm glad you brought her.

"I told you she was beautiful. So what?"

"Her face and hair alone will bring in enough to make her very, very profitable. I have someone on my list right here in the States who'd cash in half her portfolio for a head of hair like hers. But I'm not going to call the ugly bitch. I'm going to send pictures of our little Susan's head and face. The blond hair frames it so prettily." She smiled. "Some cutter who calls himself a cosmetic surgeon has a patient in need of a complete face transplant."

"A face transplant? You're out of your mind. It will never happen."

"Oh, it already has. A successful face transplant. I'll find a buyer, bet on it." She stubbed out her cigarette. "So. A transplant for the kid. If we took the second kidney from John, we'd have to terminate him. I have other plans for the lunatic before we do it."

"I'm sure you do."

"Then there's the three of us, you, me and Cranston. You believe all of us are matches for your slant-eyed, half-wit?"

Wagner bristled in spite of himself. "Save your vile, misanthropic names for someone who's shocked by them. I took a DNA swab from his cheek and from Jill. She is a match. It won't take much effort from you to confirm it and get it done." She didn't answer. He looked into her face, finding nothing of value behind her eyes. This was it. She hadn't stated it outright, but her refusal to save Sport's life with a transplant was final. He yearned to reach for the gun nestled in the small of his back and blow her head apart. Instead, he said, "Now I want you to consider something else."

His voice made the doctor sense a stronger challenge coming. She slipped off the table, standing to face him, one fist on her hip, the other holding the still smoldering cigarette.

Wagner said, "I'm closing down our clinic inDubai. It's already in the works so don't try to stop it. The Center here has served its purpose, too. We need to shut it down. We both have enough money to live anywhere in the world, in any style, in the best of styles, for the rest of our lives."

"You might be craving a ride in a rocking chair, but I'm too young to retire."

"That's more subtle than your usual attemptsto insult me. It doesn't touch me, you know. I never feel insulted unless I respect the person who's trying to do it. I imagine your favorite hobby above ground isexamining road kill to gloat over the internal organs."

She acted as if she hadn't heard. "We have the perfect setup here. Why would I leave? You can cut and run, Wagner, but I'm staying."

"The Center is old. It's deteriorating. It's a matter of time before some essential component breaks down and forces everyone out of here. Besides, the risks, not to mention our mistakes, are coming too close, too damned fast."

She crossed her arms and leaned back against theexam table. "Don't you mean *your* mistakes? Your fiasco with the hundred-thousand girl, the one named after a plant? Don't waste your concern. The Neutralizers are going to take care of her." The doctor looked into his eyes with a half-smile and said slowly,as if savoring every word, "They will also eliminate the man who took her away from you."

"You're going to have them killed?" She didn't answer. But he knew. "Your solution to any problem is to kill it or have someone else kill it. Another sign of your cowardice. Your stupidity. Our so-called partnership is over. As of right now. Good luck with getting DNA data through me or any of my contacts. I'm done. "

Doctor A's small eyes narrowed. She gritted her teeth and clenched her prominent jaw so the bones came alive under flesh pulsing with emotion. Her shriek of anger made him jump. She thrust her cigarette butt at his face. He jerked to the side so only sparks of fire scored his cheek. Her other hand struck his face, full force. He caught both her wrists, shoving her back against the table. He shifted both her wrists to his left hand. His right fist came up to punch her. Then stopped.

Even in a rage, she recognized his ability and knew not to struggle and not to strike him again. He released her wrists, shoved her away from him.

She began to babble curses, threats to kill and dismember him, disgusting words to describe his genitalia. He waited. She wouldn't wind down until she was exhausted. Then maybe she would listen to him.

Minutes later, he crossed his arms over his chest, leaned toward her and said, "If you do the transplant on Sport, I'll sell you the plane for half of what it's worth and have the pilot transfer his contract to you. And I want you to call off your assassins."

She didn't answer. Was the woman completely insane? A minute later, tired of waiting for her answer and thoroughly disgusted, he walked to the door, wrenched it open, slammed it shut behind him and entered the hub of the shelter. His breathing slowed but not the surge of anger. Now where is Cranston, that vulgar clod? He'd better not be bothering Grace again. A shock. Something fell against him, something moving. Arms and hands battered his face, fingernails raked him, pain stabbed his ear. It was Susan! He shoved her away. "Stop! Before I have to hurt you."

He wrapped one arm around her slender waist and half-walked, half-dragged her toward the padded room. He unlocked the door and pushed her inside onto the floor. Her forehead struck hard enough for him to hear it, in spite of the padding. She lay face down, gasping.

Wagner breathed deeply while he stared at her thin form, wondering what precipitated this attack. Pain in his ear. He explored the wound with his fingers. Blood. A deep scratch on one of the inner folds, bleeding freely. He tilted his head to prevent blood from entering his ear canal. Looking at Susan again, he wondered if only her fingernails had done the damage.

He bent down to grab her right hand. He uncurled her clenched fingers. A small black object fell from her palm. He grabbed it and straightened up before her other fist could reach his face. The thing in his hand was a long, pointed piece of solid plastic.

"What is this?" he demanded. "What the hell did you think you were doing?"

She turned over to look up at him. She struggled onto her hands and knees and screamed, "Trying to kill you!"

He looked at the thing in his hand. "This two-inch piece of plastic was supposed to penetrate my ear and enter my brain? You don't know much about killing people, do you? You were much more skilled at bringing me my lunch."

"You evil shit!" She struggled to her feet. The red marks on her arms made by his grasp were smaller than the red spot on her forehead. It would soon grow into a large, dark blue lump. So much for A's photographs of her, Wagner thought.

She wiped her eyes and face with her sleeve. In a more controlled voice she said, "You can't do that to people. You can't do that to Grace. She's not some animal, a cow you can pen up and use any way you want. She's a human being!"

"How did you get out of your room? It was Cranston, wasn't it?"

"Ha. He's not even here right now."

Right, Wagner though. If he were here and heard the commotion, he would have run from the kitchen or bathroom. Tired and still inwardly agitated from two physical assaults within minutes, he said, "You'll stay in here from nowon." He turned to go.

She rushed at him, striking his back with her fists. "Don't destroy her. Her heart is already broken. Let herkeep her baby." He looked into her tear-stained face and with one shove sent her back onto the floor, walked away and closed the door.

#

## Chapter Thirty

Early the same morning in Oak Bayou, Taylor's boss, the owner of the hardware store and lumber yard pulled his pickup truck into the employee parking space behind the store at seven a.m. sharp. He waved at Taylor, the signal Taylor's shift was over and he could go home.

Taylor tilted his chin at the man, unwilling to speak, unwilling to connect. Go home. He didn't want to go home. He wanted to go to Sage. At her house, in her bedroom. He wanted to take off this stupid uniform, slip into bed with her, touch the silky skin on her back, the curve of her waist, stroke the inside of her thigh....

Damn. She couldn't do this to him, dump him without a reasonable explanation, avoid him as if he carried some despicable communicable disease. He climbed into his car, turned the key in the ignition. Nothing. He struck the dashboard with his fist, once, twice. This old piece of crap! He would get a new car, one that started with the push of a button. He would....

Minutes later, after successfully getting the car running, he pulled up in front of her house. Sage's car was in the driveway. He would do this. He would convince her to see it his way, come back to him. The thought of her brought a rush of desire to his groin.

He walked up the sidewalk, noticing the man next door with a clipper, trimming a hedge. It was that guy Ben.

Ben looked up and nodded at Taylor, who ignored him and used his key in the front door.

One step inside, he felt the wrongness. Complete silence. Emptiness. His tentative erection wilted. The arousal of fear took its place. His scalp prickled. He saw the small office immediately to his right was empty, computers dark. A common wall separated the office from the living room where a sliding glass door opposite the front door opened onto the deck. Behind the office, through a short hallway, was the entry to the master suite. To his left were the kitchen and the entryway to Sage's bedroom. He took a few steps toward her room.

Seconds before the man with the gun rushed from the master bedroom a shadow or a sound warned him.

Taylor saw the gun, ducked and dodged, heard the shot that missed. He dashed for the sliding glass door before he heard the second muffled crack. His thumb pushed up on the lock. A glance behind. The gun was all he saw, Glock 17L with the long barrel.

The bullet hit him. He slammed the door left. It rebounded, grazed his arm before he was through, onto the patio. Another bullet shattered glass behind him, whizzed past his ear. He dashed ahead, dodging around large stones in the water feature, leapt over the low brick wall and tumbled downhill. A bullet struck the ground near his face. Dirt sprayed his face while he rolled over and over. Twenty yards down the weedy hill, his body hit a fence and stopped.

Adrenalin flooded his brain; instinct told him *Get up!* Roll from your back to your stomach. Onto your knees. To your feet. *Run!* His body would not obey. He struggled to raise his head, looked up. The man with the gun vaulted over the wall, aimed at him again. He flinched, closed his eyes against an impact. None. He opened his eyes again to see the man's hands were empty. He was sprinting around to the front of the house. To the street.

Taylor took a deep breath. A warm stickiness trickled into his arm pit. He looked down, saw blood oozing through his shirt. He rolled onto his side and pressed his cheek into the dirt as gently as if he nuzzled a lover's breast. Through one drooping eyelid, he saw a different man

234

standing above on the patio, a big man grasping a long gun in both hands. Ben.

* * *

An hour later at the safe house, Lee dropped the phone back in his pocket. He paced the hallway, glad the others were in the kitchen cleaning up after breakfast. Nine a.m. Already a crisis to deal with. Sage and Laura could not go home any time soon, not after what happened this morning.

The information from his Oak Bayou law enforcement contact shocked him, although it shouldn't have. His reason for hiding Sage, Laura and Wayne was fear of such an attempt on their lives. The young man shot by mistake was lucky. Lucky he was able to run. Even more lucky Ben showed up with his shotgun to chase the shooter away.

And Sage? Her police academy training started day after tomorrow. She wouldn't be safe even on the police academy campus. His local law enforcement contacts had assured him they were working diligently to track down her would-be assassin. It didn't move him. The master race cartel, now more aptly called the organ theft cartel, had connections and money enough to pay a dozen assassins.

Wayne was beginning to worry him, too. After only three night and two days here, he had begun to do pushups and sit-ups, chinning himself in doorways, working out the way a stir-crazy prison inmate would.

Lee suspected the only thing keeping him here was Sage. They were unmistakably growing closer. He often saw them talking with their heads together nearly touching. They often held hands.

Lee knew Laura was trying to be patient, watching daytime TV as if she enjoyed it. In the evening, she played cards or worked a jigsaw puzzle with Sage or with Wayne if he could sit still long enough. At odd times, Laura would look up at him with big brown eyesso similar to his own and say, "That poor girl." She meant the woman they believed was in trouble up in Georgia.

His call to Sheriff Landry had been unproductive. The word fit his mental image of Landry: unproductive, unmotivated, unimaginative.

Landry had used the information on the suicide note in Susan Barkin's apartment to dismiss suggestion of further action by his department. He emphasized that the shooting at the Stevens' household, even if meant to kill Sage, was out of his jurisdiction. He would not consider linking today's crime in Oak Bayou to the alleged Dwightsburg event involving Sage's lost phone.

Lee called his friend and agent at Interpol to ask if the Agency would investigate and intervene with the Sheriff--and possibly with Oak Bayou police. The agent replied they might, but only if a careful assessment of the situation justified it. Lee recognized the words. They placed a condition on the possibility of taking action--which later could provide an excuse.If...when...maybe....

There were too many variables, too many uncommitted or unconcerned people involved--except for himself and the three other people right here. Jurisdictions didn't bind them or rules dictate their actions. There was no fear of a boss's criticism. Negative media attention wasn't a consideration, as it was for Interpol and other law enforcement agencies.

In the kitchen, Laura sat at one end of the huge table, her cane propped against her chair, refilling saltand pepper shakers. She looked up, saw him andsmiled. Sudden shock took him, filled his chest and constricted his throat. He loved her, this daughter of Holly's, this daughter his own. He loved her desperately, more than his life. He had never expressed it to her. That shamed him. He went to her, placed one hand on her shoulder, then began awkwardly to pat it.

Wayne spotted Lee. He backed out of the open refrigerator door, holding delicatessen packages wrapped in brown paper. "Look what I found for lunch. Pastrami and roast beef."

Sage stood on a stool in front of an open cabinet. "I'm trying to find more interesting options for dinner. Last night's left me one fry short of a happy meal."

Wayne smiled at her. "I did the best I could. I'm sure your mom is the real cook here, but she's not up to kitchen duty yet."

Lee swallowed his emotions. "I'm glad you're all staying busy. Um...we need to talk again if that's okay. Can we meet in the great room after you finish here?"

Wayne was the first to walk in and drop into one of the easy chairs. Sage took the one beside it. Laura sat at the end of the long sofa so she could put both her legs up. She sighed, leaning back into the upholstered arm. They waited for Lee to speak.

Wayne grew impatient. "So, are we going back home now?"

"We can't. I have a lot to tell you." He related the events of the morning, the gist of his three telephone conversations.

Wayne said, "Well, I'm no fan of Taylor's but I've got to give it to Ben for stepping up. The guy has guts."

Sage turned, wondering how her mother was taking all this. "He's a wonderful neighbor, right Mom?" She turned to Lee. "So how is Taylor?"

"Arm and shoulder wounds. He'll recover nicely, from what I heard."

Wayne leaned forward with his hands on his knees. "What do we do now? We can't stay holed up here indefinitely."

Sage stood up to pace. "Right. We're not the bad guys so why should we hide out? I'm supposed to start my police academy training day after tomorrow. I might be safe while I'm there, but traveling there and back every day will be risky."

"It would be. That's why we're here."

Sage turned to him; her fists clenched at her sides. "I've been thinking it's not right for us to hole up here for our own safety and forget that woman--the woman on my phone--forget her screams of horror and pain. Or the fact that Otto Wagner tried to kidnap me. We don't have proof so we can't have him arrested, but we need to do something. I need to do something to find out what's going on up there."

Wayne said, "You're right. Think about all we know. Wagner tried to kidnap Sage. Today, someone set out to kill her but injured Taylor instead. We know someone murdered William Jones because he knew who killed Holly. People in the same organization tried to kill Lee decades ago. Now the organization's new generation of assassins is after Sage. And Lee—again!"

Laura scooted forward on the sofa and held her cane upright with both hands. "We know no matter how it started, it's nothing but a money-making organization now, a group of killers. They don't respect anyone's life. When Wayne brought you back home, Sage, they must have kidnapped another young woman, the one Taylor heard on his phone."

Sage said, "I've been thinking the same thing. We have a lot of information. It makes us responsible for doing something about it, even if law enforcement won't."

Wayne rose and took her elbow to stand beside her. He said to Lee, "She's right. We need to go up there. Do you agree? Because Sage and I are going."

#

## Chapter Thirty-One

Wagner had stunned himself by declaring his independence from the Center and from Doctor A. Now he needed to recover from the woman's rage and from Susan's annoying but relatively ineffective attack.

He gently fingered the wound in his ear. It had stopped bleeding. He cleaned the dried blood away and put a dab of antibiotic on the nick. Then he went to the tiny alcove off of the hub. It originally held twenty-gallon garbage cans of galvanized metal filled with canned and pre-packaged food items. Once disposed of, he had installed a door. That reserved it as his private space.

He sat in the only chair, placed between two metal file cabinets. More than anything he ever longed to do, Otto Wagner longed to walk through A's inner sanctum, into the anteroom, out the blast door, into his car and up into the sunshine, escape from this suffocating sarcophagus for the last time.

He reminded himself he was never an impulsive man. First, he must remove and destroy the contents of the file cabinets. They held records of who was brought to the Center and when. After Dr. A processed the victims, she recorded where their various parts went and to whom. She sent the information, along with sale prices, to his computer. He sent a report of his expenses to hers. Most months they calculated a net profit of over two million, U.S.

He allowed himself to enjoy the thought he would never again spend most of his days hunched over a damned computer, the ghost in the machine. He couldn't quit the cartel, but he could fine another niche in their hierarchy and another home. He would take Sport with him. To some

239

place where he would demand and get a transplant for the boy, away from this mosquito-ridden pine dump.

Without him, Doctor A would have to abandon the Center. Let her clean out the place, remove her surgical supplies and if she had any sense, fill in the deep burn pit where, along with applications of both chemicals and fire, they had turned dozens of human remains into ashes.

\* \* \*

At around the same time in Oak Bayou, Sage and Wayne sat in the back seat of Lee's late model SUV, close enough for their thighs to touch. Wayne asked, "Do you have the coordinates?"

She pulled a small bit of paper from her pocket. "I brought them. Not that I needed to write them down. I memorized them."

"It will be around one in the afternoon by the time we get there. What if we don't find anything today?"

"Then we'll find a hotel in Savannah, stay the night. Poke around again tomorrow until we do find something." She clenched her fists. They must find someone or something capable of ending mortal danger to herself and the people she loved. She longed to confront Wagner, certain he was behind the attempt to kidnap her weeks ago. When that crime didn't deliver her, he had come in person to persuade her up there, with the help of a phony story.

What it all came down to was getting answers to the questions assailing her the minute she saw the photo of Holly. She turned to Wayne. "Are you as nervous as I am?"

"Yeah, or maybe anxious is a more accurate word. I can't remember when I've felt...well, maybe when I was quarterback in college during our playoff with...."

He saw her smile. He stopped. "Yeah, the battle rightfully belongs to you, your mom and Lee. But I have a dog in this fight, too. I want you safe."

She squeezed his hand. "I wish Mom was with us but glad she's not. Lee called Ben to come stay with her at the safe house."

An hour and a half later, Lee held the scrap of paper with the coordinates on it in his left hand while he drove. They had turned off the main road; they were now on a narrow country lane. He turned to Sage, who sat beside him, "We need to turn west soon. Watch for a road on the left, maybe a dirt road."

Minutes later, she pointed to the left. He didn't see it but slowed and braked, overshooting the target. "There," she said. "I don't see a road, but there's a clearing in the undergrowth. It's giving me a glimpse of sky without tree branches."

He backed up and turned where she indicated. The SUV's tires rolled over branches and pine cones, releasing the stringent fragrance of pine sap. Ahead, the reddish soil revealed tire tracks.

"Looks like someone tried to camouflage the entrance to the turnoff." The car crept forward, following the dirt track as it rose gently in elevation. Less than a mile ahead, they came on a small clearing where it appeared a car or several cars had backed and turned around.

"This is it." They were in a sparsely wooded area without a man-made structure in sight. Loblolly pine, slash pine and black tupelo trees stood amid palmettos, weeds and wildflowers. A mild breeze stirred the tops of trees; a few large birds soared high overhead. The only sounds were the tick-tick of the cooling engine, an occasional mysterious rustle in the grass, the sudden pop and buzz of a grasshopper springing into the air. A single bird call sounded nearby.

"The back of the beyond," Wayne said. He got out, looking around. Lee and Sage joined him withoutcomment. Each stepped in a different direction, looking at the trees, the taller shrubs and grasses, the occasional dip or rise of the land.

"People have been here, that's for sure," Sage said. "Something bad happened here." They lowered the focus of their search to the ground, nudging aside weeds with the sides of their shoes, bending down occasionally to touch something in the dirt.

Sage saw a spot of color on the ground. With her fingers, she brushed away the soil until she could pick it up. She turned toward Wayne. "Look! It's part of my phone. Taylor was right. At times I almost doubted it, but a girl-- the girl with my phone--was right here."

"From what Taylor said, there was also a man or several men. Why?" He raised an arm, extending it in a half-circle. "There's nothing here."

Lee took the red plastic fragment from Sage's hand. He examined it. "*This* is here. We haven't spotted anything else but it doesn't mean there's nothing. We have to look a little closer down and a little farther off. Let's spread out but stay in sight of each other if possible. Use the top of the car or one of the trees as a focal point. Don't get disoriented. If you find something, call. Oh, put your phones on vibrate first. Let's search for half an hour, then meet back here if nothing shows up."

Wayne raised an eyebrow, his comment on the extent of the precautions. He silenced his phone anyway, as Sage and Lee did theirs. Lee said, "Oh, and becareful. There are rattlesnakes and maybe coral snakes in this kind of terrain. Could be wild pigs and coyotes, too."

They headed out. Within a few minutes, Sage noticed her shoe laces collecting stickers the size of acorns. Flat green seeds the size of sesame seeds clungto the hem of her jeans. Two rabbits flushed from cover, dashing away in opposite directions. She jumped, letting out a squelched yelp.

Five minutes later, her phone vibrated. It was Lee's excited voice. "Meet me back at the car."

Breathless from running, they reached the startingpoint. Lee said, "A couple of old wildlife cameras in the trees is what I saw first. It's what I expected. Underground. Some sort of bunker, maybe military. There's a car lift that lowers the car out of sight. It's why we didn't spot a vehicle, the reason this place wasn't discovered by casual hikers or random real estate people."

"A bunker," Wayne said. "Is someone down there? If so, who? Military or civilians?"

"Has to be civilians," Lee said. "Decades ago, maybe even during the Second World War, it could have been a munitions depot or some other military installation. It's close enough to the Intracoastal Waterway but on deep, solid ground. An ideal site. It's either abandoned military or a private citizen's bomb shelter--a big one."

Wayne wiped sweat from his forehead. "Let's go.""Wait a second. Go and do what?"

Sage took Wayne's arm. "Lee's right, Wayne. Weneed to consider the whole picture, decide what to do and how to do it."

Lee leaned against the side of the SUV, slowly lowered himself to sit on the ground, his forearms on his bent knees. Sage moved to sit facing him. She began to remove burrs from her jeans with a forked stick. Wayne kneeled beside her and sat back on his heels saying, "Powwow."

Lee spoke first. "We could call the Sheriff and getsome deputies out here."

Sage shook her head. "Don't count on it. They came and found nothing only a few days ago. They won't call out the posse again on our word alone. Will they, Lee?"

"After my conversation with the Sheriff, I have to agree with you. And Interpol sure wouldn't respond."

"Then, it's just us," Sage said. "Let's do this. If things get too far out of hand we can always call 911. We have coverage here. The Sheriff or his deputies would have to respond."

Lee nodded. "There's a hand gun in my glove compartment. I'll retrieve it. Sage, you brought yours in your purse. Why not give it to Wayne, and stay in the SUV?"

She laughed. "Not on your life!"

"Then get it. Two weapons and a pair of strong hands against--who and how many?"

Wayne interpreted his words as an argument against attack. "Sage is right. We can't leave without finding out who's in there."

Lee nodded. "But it would be crazy to go down tothem. They have to come out to us."

"Well, we could wait for them to come out--whoever they are."

He said, "Sure. Maybe they come out in the evening, go home like normal workers. We shouldn't count on it." He shifted to a more comfortable position. "Underground facilities like this have at least three features. A main entry, an emergency escape route, and ventilation shafts. I've located the main entry withthe camouflaged car lift. Right in front of it there's a metal cap like a manhole cover. I imagine it hides an access shaft fitted with a metal ladder. We can count itas a third exit but we need to find the escape hatch andthe ventilation devices."

"I get it," Wayne said. "Three of us to cover three exits."

"We have a plan now." Sage said. "Let's work it."

#

## Chapter Thirty-Two

Lee drove his car to within twenty feet of the entrance to the underground bunker. They searched. Within minutes, Wayne and Sage found two small metal objects in the ground they identified as airshafts.

Lee looked for the escape hatch without success until he noticed a peculiar shape in the thatch of weeds and wildflowers, a circle in the approximate diameter of a man's outstretched arms. He took out his pocket knife. He thrust down through the soil. A metallic sound from the tip of the blade confirmed it. Metal. The cover of the escape hatch.

He stood to consider it. At one time, someone had shoveled soil and vegetation off it to enable them to push it up and escape. No one had used it since. Now the circle was an inch lower than the ground around it. He doubted anyone could budge it from the inside but someone had to stand guard. Sage?

He hesitated. If someone managed to emerge from it and harm her he would never forgive himself. And Laura! She wouldn't be able to forgive him. Ever. Their new relationship was far too tenuous for that kind of mercy.

He rubbed his palms against his pants then swiped sweat from his face. He knew Sage would refuse to be sidelined but if the situation became menacing, it would probably be the safest place for her.

He stepped back to look from the ground into the cloud-decked blue sky, seeking--what? A sense of peace? A miracle from heaven? Neither came. He had known that pursuing unknown bad actors here would risk the safety of Sage and Wayne, two of the three people on earth he felt responsible for.

There she was, approaching with Wayne. They were holding hands like young lovers on a picnic outing. Did the cameras still work? Did the shelter's occupants have eyes topside? If someone was watching, they looked innocent enough.

The two reached him. Wayne said, "We found the air shafts. If the place is as big as you expect, we could block the shafts but it would still be a long time before anyone down there would run out of air."

"Right."

"We could block one and send car exhaust down the other."

Sage shook her head. "No way. The carbon dioxide could harm or even kill anyone down there."

"The filters would prevent it from happening. They're probably NBC--impervious to nuclear, biologic or chemical substances. "

"We could remove the filters," Wayne said.

Lee shook his head. "Those aren't bad ideas, but removing the filters wouldn't be easy and it would create a lot of noise."

Sage said, "Well then, noise it is. That would bring them out, wouldn't it? Get them curious enough to come out. Curiosity kills the cat."

Lee's forehead wrinkled. "Nothing wrong with that idea. Are you okay with staying here to guard the escape hatch?" She took the Glock from its holster at her back and held it out to say she would be ready if anyone emerged.

Lee went back to the car, started the engine, and opened all four doors and the trunk. He lifted the cover of the tire well, found the tire iron and handed it back to Wayne. He took his gun from the glove compartment, tucked it into his waistband then stationed himself behind the car lift. He motioned for Wayne to strike one of the ventilation pipes with the tire iron.

* * *

Inside the Center, the noise sounded distant and dull to Wagner. Something striking the air shaft? He wasn't alarmed, probably nothing. However, Doctor A's room was close to the inside terminus of that air shaft. To her, it must be an annoying, maybe even disturbing, sound. She couldn't call Cranston to come see what was wrong. The Center lacked both phone and internet communication with the outside world.

Grace heard the sound too. She loved it. She was thrilled by the unexpected, intriguing event. That and all the screaming and commotion in the last hour were the most interesting things in her world since they locked her down here. She hated the silence in her soundproof room. She opened her door the narrowest crack only when she figured it was safe. The interior surveillance cameras were a worry, but Cranston told her Dr. A seldom looked at the monitors and lately several had gone dark, non-functioning.

She unlocked her door to watch Doctor A enter the center room, the hub, and scream at Wagner, "Go find out what that damned sound is."

"I warned you to expect mechanical failures." The sound was persistent. He would go check it. He rose to leave. A went into the bathroom. Grace knew the doctor couldn't see the hub from in there, couldn't see her. Now Wagner was going outside. It was safe to come out for a few seconds. She stepped into the hub. Doctor A had left the door to the exam room open! The door to the outside was through there!

Without further thought or plan, she crept out of her room and stepped behind Wagner, no more than ten paces behind. Inside the exam room he quickened his step, too intent to notice his silent shadow. He keyed open the opposite door, angrily threw it back hard. It spread wide,

248

wide enough for her to rush forward and duck through before it slammed shutbehind her.

Here, what was this room? It was small, nothinghere but another door ahead. His back still to her, he was grumbling to himself, oblivious that she was here.He keyed open the door. A whooshing sound, decompression, almost made her jump and cry out. Her heart began to pound even faster. The only sound she uttered was a deep exhale of breath.

He was through, out of sight. The door was closing, closing too fast. She rushed at it. There! She caught it in time. It was heavy, so heavy. A wide bar, rather than a handle, allowed her to use both hands to hold the door ajar a few inches. She tried slipping herfoot into the crack, but the heavy door threatened to crush her instep. She pulled her foot back, her arms straining while she listened. What was Wagner doing?How would he get outside from here?

The sound of a car door slamming, the engine starting, startled her. She felt the pounding of her heartin her throat. The little body in her womb stirred. Shemanaged to peek out the narrow crack in the door. Shesaw the car rise. Then nothing. Silence, completedarkness.

What now? Let the door close and stay hereinside? The door behind her had already closed and locked. She didn't have the key so she couldn't go back. If she allowed this heavy door to slam shut, shewould have to wait right here in this tiny room until hecame back and discovered her. But if she went throughthe door.... She struggled to pull it wide enough to slip through. The effort caused a feeling of pressure at thebottom of her pelvis. The baby.

She placed both hands flat against the door. She braced her feet and turned sideways, struggling through inches at a time. She was out! She released the door, which eased closed with athump. Her fingers and wrists ached from the effort. She summoned her awareness of the baby. He was still, but she could feel his live presence.

In here, there was only semi-darkness. To her left was a deeper black and the smell of car exhaust. Stretching out both arms, she touched a wall. With shuffling feet, she hand-walked to the right. What was that? A metal bar. Groping with both hands, she touched another bar, then the vertical supports holding them. A ladder.

She placed her foot on the first rung sideways, leaving room to keep her belly away from the cold, unforgiving metal. Then, step by step, she climbed.

\* \* \*

Above, at the same moment, from behind the car lift, Lee watched the shiny new Lexus rise to the surface. He smiled a thin smile at the irony of common technology in an uncommon place. There! The man in the driver's seat must be Wagner, backing the car out. If Wagner glanced in his rear-view mirror, Wagner would spot him. He stepped to the side. The driver's window pulled even with him. He leveled his pistol at the driver's head. "Stop!"

Wagner braked, an automatic response to a command. Only then he saw Lee. And the gun. Before he could hit the gas and escape, Lee shot three times through the hood of the car, then put one through the front tire. He stepped forward, leveled the pistol inches from Wagner's head.

Wagner climbed out of the ruined car in slow motion but Lee knew the man hadn't surrendered yet. He backed away to widen distance between them. Then both spotted movements. A few feet in front of Wagner, the metal hatch rose slowly then tipped onto the concrete with a loud clang. A woman stood there at the top of the ladder. Wagner lunged forward and grabbed her, his arm holding her between her distended belly and her breasts. With the other hand he reached behind to his holster, pulled out his gun, shoved the barrel against her temple. "Drop your gun or this woman dies!"

Lee dropped his gun at his feet and raised his hands.

Wagner's lips tightened, as if to show he was in charge again. His wrist flicked, tilting the gun barrel at Lee. "Back up ten steps and lie face down."

Lee obeyed, his eyes on the pregnant girl. He knew each step brought him closer to his death. Down on his knees--his nose touched the ground. Instantly, the crack of gunshots assaulted his ears. Bullets struck, one, two, three. Dirt sprayed onto his back, into his hair. He exhaled with an involuntary grunt. He waited for the pain. Nothing. All three of Wagner's hastily aimed shots had missed.

Lee raised his head. Wagner was hustling toward the undamaged car, Lee's car, dragging the woman. He shoved her into the back, took the driver's seat and pulled away.

Lee scrambled forward and grabbed his gun.

Just then, Wayne saw Wagner in the approaching car. He stepped from behind a tree holding the tire iron. He rushed at the accelerating vehicle, swung at the windshield. The powerful blow wrenched the tire iron from his hands and propelled it through the glass. The windshield shattered. The car slowed, then stopped. The pregnant woman climbed out and ran.

At the escape hatch, Sage turned to watch the drama unfold near the shelter entrance. A sound behind made her turn. A woman had climbed out of the hatch behind her and crouched there on all fours in the dirt. An image of the black widow spider in the attic flashed through her. She stepped toward the woman. "Who are you?"

The woman stood, pointed her gun at Sage. Sage turned into a spinning kick forward at the woman's head. The woman dodged. Sage's foot hit the side of her head.

251

The woman fell, the gun still in her hand. Prone on the dirt, she aimed and shot.

Sage felt the impact, knew she was hit. She gasped, stepped forward, shot the woman twice in the chest. The woman's eyes held hers for a second. Then stilled. Went dull and dead.

Sage felt pain rip through her, searing upward into her core. She looked down at the hole in her thigh seeping blood. She looked up. Lee was racing toward her. He grabbed her upper arms, looked her up and down then focused on her leg.

She said, "I didn't see her when she first came out of the emergency exit. I should have been on it. I should have seen her."

"Sit down. Let me look." The bullet had entered her thigh an inch below the hem of her shorts. He said, "You'll be okay. It's not gushing, not spurting, so it's not an artery." He tore off his shirt, wadded it up and handed it to her. "Here. Direct pressure. Press hard. It'll hurt."

He pulled out his phone and hit 911. He spoke in a commanding tone, giving information and making requests in a voice she had never heard from him. When he was satisfied, he keyed off and walked toward the woman on the ground. "Is she dead?" Sage asked, though she already knew.

The woman's gun lay on the fingertips of her open palm. A circle of blood covered her unmoving chest. Both bullets from Sage's Glock had ripped through her heart. Lee turned toward Sage. Her head was lowered.

Then...another car approaching. Ben in his Humvee, with Laura in the passenger seat. Ben must have immediately recognized the danger. He stopped the Humvee with a screech of brakes. Sage and Lee watched as he and Laura bailed out and hunched behind the vehicle doors. Laura's hand held a pistol; Lee's grasped his rifle.

252

Lee started toward them, waving his hand. They looked around as he approached, obviously trying to understand the confusing scene.

Laura walked toward Lee until she saw Sage. Then she ran.

At Lee's ruined car, Ben was with Wayne, peering inside at the bloody mess that once was Wagner. The tire iron had gone through the windshield, smashed Wagner's forehead and dropped onto his lap. He was a gory mess.

Wayne covered his face with one hand. "Damn! I only meant to smash the windshield, to get him to stop. I'll call 911." Was there even reception out here? The call went through. It took a minute for the operator to understand where the emergency was located then she got it--not far from the old burned-out mansion.

Ben was at the driver's side door. "Looks like he's still alive. Let's get him out of there."

Together they pulled Wagner out of Lee's car and lay him on the ground. Ben stood and backed away from the inert form, staring. He glanced at the blood on his forearm. His eyes became fixed but unseeing, his fists clenched and his body grew rigid.

Wayne suspected what was happening to the military veteran. He reached, grabbed Ben's arm.

Ben flinched, brushed away the gesture and shook his head, appeared to recover. He said, "Yeah. That was then, this is now."

He knelt beside the injured man and raised his voice, "Hey, Buddy, hang in there!"

Wagner stirred. Blood had pooled in his sunken eye sockets. His lips moved.

"What?" Ben urged. He bent closer. Wagner's lips moved again, then stopped. In the next second, his body appeared actually to sink lower into the earth as the last breath of life left him.

A moment of silence broke. Wayne asked, "What did he say?"

Ben shrugged. "He said *'Sport'*."

The distant wailing of sirens sounded. Ben and Wayne walked toward the others, where Lee stood protectively over Sage and Laura. Both Laura's arms were around her daughter, whose hands still pressed the wound on her thigh.

#

## Chapter Thirty-Three

Lee watched the Sheriff's vehicle approach followed by an ambulance. The vehicles stopped but no one got out. He walked toward them with his hands in the air. Both the Sherriff and the Deputy got out with guns drawn, aiming at him. They took in the scene: a man on the ground gruesomely bloodied, probably dead, people gathered together at some distance, one with a long gun rested casually in the crook of his elbow. An obviously pregnant woman suddenly rose from behind a clump of bushes and walked unsteadily toward them.

Lee stopped with his hands still up. "Hey, I'm Lee Pendfield, the one who called you."

The Sheriff kept his gun training on Lee while the Deputy searched him for weapons. Lee had wisely handed his gun to Wayne.

Things happened quickly then. Sheriff Landry gave an okay signal. Two Emergency Medical Technicians got out of the ambulance and raced toward the body on the ground. The Sheriff followed. He soon confirmed two dead and one injured. He called the county coroner. The EMTs examined Sage and the pregnant woman then loaded them both in the ambulance.

Laura started to climb in behind them. The deputy grabbed her arm to prevent her. She glared at him. "I am her mother! I am going."

The Sheriff nodded to the deputy, who obediently backed off. The ambulance bumped away over the uneven terrain, holding both women.

Landry turned to Lee. "You have a lot of explaining to do. We're going back to the office."

"Wait. There may be more people down there in the shelter."

The Sheriff turned and walked to where Lee pointed, examined the car lift, the disabled Lexus and the shaft with a ladder descending fifteen feet down into darkness.

There below they saw the blond head of Susan Barkin. She climbed the ladder with steps hesitant enough to make the deputy behind her impatient. She looked upward to the circle of daylight. How had it happened, this sudden rescue, this unexplained redemption?

Sheriff Landry ambled over to inspect the last person to emerge from underground and instantly recognized her from his lunches at the restaurant. However, now the young woman with the beautiful face and blond hair was pathetic. Her arms, legs, and forehead were marred by purple bruises. Her face and clothes were filthy. Fear, neglect and confusion defined her.

Landry was glad he was well experienced at hiding his emotions and tamping down hasty reactions. He said,"Well, now, Sweetheart I know you. You're Susan, from the restaurant. But now, by golly, you're lookin' kind of puny." He waved the deputy away, put a gentle arm around Susan's shoulders and steered her toward the patrol car. "Let's get you fixed up, how 'bout it?"

She stopped short. "Wait. Where is Grace? The other one from down there. She's pregnant. I'm not going anywhere unless she goes too."

"She's already on her way to the hospital in Savannah, Sweetheart, same place this old grandpa is taking you."

Landry had instructed the others to go to his office in town with the deputy and to wait there for him.

There, Lee connected with Interpol agents by phone. When Landry returned, the Interpol agent in charge satisfied many of his questions and shared data for the investigation of the two dead people. The horrific story of organ theft and sale shook Landry, who thought he was too old and experienced to be shocked.

Several hours later, information obtained from all the key sources had coalesced. More importantly, the coincided. The Sheriff released Lee, Wayne and Ben. He told them most likely they, as well as Sage, would remain clear of legal charges for the deaths of Wagner and the woman called Dr. A.

\* \* \*

At the hospital the next day, her nurse allowed Susan to go to the room where Grace Williams must remain on bed rest until she delivered her baby. Grace saw Susan. She held out her arms. Susan leaned over the bed to hug her. They clung together, talking, holding hands. Then Grace moved over, patting the bed beside her. Susan took off her hospital booties and climbed in. They sat side by side, shoulders touching. Grace said, "You look different, Susan. Your face. It's more...it's softer."

"You've never seen me when I wasn't scared out of my mind."

"Yeah. Me too. But I guess I got used to it. Not showing it, anyway." Her fist went to the place between her breasts. "I still feel it in here sometimes."

"You're still afraid?"

"Yeah. If the nurse touches me real quick or the doctor comes in--barges in. Being down there changed me."

"Me too."

"But you were only down there a few days."

"Yeah, but I wasn't just scared. I was angry, angry at what they did to me, how they treated me. It was like it released a lot of anger I already had inside me."

Grace leaned her head until it touched Susan's. Susan liked the feel of it and rested into the contact. She asked, "We're friends, aren't we Grace?"

"Besties. BFFs."

Susan's head jerked back. "What does that mean?"

Grace laughed. "It means we're best friends forever."

"That's so nice." Then, "I...I have another friend I've got to reconnect with once I get out of here. Her name is Sage."

"Sage...that's a cute name." Grace didn't speak again, her face serene, while Susan's thoughts turned back to her captivity. It had tapped into a well of pain in her heart and an abyss of anger in her wounded soul. Releasing a small part of it on her captors had been cathartic.

Finally, she said, "You know, I almost didn't come out of there. I wouldn't let the Deputy touch me, even when he kept saying he was setting me free."

Grace shifted sideways to search Susan's face. "I can't imagine why you wouldn't crawl out of there on your knees if you had to." Susan didn't answer. "But then, you did ask me to kill you that first night, and I heard you say something like that to Doctor A."

"Yeah. But down there I realized I don't really want to die. What I want is peace. I want to feel peace again. I want to feel other nice things. Like other people do."

Grace's forehead creased in puzzlement. Susan said, "I remember before my grandma died, I used to go to her house every day after school. She gave me cookies and milk. Those cookies tasted so good. I remember how I felt while I ate. Then, when I was ten my mom left for a few days. I was alone in the apartment. It felt wonderful when I woke up in the mornings. I knew no one would scream at me or hit me or make me do stupid stuff. I could do whatever I wanted."

Grace grabbed Susan's hand. "You didn't deserve it. We didn't deserve any of it--what happened down there or what your mother did to you."

"I talked to the social worker about it for a long time. She said I don't have to feel so much pain and anger any more. She says underneath it all is love. Sounds nice, but I have a hard time believing it."

"Well, I can believe it. You were scared of me at first down there in the dungeon, but I was a little scared of you, too. You are a strange little beauty, but we took care of each other."

"We did, didn't we. I never realized people might see me as strange or different. If I am, it's because I--it's from a different childhood. It never sank in before, how bad it was, until I told the social worker about my mom."

"She said you need counseling, didn't she?" "Yeah. She also said she knows a wonderful place where they treat people with anorexia." Grace search Susan's face but Susan's eyes evaded hers. "Grace, what are you going to do when the baby is born?"

"I'm going to keep her. What else would I do?" She smiled and patted her baby bulge. "They did an ultrasound. It's a girl."

"Keep her? Even after...?"

"Even after how I got this way. I didn't know him from Adam but he was doing it because he wanted a baby, he and his wife. She couldn't have one. Dr. A told me that much, at least. This baby started from someone wanting a baby to love. I had never even thought about having a baby, but--well--now she's mine, she'll be loved so full of love." She rubbed her mid-section. "She's moving right now; she's kicking. You want to touch her?"

Susan smiled, shook her head no.

Grace said, "I talked to my mom and dad on the phone. I told them I'm pregnant. Oh no, not the whole story. That

259

can come later. They were just so glad to hear from me after me being missing so long. They thought I was dead. Now they have a daughter again and a granddaughter. They're flying out from California tomorrow."

\#

## Chapter Thirty-Four

John Henderson, the blind and psychotic man from the Center, lay in a bed on the fourth floor of the hospital, held down by restraints. This was the ward in which doctors and nurses medically stabilized psychotic patients before transferring them to a locked psychiatric facility. Newspapers in Savannah and surrounding areas had gobbled up the astonishing story of kidnappers and organ sellers, then spit out lurid narratives in several morning editions. The story would eventually become an investigative exposé reported nationwide.

Henderson's doctors and nurses learned how his eyes, his kidney and half his liver were taken from him and by whom. They at first could not believe it. By a medical doctor. The horror story circulated on currents of outrage through all the hospital staff. In that place long acquainted with every imaginable agony, affliction or mutilation the body could suffer, the knowledge of what a medical doctor did to him touched even those who figured they had long ago exhausted their supply of compassion. Motivated by a mutual desire to disassociate themselves from the likes of Doctor A, his attending doctors and nurses summoned all their skills in caring for the man, along with an unspoken mandate to show him the greatest care and gentleness.

\* \* \*

Sage had lost more than a pint of blood when Doctor A's bullet shattered the femur in her left leg and tore through the muscles. She was faint from both blood loss and pain as she lay in the E.R., answering questions from nurses and different questions from two law enforcement officers.

At some point, the emergency room doctor examined her, reviewed the x-rays, ultrasound and labs. He came to stand over her with his arms crossed over his chest. He informed her she didn't need a transfusion; the symptoms of blood loss would soon resolve on their own. However, she did require surgery on the leg--urgently. She didn't respond. He repeated the word several times. Then she shook her head. He pulled a permission form from the clip board in his hand, thrusting it at her. She batted it away without fully realizing why. The irrational thought dimly swirling in her mind was that if she didn't have surgery, she would still be able to enter the police academy--day after tomorrow.

The E.R. doctor called in an orthopedic surgeon. Men in that specialty were not known for their bedside manners. This doctor was especially blunt. He told Sage he was the best orthopedist in southeast Georgia. She was lucky he was offering to attend to her injury. She shrugged. He told her he would give her half an hour to give permission and sign the form. If she didn't, he was out of the picture. He left the room in a huff, sending the head nurse in behind him.

Three days after performing her surgery, he discharged Sage from the hospital. Wayne was there to drive her home in Ben's Humvee, playing chauffeur and nurse. The vehicle's wider back seat allowing Sage to lie down. A thick cushion of memory foam bore the weight of the huge cast on her leg, while her head rested on a small pillow.

She was not in the mood to talk with Wayne. They rode in silence for almost an hour. Her only utterances were an intake of breath or a muffled grunt when the car bumped over potholes or jolted over train tracks. Halfway there, Wayne looked for a roadside rest stop. Soon he found a small pullout with two picnic tables but no restroom. It was deserted. He pulled over, hearing her sigh of relief as the Humvee came to a stop. He got out and opened the rear door. He looked down into her face. "Okay officer. No loafing. Time to hit the pavement!" It earned him a wan smile. He raised an eyebrow at his own bad joke. Then another: "Wait here."

He went to spread a blanket at the far edge of thegrassy sward, in the shade of a tulip tree where a multitude of fallen greenish-yellow florets decorated the grass. He went back, retrieved her cane and propped it against the fender while he helped her out.

They walked across the grass together very slowly to accommodate her limp. She sat down on the blanket with both legs straight out in front of her. On the injured leg, the nurse had cut off the hospital scrub pants Sage wore an inch above her cast. It exposed all the bruises and swellings from the brutal injury and the equally brutal surgery.

She sank back to look up into the tree. "This thingmust be almost two hundred feet tall; it's almost like a poplar."

He sat down beside her. A blossom fell near her. She picked it up to look at it closely. Inside the cup of pale greenish petals was a daring tinge of orange. She touched the feathery top of the center stile, then circled her finger around the tops of the soft green filaments and lowered her nose into the cup. She sniffed. "They smellnice--but subtle. Mild but complex."

He watched her.

She said, "Haveyou noticed you have to be ready to see beauty beforeyou can actually perceive it? When you look, you findit in the most unexpected things."

He hesitated before he spoke. "Love is like that too. You have to open yourself to it. You have to surrender before it can capture you."

He reached down to brush her forehead and finger a strand of her hair. "Ummm. Your hair is beautiful spread out around your face like that. The reddish highlights in the brown areso deep, so rich. Strong, like the rest of you."

"I don't feel very strong right now." She looked down at the cast. "This is the pits. And it will be for the next six weeks. I'll have to take up knitting or crocheting or...something."

He lay down on his side facing her, his head propped on a hand. "You're going to have trouble staying down, aren't you?"

"Yeah. One good thing about the whole mess is that it saved Susan. How weird is it that she was the one Taylor heard screaming on my phone? I talked to her early this morning before I was discharged. She apologized for pretending not to recognize me at the restaurant. And for not trying to return my phone the minute she found it."

"If she had, Taylor wouldn't have heard her screaming. We would never have gotten into the action. They might actually have...."

"Stop! I don't even like to think of her in that repulsive place. We had a good conversation. We're going to stay in touch. She won't ghost me this time."

She took a deep breath and raised her arms toward the innards of the tree, relishing her intimacy with it. After a moment she looked up at him to answer his earlier question. "It's not easy, but when I do pause and stay down like this, I know things. Like I'm connected to this tree somehow. Not only to it--to everything. We're all connected to everything. Everything and everyone. Especially to you." She looked into his eyes. "I never thought that way before. Or felt this way."

He kissed her forehead then settled onto his back. "We're lucky to be here. Legally free. I'm surprised the County Attorney in Georgia was able to get a grand jury together like that--in record time."

"Right. In spite of the complex details, the totally weird circumstances they heard about, it was enough for them to clear us both. Thank God for small and great favors."

"Speaking of gratitude, I'm especially glad for you, Sage. You've been through enough."

She shifted her position which brought a small grunt of pain. "I feel like I've been through *too* much." He touched her arm, stroked it, then looked at the cast on her leg. He said, "As much sports as I played in school, I never had an injury like that. It should have been me."

"Never say 'should have,' Wayne. It makes reality a mistake and as much as we may dislike reality, it is what it is. Besides, the doctors say I'll be fine in six weeks." She took a deep breath. "Yeah. But I don't know if I'll ever hit the pavement as Officer Stevens."

"What?"

She hesitated. "I called the Academy to let them know I was injured and of course they confirmed with the hospital. I got a conditional acceptance to the *next* Academy--if I can pass a new physical. That gives me more than six months to heal and get back into shape. No problem."

"Then what is the problem?"

"I can't stop thinking about that woman."

"Who?"

"Who do you think? The one I shot!"

"What is this, guilt? You feel guilty? She shot you first, Sage. It was self defense."

"Yeah. I killed her because she was going to kill me if I didn't kill her first. That made it legal--by the legal definition. But it doesn't feel legal. It feels like maybe there's another rule or law that makes it wrong."

Hearing the pain in her voice brought a flush to his face. "If anyone needed to be killed, it was that woman! She kept innocent people as prisoners; she tortured, mutilated then killed them. You did the world a favor."

"Maybe. I guess you're right. But as a police officer, I might have to kill someone again--someone not like her."

"You knew that from the start, Sage. And you knew that most cops don't pull their weapon during their entire career, much less kill someone."

"Yeah. But now I know how it feels."

He blinked, remembering. Then, "Me too. I didn't intend to kill Wagner. When I replay it in my mind I feel like shit. Did I have to throw the tire iron through the windshield? I want to stop asking myself that. I'd rather not think about it at all."

She turned on her side to look into his face. She reached to stroke his hair and his cheek then lay back again. "For me, as a police officer, whenever I strap on a gun I'll see the look on her face in the second she knew she was dying. I have to come to terms with it. Or give up on law enforcement."

"Hey, you have time. I'll help you figure it out. I'll be there for you as much as you'll let me."

Tears filled her eyes. She blinked them away and held her arms up for an embrace. He slipped his hands under her back, lifted her and held her close. He kissed her, deep and slow, so slow. The kiss ended but the desire that sprang up pulsing between them was palpable. She collapsed back onto the blanket. "I want you."

"Hey, I want you too. Have you ever doubted it? Can you feel it?"

She smiled and caressed him. "No doubt there at all. But I have no idea how we could manage to be lovers now, with this thing on my leg."

He looked around. They were still alone in the rest area. He touched her breast under the thin top she wore, then rubbed in a circle. She arched her back into his hand, feeling her nipple harden. She wasn't wearing a bra. He rubbed, slow and gentle, then firmer, squeezing. She gasped. They kissed again. She stroked his cheek and his neck. A breeze sprang up, caressing them, stirring the trees. Unexpectedly, wilted tulip flowers fell like rain drops around and onto them, onto her upturned, smiling face.

He placed his palm over her stomach. She didn't object. He slipped his hand under her elastic waistband to gently rub her belly. Her throaty murmur, encouraged him. His hand moved down to the subtle swell of her pubic mound. He kneaded the soft flesh then cupped her, his fingers curling down to probe and stroke, gently, slowly, persistently. He felt her surrender, then with a groan, she climaxed.

He leaned down and whispered in her ear, "That's one of the ways we'll manage it--when you're not wearing these damned clothes."

Her breathing slowed. She reached up to smooth her hand over his forehead. "But what can we do for you, my love?"

He reached down to adjust himself. "Don't worry about me. We kindled this spark when we were sixteen. We can wait until the right time--the perfect time—to ignite it."

#

## Chapter Thirty-Five

They reached her house to see Laura and Lee waiting on the porch for them. Sage started to climb out of the Hum-V. Laura rushed down the walk to hug her then walk side by side with her arm around her daughter. Lee stood on the porch and watched. Sage shook off her mother's and Wayne's helping hands to maneuver into the house on her crutches. "There. See, I'm not helpless."

They went into the den. Wayne and Sage claimed the easy chairs and accepted the soft drinks and snacks Laura offered. She and Lee sat on the sofa. For long peaceful minutes no one spoke, satisfied to enjoy each other's company again.

Then Sage lifted her face, sniffing. "What's that I smell?"

Laura said, "I'm cooking your favorite--roast beef with carrots and potatoes. I can do a lot more now my cast is off. Oh! Mine came off while yours went on. I'm so sorry, Sweetheart."

"I know, Mom. Thanks for the roast beef. I've missed your cooking so much." Sage finished her drink. She glanced up at the door to the kitchen and did a double take. A big calico cat strolled into the room. Four kittens scrambling behind her.

"Mom! What is this?"

"Sage, your leg is injured, not your eyes." "You adopted a cat and four kittens?"

"Actually, the mother adopted me. It's an interesting story."

Wayne laughed. "I've heard this kind of story. I told one like it myself when I was a kid. About a dog."

Laura tilted her head, a hint of defensiveness. "She came onto the deck one night and hung around. She was still there in the morning. I could see how skinny she was. I couldn't let her starve. It wasn't until a week later that I saw the four kittens. She had been hiding them under the deck. What could I do? I fed them and took them to the vet."

"I'm glad," Sage said, "But five cats in the house?"

"Ben came to have dessert and coffee last night. He's been so good to our family, hasn't he? Anyway, he saw the mother and for some reason she took to him, jumped on his lap without so much as an invitation. Surprised all of us. She'll go to him once she weans the kittens."

"Nice. Ben over there by himself probably needs some company. What about the kittens?"

"Other people have spoken for three of them. I'll keep one if you're okay with it."

"Mom. You don't need to ask. But I'm more than okay with it." Sage scooped up the yellow kitten climbing the fabric of her uncut pant leg. With her other hand, she picked up the black kitten her mother had placed on her lap. She held up the two warm, squirming kittens to rub their fur against her cheeks.

"What do you call them?"

"The tabby is War, the calico is Famine, the lack one is Death. The one you're holding is Pest, short for pestilence. "

"Uh---War, Famine, Pestilence and Death? The four kittens of the Apocalypse?" Sage's head tilted back in open-mouthed, delighted laughter. It ended with a snort.

Laura said, "I was kidding about the names. But I love it when you laugh that way, Sugar."

"I love it when you call me Sugar. You're the only one who's allowed to."

Wayne lifted an eyebrow at Sage. His eyes gleamed with sudden understanding, and then with love.

*Friend, you have read enough.*
*If you desire still more,*
*Then be the story yourself,*
*and all that it stands for.*
*Angelus Silesius*

## Acknowledgements

My sincere thanks to the people who contributed to the creation and development of this book, chief among them Carelyn Parr, my beautiful sister. Carelyn was the catalyst for imagining this story.

My inspiration began with a photograph of Carelyn as a young woman, wearing a gold necklace with the word *Perfect*. The photo of Carelyn, her surroundings and the stars in her eyes match my description of the fictional Holly Wallace. The single other feature my character and Carelyn have in common is that both worked as airline stewardesses many decades ago.

Warm gratitude goes to Nathan Bransford, my developmental editor. This book is a different and improved creation as a result of his wisdom and sage advice.

Also, many thanks to Dan Owens and Lou Pearson of DeFuniak Springs, Florida. Their patience in reading and commenting on an incomplete and messy manuscript was invaluable.

My heart is filled with gratitude and love for Peggie Torres and Kaylee for their contributions. I also appreciate Chance Alexander, who helped with smart-phone technical details.

Finally, I am so grateful for information about police procedures generously shared by Constable Thomas Schenek, elected Constable of Pima County, Arizona. Constable Schenek is a former Tucson police K9 Sergeant and before that, a member of the U.S. Marine Corps. His history of service, his bravery, family and Christian values, as well as his character are inspiring examples for us all. When I am tempted to picture him with a superhero cape billowing over his Constable uniform, I replace it with a truer image: he is on horseback in the Arizona out-back, his face shaded from the glaring sun by a black Stetson.

Dear Reader,

Thank you for reading **_Perfect!_**. I hope you enjoyed it and that you will take a few minutes to review it on line. Just a few words can recommend it to others. If you've never reviewed a book on Amazon, you can find directions on my web site at https://sharonsterling.net.

# Perfect! A Story of Love and Suspense

Made in the USA
Columbia, SC
28 April 2024

34994445R10153